Rough and Ready

ITALIAN STALLIONS
BOOK THREE

MARI CARR

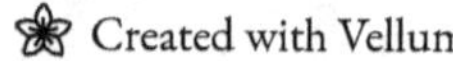 Created with Vellum

Rough and Ready

Gio is blessed with a big family and lots of friends. Unfortunately, there's an unspoken code amongst his buddies...one where sisters are off-limits. That wouldn't be a problem if he and his best friend, Rafe, could stop thinking about Kayden's vivacious, fun-loving little sister, Keeley. They have always been stand-up guys, but Keeley is so tempting, so sexy, that they're in danger of breaking all the rules.

Keeley's not exactly batting a thousand when it comes to life. She just lost her job and her only true talent seems to be picking the worst guys on the planet from online dating sites. However, her uneventful life takes a turn for the steamy after Rafe hires her to work for him and he and Gio start crashing all her bad dates.

When one kiss lead to a second and then to something much, much more, the lovers are left to decide if they're engaging in a fun fling or embarking on forever.

Chapter One

"Damn. I'll have what she's having," Keeley mused as she watched Penny Beaumont slow-dancing with Gage Russo. She leaned back in her chair and sighed heavily.

She was jealous as hell.

When she'd helped plan this birthday party for Penny, she had no idea her quirky, sweet friend would be swept off her feet by her hot-as-sin, billionaire boss. And while Keeley was over the moon for her, she desperately wished *she* could find someone like Gage.

Not a billionaire. She wasn't that type of woman.

No. What she wanted was a man so filled with love that he would crash her birthday party and claim her right there and then, in front of God and everybody.

Her mother would have loved it, would have called it wildly romantic. And it was. It really was. If there was one thing she'd gotten from her mother—well, except for her dark brown eyes and less-than-bountiful tits—it was her hopeless romantic side.

"I want it too," Liza said, agreeing. "Even if he *is* a Russo. I mean, how hot is that dance?"

Keeley had been friends with Liza long enough to know she

wasn't the only woman at the table with a green-eyed monster sitting on her shoulder.

The last strains of John Legend's "Conversations in the Dark" played out as Gage kissed Penny with such passion, Keeley swore she felt it all the way across the room.

Their other girlfriend, Gianna, left the dance floor right after the slow song ended. Her boyfriend headed to the bar while she reclaimed her seat next to Keeley. "I swear to God, that is the dreamiest thing I've ever seen. Penny with Gage Russo! Who would have guessed it?" she gushed excitedly.

Unlike Keeley and Liza, Gianna didn't have a speck of jealousy in her tone. Why would she? She'd been dating her super-sweet boyfriend, Sam, since they were both sophomores in high school. She'd had her life mapped out and planned down to the very second ever since she was fifteen years old and fell head over heels in love with Sam Mannarino.

Gianna had never spent a single second out there in the cold, cruel world, traveling from one meat market to the next, trolling online dating sites, and kissing frog after fucking frog, all in the hopes of finding the one.

Mr. Right.

It was a depressing task. Not that Keeley would ever give up or stop looking. Her prince was out there, and she was bound and determined to do whatever it took to find him.

And, of course, because karma liked to kick her in the ass from time to time to keep her humble...a prince she *couldn't* have decided to make his appearance at that very moment.

Gio Moretti, like all the Moretti men, was the living embodiment of tall, dark, and tatted-to-perfection handsome, and as such, he'd starred in pretty much every fantasy—romantic, sexy, and kinky—that she'd had since puberty.

Gio approached their table, scowling, and Keeley didn't even bother to hide her grin. She knew why he was pissed off. And it amused her to no end.

"Down boy," she said when he was within hearing distance.

"Did you invite Gage Russo?" he asked.

Keeley shook her head. "No, but Penny might have."

Gio grimaced. "Yeah. She said she did. What's going on with those two?"

Liza snorted. "Come on, cuz. You can't be *that* thick. I think it's pretty obvious what's been going on between them."

"Did you know about this?" he asked the table in general.

Keeley shook her head. "Not really. They danced together once when we were all at Enigma, but Penny never alluded to anything between them. She definitely didn't tell us she was sleeping with him, but...wowza. I think that's pretty much a given."

"Why were you at Enigma?" Gio plopped down in the empty chair next to her.

Keeley gave him a "seriously?" look. "Where else would we be? We're single ladies on the hunt for a man."

"Something incredibly difficult these days. There are no men worth dating in Philly. Period. End of story," Liza chimed in.

While Keeley was still optimistic about her chances of finding the perfect guy, Liza was a lot more jaded. So jaded, in fact, that she joked her skin fairly shimmered with the blue-green hue.

Gio smirked. "You always say that, and yet I have countless friends, brothers, and cousins who are great guys."

Liza rolled her eyes. "Fat lotta good that does *us*. None of you guys will ever go out with Keeley because you've shoehorned her into the eternal kid-sister role. And I'm related to most of those yahoos you speak of."

"Just say the word, Gio, and I'd be yours forever," Keeley teased, running her fingers up and down his tattooed arm. God, she was a sucker for tats. "Don't mean to brag or anything, but I'm awesome in bed."

He was completely unaffected by her flirting. "I'll take your word for that."

"Smart-ass," she muttered.

Gio had never crossed the line with her, despite the fact she'd flirted with him for years. It was a harmless game she played with her brother's friends because they were all stand-up guys. And just as Liza said, they'd never see her as an available woman because she would always be Kayden's little sister.

Kayden, who was sitting at a table nearby, yelled out, "Behave yourself, Kee. Leave poor Gio alone."

His words had the same impact as a dare, so she shifted her chair two inches to the right, ensuring that she was sitting even closer to Gio. She gave him a wicked, come-hither smile, purely for her brother's benefit. "Break the bro-code. I'll make it worth your while," she cooed in her best sex-vixen tone.

"Jesus." Kayden gave up, shaking his head as he turned his attention back to the people at his own table.

Gio smirked, and then, because he was as shameless and accomplished as she was when it came to teasing, he rested his arm around the back of her chair.

"I took no vow, little one," Gio said, winking at Keeley in that charming way of his.

She wanted to be annoyed when he called her "little one," but in truth, it got her girl parts purring like a well-loved kitten. Unwilling to let him claim the upper hand in their game, she shrank the distance between them by another inch or two. "Just one kiss?"

Gio snorted. "You can't handle me, minx."

Keeley relented, moving back and crossing her arms. "All you're doing is proving that Liza's right. She and I are doomed to forever be the sister mascots for your merry band of men."

Gio didn't deny her comment. Instead, he offered a one-shoulder shrug that gave her the tiniest bit of hope he was serious about taking no vow.

Yep. Optimist. That was her.

Back when she was younger, she'd suffered serious crushes on both Gio and his best friend, Rafe Baros. The two men had solidified their places in her heart the night her parents died.

However, over the years, she'd learned to accept that she

would always be—for all intents and purposes—untouchable. Not that it stopped her from flirting...and hoping. She'd just gotten to the point where she considered all this playful teasing to be practice for guys she actually stood a chance with.

Unfortunately, as far as single men went in Philly, Gio was right. His friends and male relatives were all very good, very decent men, sexy as sin...and the ideal she'd been using as a yardstick when measuring the men she dated.

Sometimes she considered breaking that stick in half—maybe twice—if she hoped to find someone worthy of a second date, but in the end, she refused to lower the bar. She knew what she wanted, and she was determined to find it. She wouldn't stop trying to find *him*—the one man who was perfect for her. Just like her dad had been perfect for her mom.

Gio glanced back toward the dance floor. The music was faster now. Justin Timberlake's "Can't Stop the Feeling" blasting from the speakers. Penny and Gage were dancing like lunatics, laughing their asses off, and even Gio couldn't manage to hold on to his scowl, grinning reluctantly at their silliness. "She looks really happy."

Keeley studied Penny's face and agreed.

She'd thought the slow dance and kiss had been hot, but there was no denying the friendship and fun Gage and Penny shared looked just as amazing. It seemed Penny had scored the dating trifecta—romance, friendship, and set-the-sheets-on-fire sex.

Meanwhile, Keeley was zero for three in that department.

"Yeah. She does." Keeley's jealously tripled, and she sighed again.

The sound captured Gio's attention. "You okay, Kiwi?" he asked.

She narrowed her eyes. "Thought we agreed we were going to let that nickname die."

The Moretti family was huge, several generations deep, with most of them still living in Philadelphia. Billy, one of the youngest generation, had struggled with her name when he was learning to talk, only managing to call her Kiwi, something the Moretti men had found completely hilarious.

For the past five years, she'd stopped being Keeley and had instead been dubbed with the ridiculous fruit moniker. And it wasn't even a good fruit. Those fuckers were impossible to peel.

Gio gave her a devilish grin. "Again...I never agreed to anything."

"Dick," she murmured.

"Bitch," he retorted playfully.

"Fuckrod." This exchange of name-calling between them wasn't new. In fact, it was so standard, it bordered on tired. She couldn't recall the last time they'd had a conversation that didn't end this way.

"Here we go," Gianna said with a laugh. "You two need to find a new schtick."

"Karen," he returned, ignoring Gianna's joke.

She scowled, though she didn't feel the slightest spark of anger. Just the opposite. Still, she fought to hide her grin. "Too far," she chastised.

"You started it." He reached over to ruffle her hair in a brotherly way, and she smacked his hand.

"You're messing it up and it took me ages to get the curls just right." Her chestnut hair—streaked with dark auburn highlights —was painfully straight. And as was the custom with women all around the world and throughout history, she hated her hair, always longing for what she didn't have. In her case, curls. Or hell, she'd settle for a wave or two.

"Seriously though," he said. "Why the heavy sigh?"

Keeley shrugged. "I think I'm entitled to a little depression here. I mean, I lost my job, the landlord just raised my rent— which doesn't matter because without a paycheck, I can't pay him anyway. And I'm this close," she pinched her thumb and forefinger together, "to having to move back in with my brother, which I think we can all agree would end badly."

Liza feigned a horrified gasp. "One of you would definitely kill the other. No question about it."

Keeley loved Kayden more than life itself, but their relationship had gotten a gazillion times better after she'd gone off to college and moved out from beneath the ever-present thumb he'd kept on her while she was growing up. Not that she could blame him for his overprotective nature. After all, Kayden had basically stopped being a big brother when he was twenty-five, forced to take on the role of surrogate mother and father instead, stepping in to raise her after their parents had been killed in a plane crash.

Her father, a former pilot in the Air Force, had continued to fly small charter planes after retiring from military service. When she'd been younger, she would swear she spent more time in the family's single-engine Cessna 172 than in their Buick. Her dad was airplane crazy, never so happy as when he was in the air, soaring with the birds, as he liked to say.

Sadly, the plane had gone down when an unexpected storm caught up with him and Mom as they were returning from an anniversary trip to Nantucket.

Keeley had been fifteen and, even now, ten years later, she missed them more than words could say. Not a single day passed when she didn't long for one of her dad's big bear hugs or wish she could talk to her mom.

"And," Keeley added, "if the job situation wasn't bad enough, last night's date ended with the same whimper as the previous forty-seven. I really, *really*," she stressed, "need one to end with a bang."

"Pun intended?" Liza joked.

"Absolutely," Keeley replied.

"Hey, Gee," Sam called from the dance floor. "They're playing our song."

Gianna hopped up with a laugh, joining her boyfriend as "I Like Big Butts"—which was definitely *not* their song—started to play.

However, it did appear to be Keeley and Liza's song, as they both broke loose, singing all the lyrics at rapid pace, never missing a single word and shouting, "You get sprung!" at the top of their lungs, while Gio merely shook his head in amusement, claiming, "You two have issues."

"Hey, Keeley," Rafe called out, interrupting their impromptu concert as he approached the table. He dropped down into the chair Gianna had just vacated.

"Hiya, Rafe. You're in luck. Gio turned me down for the night. The path is clear for our lust-filled evening of passion. If you're nice, I'll even let you pull my hair."

"Keeley." He gave her *that* tone, the one seemingly reserved for her that said "cut the crap." And he managed it by just saying her name in that patient/exasperated tone.

"Please don't tell me you're going to break my heart too."

Rafe ignored her joke, which was not particularly surprising. While Gio teased back, Rafe simply pretended she wasn't flirting at all. "Kayden just told me you lost your job."

"Yeah, I did." She hadn't shared that information with Rafe because he'd spent the last month dealing with the aftermath of his grandfather's death. She didn't feel right complaining about her problems when he was genuinely grieving.

"Why didn't you tell me?"

She let her sympathetic smile answer for her.

Rafe rubbed his chin. "I've been too wrapped up in my own problems."

Keeley reached out and placed her hand on his. "You lost your grandfather, Rafe. I just lost a stupid job I didn't even like." She'd been laid off in "last hired, first fired" style when the office supply company she worked for had been forced to scale back. Online shopping conglomerates were hell on the little mom-and-pop businesses.

"Even so...I'm kind of hoping I can solve both our problems. If not forever, then maybe for a little while."

She frowned, confused by his comment. "What do you mean?"

"I'm dying on the vine, Kiwi. I need you." Rafe flipped his hand over, clasping hers.

Her heart skipped a beat or three as she purposely let herself misinterpret his words.

He needed her?

She wished.

"Need me how?" she forced herself to ask, ignoring the sudden heat growing between her legs. She wasn't kidding about needing to get laid. It had been a while.

Scratch that. *A while* indicated months.

She'd drifted into *forever* territory, as she hadn't gone to bed with a guy in well over a year.

"I want you to come work for me."

She laughed for just a split second...before she realized he was serious. It was hard for her to get used to the idea of Rafe being his own boss. For the past decade, he'd been working as a finance manager for a large international company whose home base was in Philadelphia, but he'd taken a leave of absence after his grandfather's terminal cancer diagnosis, wanting to spend as much time as he could with the beloved man before his passing.

He didn't go back to the job after his grandfather's death because he'd discovered he was the sole heir to what turned out to be a legit fortune. Like, an overnight-millionaire kind of fortune.

According to Gio, Rafe had expected his mom to inherit his grandfather's wealth and vast property holdings. Apparently, his mother and the latest in a long line of stepfathers—Keeley thought this might be husband number four or five—had thought the same. And they'd caused one hell of a scene in the lawyer's office. His mother had broken into loud sobs, while his stepfather insisted they would contest the will and that Rafe hadn't heard the last from them, before storming out.

"Rafe—" she started, shaking her head, certain his job offer was one of pity.

"Hear me out," he interrupted, still holding her hand, a fact that was making it difficult for her to process what he was saying.

He had a large, warm hand, and it made hers seem tiny in comparison. "I'm in over my head right now. I hate to admit that, but it's true."

Keeley didn't doubt for a second he detested saying those words out loud. Rafe was the "never say die" type, the kind of guy who rarely asked for help, certain he could do everything on his own. To hear him say he was in over his head was...well, shocking. Because she'd never heard him admit defeat on anything.

Rafe continued, "Grandpa was old school—like, *severely* old school. He didn't trust computers, so all of his business information is stored in countless handwritten ledgers."

Keeley's eyes widened. "Holy shit. You've gotta be kidding me."

Rafe shook his head. "And to add insult to injury, he was a bit of a hoarder. Not a gross, piles-of-trash, dead-pet-remains hoarder, but I swear to God I think the old guy kept every single piece of paper he'd ever touched. He has so many boxes of paperwork, I can't possibly count them all. They're stacked floor to ceiling in three rooms in the haunted mansion, and his office at Eclectic—that's the nightclub he owned—isn't much better."

Keeley had gone to the reception held at his grandfather's home, after the funeral, and Rafe's nickname for the place was pretty accurate. It was dark and dusty and creepy as fuck. Several rooms were decorated exclusively in large drop cloths, covering God-only-knows-what kind of furniture.

"Is the paperwork stuff you need? Can't you just pitch it?" Gio, who'd been listening, asked the question.

Rafe rubbed his eyes wearily, and Keeley noticed the dark circles and lines caused by tension that never used to be there. Rafe was nowhere near as easygoing as Gio, which made their friendship one of those opposites-attract sort of relationships.

Rafe was the type of friend who seemed content with always standing on the sidelines, while Gio, with his larger-than-life personality, took center stage. Gio was quick to tease with a loud, blow-your-eardrums-out laugh, while Rafe had a tendency to take life too seriously. Gio was one big ball of emotions, all of which showed on his face and in his voice and hands, which—as was true of most Italian men—were an extension of his words and always moving, while Rafe was the very definition of stoic, never revealing any of his feelings.

However, Rafe's stone-cold, rock-solid nature was absent tonight. She'd never seen him looking quite so...on edge.

"I wish I could toss them out," Rafe said, "but I went through a couple boxes...just to see what was in them. Buried amidst a lot of crap that *was* trash, I found the title to a boat I didn't know he owned and...Jesus, get this...over three thousand dollars in cash. Apparently, he didn't trust banks much more than computers."

"Hot damn!" Gio exclaimed. "A boat. We need to go fishing."

Rafe rubbed his brow. "I'd love that, but the truth is, I don't have a clue where the boat is docked."

Everyone at the table, with the exception of Rafe—who really was stressed to the max—laughed.

"Basically, there's no way I can just take the boxes to the shredder. I have to go through all of them. And I can't stress this enough...there are a *shit ton*. Plus, there's a goddamn safe in his office, but I can't find the combination. I'm hoping that's in one of the boxes as well." Rafe looked at Keeley. "That's where you come in. I want you to help me go through the hoard."

"If this is as bad as you make it sound," Keeley said, "it could take me months to help you."

"I know that. But, well..." Rafe shrugged, rubbing the back of his neck. "It could be a part-time project—that I'll pay you for—if you want to keep looking for another job. Or I'm in a position to make it a permanent one, if you prefer. I'm okay with running Grandpa's businesses from a financial point of view, but I'm no marketing expert."

Keeley perked up. She'd earned her bachelor's in writing and digital media, and a master's in marketing at Penn State before coming back to Philly. She'd worked hard to finish all her course-work in five years. She'd thought her majors made her fairly marketable, but finding her first job had been a challenge. She'd known the office supply company wasn't going to be her forever career, but they'd been the first to offer a position, so she'd taken it for the practical working experience it would add to her resume.

"Rafe. Listen…" Keeley wasn't sure what to say. If his offer was sincere, this could be her dream job. Because he would certainly be her dream boss…and she didn't mean that in a sexual way. Rafe was a really nice guy. He wouldn't be condescending like her last boss, who also managed to creep her out by calling her "sweetie" and leering at her all the time.

"Let's make some time on Monday morning to sit down and talk about it," Rafe said, when she didn't finish her thought. "I don't want you to think this is a spur-of-the-moment decision. I realized immediately I'd need to hire someone to help with the boxes *and* the businesses. I was going to chisel out a job description and upload it to Indeed and LinkedIn. Then Kayden said you were looking for a job and…it felt like fate had led us both to this same place at the same time."

Rafe gave her a brazen grin that proved he had her number. She was a big believer in karma, and not a day went by that she didn't read her horoscope.

"Nicely played, Rafe," Gio murmured, while Liza giggled.

Rafe continued, clearly not finished trying to plead his case. "We've known each other for years, and I have a feeling we'd work really well together. You won't cry when I bark."

She grinned. "You don't bark. But if you do, just know that I'll bark back."

He raised his hand as if she'd just made his point. "Which is exactly what I want. That, and your upbeat personality. That dark, dreary house is starting to get to me. I need your sunshine."

Keeley smiled, touched by his compliment. "I would love to talk to you about the job. What time Monday?"

"Why don't you come by that creep show of a house of mine around nine? I feel like I owe you full disclosure. You really should see how many boxes I'm talking about first, before we take the discussion any further."

"That sounds good. Are you sure Kayden didn't put you up to this? Call in a favor or something?" she asked, kicking herself for looking this gift horse in the mouth. Because she wasn't sure she gave a shit if this was a kindness for her brother or not.

Rafe shook his head. "No. He doesn't even know I'm over here making the offer. You've got a good work ethic, Keeley. I know that. I've watched you bust your ass the past few years, showing up every day and putting in the hours, even though you didn't love the job."

"That's an understatement," she muttered.

"And if you decide this isn't for you, that's cool too," Rafe said.

"I'm going to help you with the boxes regardless," she said.

"Hell, *I'm* probably going to help with the boxes. There's a boat to find," Gio joked.

Rafe looked at him with tired but amused eyes. "Yeah. Damn boat."

"Rafe," Keeley said, feeling a thousand pounds lighter than she had a few minutes ago. She had a job prospect. One that she was super excited about. Maybe she wouldn't have to move back in with her brother after all. "Thanks."

"Don't thank me yet. You haven't seen the hoard. I'm afraid you're going to take one look at it and run screaming into the hills."

Keeley's eyes widened. "You're kidding, right? A treasure hunt for a lost boat? The combination to a safe? Hidden cash? Sounds like an amazing adventure."

Liza, who'd been eavesdropping the whole time, laughed. "It sounds awesome to me too."

"Now," Rafe said, pointing to the dance floor. "What's going on out *there*? Isn't that Gage Russo?"

"Yeah," Keeley said wistfully. "Looks like Penny found her prince."

"Lucky bitch," Liza muttered.

"Apparently, Liza and Keeley are operating under the impression that there are no decent men in Philly to date," Gio explained to Rafe.

"Really?" Rafe said, somewhat surprised. "I know lots of single guys who are great." Then he looked at Liza. "Of course..."

"I'm related to all of them," Liza finished for him.

Rafe chuckled. "Yeah. Pretty much."

Gio leaned forward. "You know, maybe the problem is that you're both setting unreasonable expectations. What are you looking for in a man?"

Keeley shrugged. "I guess I'm looking for someone like my dad and Kayden. Stand-up guys with a sense of humor, devoted to their family. He also has to be someone who'll put me on a pedestal, worship the ground I walk on, and live only for my happiness," she joked. "That doesn't feel like too much to ask for."

Rafe shook his head. "I think I'm beginning to understand your difficulties."

They all laughed.

"And you're searching the online dating sites to find this perfect match?" Gio asked.

She and Liza nodded.

Rafe rubbed his chin. "Do you really think you're going to find an amazing guy on Tinder or Bumble or Hinge?"

Keeley shrugged. "We haven't had much luck so far, but when you get to be our age, that's how this is done. We didn't meet our true loves in high school like Gianna."

"And we didn't meet guys at college, and neither of us have met prospects at work," Liza added.

Keeley nodded. "I've even tried the blind date routine a few times, set up through girlfriends who were *sure* they knew 'this great guy' I'd love. They were wrong."

Rafe and Gio seemed to consider their dilemma, as if they genuinely wanted to help them figure this out. Which would be sweet, if it didn't drive home just how off-limits she really was when it came to both men. Unfortunately, and despite her best efforts, they snuck into her fantasies way too often. Apparently she was an emotional masochist, her own worst enemy.

"Maybe your problem isn't the men, but where you're going on the dates. Seems to me you're always going to places like Enigma. Isn't it hard to get to know someone in a nightclub?" Gio asked.

Keeley took a sip of her wine. "That's not the issue. I've gone to movies with guys, out to dinner, coffee dates. It's just...either the conversation is awkward, or the guy has strong political beliefs—that are completely opposite of mine—or they're a mansplainer or a chauvinist or a racist or a commitment-phobe or a homophobe or mama's boy or a guy just looking to get laid or..."

"A married man," Keeley and Liza said in unison.

"Married?" Rafe asked, frowning.

Keeley wrinkled her nose. "I managed to land dates with two of those cheating assholes. The dating game is a tough one. Requires a lot of patience and persistence."

"Preach, sister," Liza said, raising her hands to Heaven.

"Shit," Gio said. "You're starting to convince me you're right. Didn't realize there were so many pricks in Philly."

"Or it could just be that we have exceptionally bad luck," Liza said.

"I can see you've both given it serious effort though," Rafe said.

"We've been out there awhile," Liza said. "Gives a girl too much time to try to figure out where the hell she's going wrong."

"Amen," Keeley said, sighing once more.

"Neither one of you is doing anything wrong," Gio said with a confidence that touched Keeley deeply. He placed his hand on the back of her chair, closing the distance between them.

"You're gorgeous, intelligent, and independent. Both of you," Rafe added.

Gio ran his finger down the line of Keeley's nose, bopping it on the tip. "Any man who doesn't see that doesn't deserve you."

Keeley blinked a couple times, waiting for a punch line, because it was Gio, and teasing each other was their schtick.

It didn't come.

So she decided that was the nicest thing Gio or Rafe—or hell, anybody—had ever said to her.

"Wow," Keeley breathed. "Thanks. I needed that pep talk."

She smiled widely, well aware her fantasies tonight were definitely going to include one of the guys currently sitting at this table.

The thing was...she couldn't decide which.

Chapter Two

Gio left the back alley, reentering the restaurant through the kitchen door. He hip-checked Keeley, who was drying dishes. She laughed, then went back to work.

"I took the rest of the trash out to the dumpster," he said to Rafe, who was putting the last of the tables back in place in the main dining area.

His family had stuck around after the party, everyone pitching in to clean up, but eventually they began heading out one by one, all of them wanting to get home before the coming storm hit. He, Keeley, and Rafe were the last ones there.

"I'm finished too." Keeley followed him out of the kitchen and walked over to retrieve her purse.

"What's the deal with you and that hippie bag?" Rafe asked curiously. "I never see you without it."

Keeley hugged the bohemian-style hobo bag to her chest. "It belonged to my mom. She loved it and carried it all the time. I thought...well, I was surprised to find it in her closet when we were cleaning out her things after she died. I would have expected her to take it with her, so I assumed it was lost in the plane crash."

Gio smiled. "I can see your mom carrying that. She was super cool. Made the best Italian hoagies on the planet." He studied

Keeley for a minute, then added, "You know...you look and act a lot like her."

Keeley lit up like he'd just crowned her Queen of the Universe. "Thanks."

"You should be proud of yourself. It was a great party, Kiwi," Rafe said.

She smiled widely. "Yeah. It was. And damn if Penny didn't get one hell of a great present."

Gio narrowed his eyes, though he didn't feel any real annoyance. The Morettis and Russos were famous in Philadelphia for their Hatfield-and-McCoy-style feud, battlelines drawn four generations earlier. Gio's dad and nonno still held grudges against the older Russo men—who were all dead now—for long-ago slights, something they'd worked hard to instill in Gio and his brothers. Some of the disdain had held. Some hadn't. Because while he was no fan of Matt Russo, Gio had no real beef with his younger brother, Gage—who'd stormed in here tonight and swept Penny off her feet—or the other brother, Conor.

"Bet she's getting lucky tonight," Keeley mused, and Gio couldn't help but laugh at the obvious jealousy in her tone. "You find my lack of sex life funny?"

"Apologies. I didn't mean to rub salt into that particular wound," he said, bowing at the waist dramatically.

"You know," she drawled. "If you want to make it up to me, one of you could kiss me good night. I would kill for a decent good-night kiss."

"Keeley," Rafe said, in that patient way of his, gently letting her down without actually saying the words.

"This isn't me flirting," she argued. "It's an honest request. Do you know how long it's been since I've had a *good* good-night kiss?"

"How hard is it to kiss someone goodbye?" Gio mused.

Keeley scoffed. "Apparently, very hard. In the past year, I've had dry kisses, sloppy, disgusting kisses, tastes-like-cigarettes kisses, short kisses, and ones that lasted way too fucking long.

And there was the guy who bit my lip and made it bleed, then proceeded to tell me he was part vampire on his mother's side. A special kind of crazy he didn't reveal to me until that point in the date."

"Wow." Rafe shook his head.

"Not to mention the guy who sucked on my bottom lip. Nothing else. Just sucking. Or the guy who ran his tongue along every single one of my teeth like he was doing a fucking dental exam."

Gio held his hands up in surrender. "Keeley. Jesus. You gotta stop. You're killing me."

She crossed her arms and gave them a smug grin. "And those guys didn't even break into my top five worst kisses ever."

"Given the things you've told us tonight, I don't know why you'd ever go on another date," Rafe said.

"Or haven't consider playing for the other team," Gio teased.

"Oh, believe me, I figured out a long time ago I'd probably be a lot happier if I was into women, but—"

A bright flash of lightning cut through the night sky.

"Shit!" Keeley jumped, cursing in surprise.

"Doesn't look like we beat the storm," Rafe mused, glancing out the front windows. The wind had picked up, the rain suddenly coming down hard. Thunder rumbled, filling the quiet night with something equivalent to the roar of a pissed-off giant.

Lightning flashed again, and once more, Keeley cried out, "Son of a bitch! That was close."

Gio grinned...until he realized she'd suddenly gone pale. "You okay, Kiwi?"

Rafe crossed the room when a loud peal of thunder shook the front windows. "It's only a little thunder," he reassured her when she covered her ears.

"I know. I just...God, I hate storms!"

Gio stepped next to her, taking her purse from her shoulder and placing it on a table before pulling her in for a hug. "I didn't know that."

She nodded shakily. "Ever since..."

Gio cursed himself. He wasn't thinking. Of *course* she was afraid of storms. She'd lost her parents when they got caught in a nasty thunderstorm, their small plane crashing and killing them both. "Oh, Keeley," he said, continuing to hold her. "I'm sorry. I should have realized."

Keeley closed her eyes tightly, pressing her face to his chest, her muscles tensing when another lightning strike lit up the outside sky.

This time, it was followed by a loud crack, then a sizzle. The bolt had hit something nearby.

When the lights in the restaurant flickered, then went out completely, he realized it was probably a power pole. And a quick glance out the front window proved they weren't the only ones without power. The neighborhood outside was pitch black.

With the restaurant plunged into darkness, Keeley clung to him tighter, her whole body shaking. She had downplayed her dislike for storms. This wasn't disdain...it was terror.

"Hang on." Rafe used the flashlight on his phone to guide him as he walked back to the kitchen.

Gio carefully led Keeley around a couple tables to the circular corner booth, pushing her onto the cushioned seat before claiming the spot next to her, wrapping his arm around her shoulders and keeping her close.

"Let's ride out the worst of the storm here. There's no way we could make it to our cars without getting completely drenched, and I don't like how close that lightning strike was."

"Okay," she said. "I wasn't planning on leaving right now anyway. I don't...I couldn't drive in this."

Rafe returned with a couple of candles and a lighter. He placed them on the table, lit them, then slid into the opposite side of the booth, claiming Keeley's other side. He reached out for her hand. "You okay now?"

She shrugged. "Sorry for acting so silly. I swear storms never used to bother me."

"I get it, Keeley. We understand why," Rafe said quietly.

Gio shared a look with his best friend, over Keeley's head. He knew Rafe was recalling the same night he was, ten years earlier. The two of them had been out with Kayden, sharing a pitcher of beer at a sports bar, watching Gio's cousin Elio play in a pro hockey game on the big screen. It was his first season in the NHL and they were all proud as shit, excited to see him in the rink.

A storm warning scrolled across the bottom of the TV screen, announcing the imminent bad weather rolling in off the coast. Gio had been sitting there wondering if he'd left his car windows cracked, when Kayden's phone rang.

Within seconds of his friend answering, he knew the news was bad.

Really bad.

"You know," Keeley said softly, "I don't think I ever thanked you guys for...that night." She didn't have to specify which night. "For what you did for me and Kayden," she added.

Gio tightened his grip around her shoulders, taking note that Rafe still held her hand. Ever since the night her parents died, Gio had felt some level of...

God, he wasn't sure what word to use. Responsibility? Protectiveness? Possessiveness?

All he knew was, he'd started watching Keeley a little more closely after that, and Rafe had as well. When she'd been high school, it had definitely been in big brother fashion. But after she graduated from college and returned home...that changed. She'd always been pretty and confident and independent, and those attributes had only become more amplified as the years passed. He'd started taking notice a few years ago, and not as an overprotective brother figure.

"You don't have to thank us for that, Keeley."

She shrugged, and Gio could tell she was recalling that night too. He'd played it over in his mind more than a few times himself over the years.

He and Rafe had driven Kayden home. Not to the apartment

Kayden shared with Aldo, but to his family home, the one he'd moved out of on his twentieth birthday when he'd achieved his dream of becoming a Philadelphia police officer.

It was just after midnight when they arrived, and they could see the living room lights on, the TV flickering. Gio recalled smiling for a split second, realizing that—of course—Keeley, queen of the night owls, would still be up. That smile faded soon enough...

Keeley looked up from the TV when he, Rafe, and Kayden walked into the house, clearly surprised to see them. Kayden hadn't lived at home in five years, and it was way too late to stop by for a visit.

No doubt, she'd been waiting up expecting to see her mom and dad walk in, full of stories about their anniversary weekend on Nantucket.

"What are you doing here?" she asked, her gaze traveling from Gio to Rafe, before it locked onto Kayden's face.

Kayden was trying to school his expression, but Gio could see the shattered devastation in his friend's eyes. He'd been quiet in the car on the ride over from the bar. No talking, no crying, just steeling himself for what came next.

Gio knew telling Keeley their parents were gone would be the hardest thing his friend would ever do in his life.

"Kayden?" Keeley said, rising slowly from the couch.

Kayden swallowed deeply and took a shaky breath. Keeley saw the tears in her brother's eyes—and suddenly she was crying too.

Quietly. Without sound. Nothing but shiny lines of tears streaming down her pale cheeks.

She quickly wiped them away, waiting for the inevitable. She was smart and observant, with a heart the size of Texas.

She doesn't deserve this, Gio thought. Neither of them did.

"Say it," Keeley croaked, before clearing her throat. "You can say it, Kayden. It's okay."

She knew what was coming, and the incredibly brave girl didn't cower, didn't scream, didn't try to deny it. Instead, she found a way to give her brother the strength to speak the words.

"Mom and Dad aren't coming home. Their plane...the storm..." Kayden said.

And then, as if he'd bid it to come, lightning pierced the sky, followed by a loud peal of thunder.

Keeley flinched, and Gio crossed the room to her while Rafe stepped closer to Kayden. He eased her back down to the couch, afraid her trembling body wouldn't support her for much longer.

Kayden came and sat on the other side, reaching out for her, and the two of them sat there, locked together, crying out their grief for hours, the storm raging outside, as he and Rafe silently stood sentry by the couch.

"I know it's stupid to be afraid," Keeley said. "I mean...we're perfectly safe in here."

"It's not stupid," Rafe assured her.

Gio didn't like how pale she'd gone. What she needed was a distraction. "We all have irrational fears. For me, I'm afraid of hospitals," Gio admitted.

Keeley smiled slightly. "I don't think anyone likes hospitals, Gio."

He chuckled, though the sound held no mirth. "Yeah, well, I think it's a little more than dislike. I was thirteen when my mom died of cancer."

"Thirteen?" Keeley asked.

He nodded. "I spent the better part of my eighth-grade year at Hopkins, either waiting while she went through treatment, or sitting next to her hospital bed whenever she was admitted due to complications. I hated the sounds—the constant beeping of machines—and the bright, relentless fluorescent lighting, and the smells. God, they were the worst. Antiseptic and bleach and...sickness."

Rafe still held one of her hands, so Keeley placed the other on his thigh. She gave his leg a squeeze. Another flash of lightning lit up the restaurant, and Keeley jumped.

He placed his hand on her nape, gently caressing the soft skin beneath her long hair, hoping it would soothe her. "Nowadays, I avoid hospitals like the plague. I couldn't tell you the last time I stepped foot in one."

"I never knew all that," Keeley said. "I mean, I knew your mom passed away, but I never knew how. I should have asked long before now."

Gio waved away her guilt. "We lived in Baltimore at the time. I didn't meet Kayden until we moved back here shortly after, just before my freshman year of high school. And you, little one," he said, chucking her under the chin, "were barely in elementary school and too young to remember any of that anyway."

"Yeah...but still," she said.

They sat quietly for a few moments, simply listening to the sound of the rain beating on the roof. If he wasn't mistaken, he could hear hail pelting the windows as well. It was a violent, nasty storm, but sitting here with Rafe and Keeley, he could almost forget about it.

With anyone else in the world, Gio might have tried to fill the silence between them, kept the conversation going with light chatter. This lingering quietness would have felt awkward in a different crowd, but right now, with them, it felt peaceful.

"What are you afraid of, Rafe?" Keeley asked after a few minutes.

The dark room, lit only by the flickering light from the candles and the occasional flashes of lightning, created an almost... well, if he was the fanciful sort, he'd say romantic atmosphere. There was something about the coziness and the closeness, the three of them huddled together in the booth, that seemed to invite the sharing of deep secrets and the kind of intimate conversation that could only be shared between friends who'd known each other forever.

"I'm afraid of the ghost currently haunting that house I'm living in," Rafe joked.

Or at least Gio thought it was a joke.

He and Keeley laughed.

Rafe did not.

Keeley leaned toward Rafe, nudging his shoulder with hers. "Seriously?"

Rafe winked, finally breaking into a grin. "No. Not really. I mean, I hear a lot of bumps and creaks in the middle of the night. Personally, I blame Grandpa Albert for planting the ghost story seed."

"Sounds like your grandpa," Gio observed. "I loved the guy, but he was definitely..."

"I think the word you're looking for is eccentric," Rafe finished for him.

"I thought he was awesome. He always had cinnamons in his pocket, and he said I reminded him of his wife. Said she was a looker too," Keeley confided with a fond smile.

"I never met Grandma Marta, but I've seen plenty of pictures. She was very beautiful...just like you," Rafe said, brushing a stray hair away from Keeley's face.

"Why did he think his house was haunted?" she asked.

"Grandpa Albert lived in that mausoleum of a house for nearly fifty years. He bought it for Grandma Marta as a wedding gift."

"A house as a wedding gift. How sweet," Keeley gushed.

Gio grinned. She had a romantic streak a mile wide, and he vaguely wondered if that was why she'd always had such a hard time finding a boyfriend. None of the yahoos she and Liza had ever dated seemed capable of sweeping a woman off her feet. Not in the way Keeley deserved.

"You've seen the house. If you think *that's* romantic, then sure," Rafe teased. "Anyway, Marta died a few years after the wedding, in childbirth with my mom."

"Oh no. That's so sad."

"Yeah. It is. But Grandpa always insisted Marta never left the house, or him. That her spirit remained behind, waiting for him to join her."

Keeley was completely enthralled by the ghost story. "And now they're together."

"Suuuure they are," Rafe replied sarcastically.

Keeley gave Rafe a wide-eyed, exasperated look, as if he was missing the obvious. "Of course they are. They're living in their mansion—the home he bought for her—together at last, forever, in the spirit realm."

Rafe lifted one shoulder casually. "That could be true. Or maybe this just felt like the right time and place for a ghost story."

Gio laughed. His friend wasn't wrong. With a little imagination, it wouldn't be hard to pretend they were all sitting around a campfire.

Rafe continued, "I'm pretty sure if Grandpa had left the house to Mom, she would have had the thing knocked down five minutes after his funeral. She's always hated the place."

"That's probably why your grandpa left it to you," Keeley said. "He knew you'd keep his and Marta's home safe."

"I'm going to regret telling you that story, aren't I?" Rafe joked.

"Your mom calmed down yet?" Gio followed up. "Still upset about the will?"

Rafe shrugged. "I haven't talked to her much since he died. The whole thing just...caught us both unaware. Though now that I've had time to think about it, I understand why Grandpa did what he did. He was a workaholic who'd given his life to building up his business. Meanwhile, my mom has maxed out her credit card no less than twenty times in her life."

"Twenty times?" Keeley asked, aghast.

Rafe nodded. "Mom's not good with money. She's spent the last thirty-five years as a secretary. She makes an okay salary, but none of it stays in the bank for long. In my mom's mind, the way to a man's heart is either through his stomach—hence an overstuffed fridge of food—or with toys, like computers or big-screen TVs or PlayStations. As a result, her problem with spending was usually the source of her divorces. The first three guys couldn't handle being buried under her heaps of debt. The fourth one left when she ran out of money to support him."

"That's terrible," Keeley said.

"Yeah. Things would get bad, my stepdad of the moment would cut and run, and then she'd go to Grandpa for help. And he always bailed her out. So I'm sure he was afraid that if he left his estate to her, she'd squander all the money and his legacy would be gone in an instant."

Keeley shook her head in disbelief. "That's kind of..."

"Sad," Rafe filled in for her. "And you're right. It is."

Gio looked at the front window. Though the thunder and lightning had died off, the rain was still coming down in sheets. "Doesn't look like the storm is going to let up for a while."

Rafe stood and walked over to the bar. Tucking a bottle of wine under his arm and a corkscrew in his pocket, he grabbed three glasses and returned to their table. "I don't mind hanging out for a little longer."

He deftly opened the wine, pouring each of them a glass. "Sort of cool owning a restaurant," Rafe admitted. "Unlimited booze...and cheese fries."

Keeley narrowed her eyes, pointed a finger at him, and launched into a fake lecture. "If I come to work for you, there will be none of that. You, Mr. Finance, know what it would do to the bottom line if you started feeding this one," she said, crooking her thumb toward Gio. "He'd eat you out of house and home."

"Take the *if* out of that threat," Rafe said. "You *are* coming to work for me, Kiwi."

She didn't deny Rafe's assertion because it was clear she wanted the job.

Gio was happy for the two of them, pleased that Keeley would have a good job and Rafe would have the help he so desperately needed.

However, the job would ensure that Rafe and Keeley were together all day, five days a week. And there was a small, silly part of him that felt...left out.

Keeley lifted her wineglass. "To Albert and Marta. Together again."

The three of them tapped their glasses together and took a sip.

"I miss that old guy," Rafe confessed.

"He was a character." Gio had always been fond of Rafe's grandfather.

Rafe toyed with the stem of his wineglass. "He changed my life. And I don't mean with the inheritance."

Gio was surprised to hear Rafe admit that out loud.

He knew quite a bit of Rafe's history...the issues with his mom and her revolving door of husbands. Gio had been around Rafe enough in high school to see the toll it took on his best friend. And the long-lasting impact it had on Rafe's own ability to forge lasting relationships.

His surprise stemmed from the fact Rafe was sharing any part of it with Keeley. Rafe didn't like to talk about himself, and the only reason Gio knew as much as he did was because he'd been around for it, the two of them spending a lot of time in each other's houses in high school.

"What do you mean he changed your life?" Keeley asked.

Rafe looked at her for a moment, and Gio realized that his friend *hadn't* meant to say anything out loud. Rafe didn't reply immediately, and Gio expected him to backtrack. But he didn't.

"College wasn't something I'd ever considered for myself. Like I said, Mom never saved a penny in her life. Grandpa, when I was younger, wasn't around much, always busy with his business, working long hours. He chased the almighty dollar, while Mom spent most of her days looking for love in all the wrong places."

Gio started humming the old country song, and the three of them laughed at the familiar tune.

Rafe continued, "Like I said, whenever Mom dug herself into a deep hole, Grandpa would help her, but it was always issued with his standard 'money lecture.'" Rafe finger-quoted the last two words. "And while his lessons on fiscal responsibility didn't work on Mom, they definitely worked on me. I hated the way my mother always took the easy way out. Getting Grandpa to write a check to make all her mistakes go away. I refused to be like her. So I worked all through high school at a fast-food place, and for Moretti Brothers in the summer."

"Your grandpa didn't give you money like he did her?" Keeley asked.

"He tried. But I was a prideful little fucker, and stubborn to boot. I refused to take his 'charity.' That was what I called it. So I worked to buy my own clothes and hockey equipment and shit like that."

Keeley grinned. "That sounds like you."

Rafe ruffled her hair, and she swatted his hand away. "I wasn't planning to go to college. Instead, I was saving every penny to move out after graduation because I knew I'd go crazy if I spent one more minute living with my mom and stepdad number four, who was a complete douchebag."

"How long did douchebag last?" Keeley asked.

Rafe grimaced. "Longer than most. Six years. He was a total slob, an out-of-work drunk who sat on the couch in his underwear all day, scratching his balls. Unfortunately, my mother loves taking care of people, so Douchebag fit the bill to a tee."

"Sounds like a real prince."

Gio held up his hand. "Don't get him started on Douchebag or we'll be here all night. I've heard enough of the horror stories surrounding that guy to last me a lifetime. Tell her how your grandpa changed your life," Gio prompted. "That's a better story."

"Fine," Rafe said. "Grandpa Albert came to graduation, and he pulled me aside after the ceremony. He handed me an envelope. I figured it was just a card, maybe a few bucks, you know."

Keeley nodded.

"It was an acceptance letter to Temple University."

"What?" Keeley's eyes widened.

Gio had been there when Rafe's grandfather handed him the letter.

"He told me he was proud of the man I'd become. Then he did that thing Grandpa Albert was good at."

"What was that?" she asked.

"Guilt."

Keeley snorted. "What?"

"He said he was an old man who'd spent too much of his life worrying about work and money. Said he regretted missing so much of my childhood, only visiting occasionally. According to him, he'd worked his whole life with precious little to show for it. Except me and Mom. Said the greatest gift I could give him would be to take his money, go to college, choose a career I was passionate about, and continue to make him proud. He had applied to the college for me, but said the decision to attend was mine."

"Whoa," Keeley breathed. "I always liked Grandpa Albert, but now I love him."

Rafe nodded, clearly pleased by her words. There was no denying Rafe thought his grandfather walked on water.

"But I'm confused," Keeley said. "Your dream job was to become a financial manager? You couldn't find anything more boring?"

Gio laughed loudly. "An excellent point."

Rafe narrowed his eyes. "My dream career was one where I could make money. Please refer back to my earlier comment about my mother's mountain of debt. She might not have felt the stress of that, but I always did. My first stop on campus was the library, where I researched which major offered the best chance at landing a good-paying job after graduation. I've always loved math and numbers, so that path felt like a decent fit. Of course, the best part of the college deal was Grandpa had given me an instant place to live...away from Douchebag. I stayed on campus, living in the dorm. I took a job as an RA during the school year and kept the summer job with Gio's family, so I could buy my own food, pay for textbooks, stuff like that. I still had a little pride, I guess. But Grandpa covered the rest."

Keeley took a sip of her wine and gave Rafe a mischievous smile. "Now you *have* to let him and Marta stay in the mansion. You owe him."

Rafe sighed. "Yeah. I guess I do."

The three of them finished the bottle of wine, talking until the wee hours. The storm had ended well before they decided it was time to call it a night.

He and Rafe walked Keeley to her car.

"See you Monday morning?" Rafe asked.

She nodded. "Yep." Then she accepted the hug Rafe offered.

Gio watched their embrace, Rafe's hand gliding up and down her back slowly.

He reached for her the moment Rafe let go, adding his own hug to the farewells. "You going to be okay getting home?"

"Yeah," she said, returning his hug. "Thanks for tonight. If I'd gotten home before that storm hit, I would have been riding it out with my head buried underneath my pillow, praying for it to end. Being with you guys really helped."

Gio started to let her go, then changed his mind. Instead, he cupped her cheeks. "Keeley."

"Yeah?"

"This doesn't mean anything," he said firmly.

"Wha—" she started to ask, but he cut her off with a kiss. He took his time and made sure to do it right. She remained frozen for a split second, but Keeley wasn't shy, wasn't timid, or easily spooked...unless it was a storm.

Her lips softened and she returned the kiss, her lips parting on a sigh, giving him the chance to swipe his tongue inside. The kiss lingered as Gio turned his head slightly, seeking to deepen it. She was soft, her breath sweet like the wine they'd shared. Her hands remained at her sides...and all he could think about was how much he wanted them on him.

Through it all, he felt the weight of Rafe's gaze, and it added to the intoxicating quality of their embrace.

When they parted, he was pleased to see the paleness of her face replaced with a healthy flush.

"There," he said, painfully aware that he hadn't been as unaffected by the kiss as he'd expected. "Now you've had a *good* goodnight kiss."

She gave him an adorable breathy laugh, and then, because she was Keeley, she asked, "How do you know it was good?"

Gio tugged her hair playfully. "Minx."

"Next time you're afraid, Keeley, call us. We'll come over," Rafe said, his invitation not only surprising Keeley but Gio too.

"I might take you up on that." There wasn't an ounce of flirtation in her voice. Just gratitude. She gave them both a sweet smile, then climbed into her car. He and Rafe watched her drive away before turning to walk to their own vehicles.

"Quite a kiss," Rafe observed.

Gio gave his best friend a sideways glance, making sure he saw his cocky grin.

"You think that was smart?" he asked.

He considered the question, then shrugged. "I've done dumber things."

Rafe laughed. "Yeah, you have. But just the same, you might not want to do that again."

"Why? You think Keeley will get the wrong idea?"

Rafe shook his head. "Nope. I think *you* will."

Chapter Three

Rafe pushed his desk chair away from the computer and rubbed his eyes wearily. He'd been looking at the screen for so long, the numbers were starting to blur. Grandpa's dog, a five-year-old Chihuahua named Cricket, lifted her head from where she lay on the floor near his feet. Cricket didn't weigh eight pounds soaking wet and looked more like a scruffy, oversized rat than a dog, but she'd been completely devoted to his grandfather, and it was obvious the sweet animal missed him.

"Should we take a break?" Keeley asked, looking over at him from the table they'd set up on Monday afternoon as her temporary workstation. "Or call it a day? It's nearly five. I could check with the boss, see if he's okay with us knocking off a bit early for the weekend."

He grinned at her joke. Keeley had shown up Monday morning at nine on the dot, and the two of them had created a list of job duties, negotiated a salary and benefits, and come up with a job title as well. She was now officially the Marketing Director for Baros Corporation, a small company that consisted of a restaurant, a nightclub, a used bookstore, a flower shop, and three apartment buildings.

There was no rhyme or reason to his grandfather's ventures. It felt as if all his business decisions were based on impulse buys. He saw something he liked, and he bought it. A workaholic widower, Grandpa had filled his days—and coffers—by acquiring struggling businesses that he'd managed to revive.

Of course, it helped that Grandpa had the Midas touch. Every business he'd bought now operated well within the black, turning huge profits and adding to his fortune.

Or at least they had. Until Grandpa's cancer diagnosis and subsequent illness. His grandfather had attempted to manage work affairs from his bed the last four months of his life, but pain had distracted him, left his brain too fuzzy to fully concentrate.

So the majority of the day-to-day operations had been handed over to the managers of each business. Without guidance, things had been allowed to slide, slip into disarray. After crunching a few numbers, Rafe was even starting to suspect the manager at Eclectic was skimming money off the top—which was why he'd given Keeley his grandfather's office there for her marketing work. Not that she spent much time there—yet. Until the hoard was beaten down, she was spending most of her time at the mansion.

He'd asked Keeley to try to get a feel for Rick, the manager, when she did work from that office because she was very good at reading people—something he struggled with—and he trusted her instincts.

Grandpa had been gone six weeks, and it was well past time for him to step up to the helm properly, rather than riding along on a wing and a prayer.

When Rafe first learned he'd inherited the company, he'd felt completely overwhelmed and out of his element. He wouldn't say his stress was gone, but with Keeley on board, he had someone he trusted to consult, and what had felt like a never-ending pressure on his chest had lessened. In just the last few days, she'd already helped him see past the mounds of work, suggesting ideas for the future and ways to expand Baros Corporation.

Keeley hadn't looked at the business and seen an obligation.

She'd seen potential—and she'd opened his eyes to it as well. He suspected he would have gotten there eventually, but grief and stress had been standing in his way.

"I think the boss could be convinced," he said, reaching back to rub some of the tension out of his neck. Maybe he should consider getting a massage...or seeing a chiropractor.

"Phew, good. Because while I was ready to offer sexual favors to get my way, I'm feeling a bit grungy from all the dusty boxes."

Rafe laughed, realizing that was the first time this week she'd reverted back to old Keeley, the one who was a constant, funny flirt. "We've made a lot of headway this week. I can't believe how much, actually. I couldn't have managed half of this on my own, Kiwi."

"This probably makes me sound like a lunatic, but I think it's actually fun work. Every box so far has hidden a golden egg. I can't wait to go through the rest to see what else we find."

She wasn't kidding about the treasure. In addition to the cash they'd pulled out of every single box—which had so far added up to tens of thousands—they'd discovered the title to a house in the Outer Banks, a key to a safe deposit box—which they hadn't had a chance to go to the bank to open yet—and five hundred shares of original Microsoft stock. Grandpa had attached a handwritten note to the stock, explaining that he'd won it in a bet but considered it worthless because...computers.

Every single box had yielded something fun and valuable.

Rafe looked around his grandfather's—no, *his*—office. They'd started working their way through the boxes in here, determined to clear it out so that they would have a decent work space for the two of them. After this room was finished, they were starting on the other three "box rooms," as they'd begun to call them.

At some point, he'd move the operation of the business out of this house—rent or buy proper office space—but for now, it was easier to tackle everything here, since everything *was* here. While his grandfather had kept an office in every single one of his businesses, he'd always done the lion's share of work right here from the house.

Keeley rose and walked over to his desk, leaning her hip against it.

"I think we make a good team," she said.

"We do," he agreed readily.

Over the past week, he'd learned a lot about Keeley he hadn't previously known. He'd spent the last decade accepting her proscribed role in his life. She was Kayden's little sister. She loved to tease and had a fun personality. Her laugh was always the loudest, and her voice was the one he always heard over the din. She flirted with him and Gio because, one, it drove her brother insane—which ranked very high on the list of Keeley's favorite things to do—and two, it was safe. She could say audacious things, wink, giggle, flip her hair, and generally be her silly self because neither he nor Gio would cross the line.

But since Saturday night, after the party, Keeley had put the flirting away and revealed two new sides to him. That night, the confident woman had revealed a vulnerable side...and it called to him in a way he'd never experienced before. He'd wanted to reach out and hold her that night, just take her in his arms...and never let her go. That was the part that had shaken him. He'd never looked at *any* woman and felt the slightest inkling of possessiveness.

And throughout this week, she'd shown him her professional side as well. She was seriously smart and creative and driven. Every single day, she'd found a new way to impress him.

When she'd questioned his decision to offer her a job at Penny's party, he had claimed to need sunshine in his life. He could see now just how true that was. They'd worked side by side for hours this week, and it was the first time in ages that he'd felt... God, the only word he could think to use was *happy*. Though he wasn't quite sure what that emotion felt like. He'd always been too serious, a big ball of anxiety since birth. Happiness didn't come naturally to him.

But with Keeley...

She was easy to be with, and while they'd done nothing but work, it hadn't felt like that because she'd been there, sharing the load, telling him all her dating stories, singing along to the music she always had playing in the background, and making him laugh with her quick wit and humorous observations about the world going on around them.

He rose, trying to ignore the pain in his back that told him he'd been sitting too long.

Suddenly, his desk slid several inches to the left.

Keeley, who'd still been leaning on it, was caught off guard, her arms flailing as she fought to keep her footing.

He caught her, gripping her waist before she tumbled to the floor. Keeley clenched his upper arms, steadying herself.

"What the hell?" she exclaimed. "I wasn't even leaning on it that hard."

Rafe had observed the same thing. More to the point, the desk was heavy as fuck...yet it slid away from her like it weighed practically nothing.

"Strange," he observed. Then he realized his hands were still on her waist. And she'd lied about being grungy because in truth, she smelled fantastic, like citrus and flowers.

Keeley tilted her face up to his, and for a moment, it felt as if she was inviting him to kiss her. They were standing closer than normal, but they didn't step away, and he felt her breath on his face. She'd found a stash of his grandfather's cinnamons, and he could smell that spicy, sugary sweetness as well.

He waited for her to make one of her flirty jokes. Actually, he *needed* her to make one. Because right now, he was thinking things he shouldn't be thinking.

He closed the distance a scant inch more, recalling the way Gio had kissed her. How hot he'd gotten from watching the two of them, how much he'd wanted to step forward when Gio stepped away, to steal his own kiss.

Keeley didn't move, her eyes locked with his, and he realized both of them had stopped breathing.

He lowered his head, his lips just about to touch—

"Hey! You guys in the office?" he heard Gio yell out from the front door. He and Keeley moved apart quickly, but not before Rafe noticed the flush on her cheeks that proved he wasn't the only one affected by what had just passed between them.

"Sorry," she whispered hastily, the spell suddenly broken.

"No," he said. "That was on me."

Gio's arrival prompted a flurry of barks from Cricket. Not that the dog would be a bit of help if an intruder ever broke in. Her home security technique consisted of barking her head off until the guest appeared, then dancing around them until they picked her up so she could slather them with sloppy puppy kisses.

"Yeah," Rafe called out, taking a deep, steadying breath. "Come on back."

A moment later, Gio walked in. "It's Friday. Let's kick this weekend off in style."

Gio had stopped by a few times this week after work to see how things were going with the hoard, jokingly inquiring about the status on the boat...which was still missing. Rafe wasn't used to seeing so much of him, and he'd begun to suspect it had something to do with Keeley's presence in the mansion.

Cricket, now used to him, jumped up on her hind legs, pawing at Gio's knees until he picked her up so she could lick him to death.

"Cricket," Rafe said sternly, but Gio waved away his attempts at training the dog.

"Leave her. This is the most action I've seen in months," he joked. "Did you spy any ghosts today, Cricket?"

"She did!" Keeley excitedly proclaimed, pointing to a battered recliner in the corner of the office. "Sat beside Albert's old recliner for nearly an hour, staring at the same spot the entire time. I swear I think his ghost was sitting there, talking to her. At one point, she rolled over like someone was stroking her belly."

Then, Keeley's gaze flew to the desk before lifting to capture Rafe's, her brows raised. Rafe knew exactly what she was thinking because there was a small part of him that wondered the same thing.

Something had moved the desk—and he was certain it wasn't Keeley.

But he wasn't about to fuel that flame because Keeley was way too obsessed with the ghost story, so he shook his head dismissively. "Cricket was a weird dog before Grandpa Albert died. She's not seeing ghosts," he insisted, even though he was secretly skeptical. The longer he lived here, the harder it was to hold on to the assertion the place wasn't haunted. There had been a few too many bumps in the night, creaking floorboards, and things he was certain he'd left in one place, only to find somewhere else later.

"Well, if anyone was going to haunt a house, it would be Grandpa Albert," Gio said. "Simply because I'm pretty sure he'd take a lot of pleasure in messing with you from the Great Beyond."

Rafe grimaced. "You're not wrong about that."

His relationship with his grandpa had changed after Rafe graduated from college. The old guy—true to his word—did seem to regret his workaholic ways, so for the last decade of his life, the two of them had met up for drinks and dinner every Monday night, talking about everything under the sun. Rafe had shared stories about work and his mom, about his buddies and his high school and college adventures, while Grandpa told him about his own life, about Marta and what his mother was like when she was younger. Grandpa admitted he saw a lot of himself in Rafe, so he'd done a bit of preaching, telling him that while hard work was all well and good, he also needed to stop and smell the roses.

Rafe missed those weekly dinners more than he could say.

"I'm afraid I'm out on happy hour," Keeley said, reaching for her oversized purse. "I need to go home and get ready for my date."

Gio frowned. "Another of your online guys?"

Keeley nodded. "Yep. Although, I think this guy might have potential. We've chatted on FaceTime a few times. He's cute, appears to have a sense of humor, and best of all, he has a real job and an actual apartment—unlike the last two guys, who were still living in their parents' basements and trying to break out as videogaming stars on Twitch. Plus, my horoscope promised that romance would go beautifully for me today." She smiled brightly. "All I have to do is communicate openly and honestly."

"Well, if your horoscope says it, it must be true," Rafe said dryly. They'd started every single workday this week with Keeley reading his horoscope to him. It was getting to the point even *he* was starting to take them seriously. His horoscope for today promised vast changes were coming, and he'd spent more than a few minutes wondering what the changes could be. "Where's he taking you?"

Keeley crinkled her nose. "We're starting with dinner at Saloon and then—no judgment, please—we're going to Enigma. He said he likes to dance."

Gio scoffed. "He likes to cop a feel, is more like it. Why don't you just do the dinner part tonight and leave the bump and grind for a future date?"

"Wow, Gio. I've never heard you manage to channel my brother so perfectly. When did you turn sixty, by the way?" she asked. "I must have missed a few birthdays somewhere."

"Smart-ass," Gio said.

"Old man," Keeley retorted.

"Come on. We're not starting that shit again," Rafe said, cutting off their standard name-calling game. "I'm in for happy hour, Gio. And dinner too, if you don't have any plans. Haven't had time to hit the grocery store lately, so the cupboards are bare. How about cheesesteaks at Founding Fathers?"

Founding Fathers was a local bar, and a hidden gem as far as Rafe was concerned. He and Gio had spent countless evenings there, watching whatever sport was in season with the other regulars.

"Dinner sounds good." He turned to Keeley. "You sure you don't want to jump to the inevitable and give this loser the heave-ho *before* the date instead of after? I'll pay for dinner."

"He's not a loser. I'll stick to my plan and continue to hope for the best, since you guys keep rejecting me." She flipped her hair over her shoulder dramatically. "Besides, Baby is lonely," she said, pointing downwards, making it clear the nickname was for her vagina. "I don't put out on the first date," she added, "but if this guy is cool, I wouldn't be opposed to setting up a second date that includes heavy petting. I'm getting bored with my vibrator."

"So the end goal on all this dating is just sex?" Gio asked.

Keeley shook her head. "Of course not. Well, not *entirely*. I mean, I like a good time as much as the next person—and don't you guys dare pretend that you're not the same. I've been around long enough to overhear plenty of your locker room talk."

Gio grinned. "I don't believe in the double standard, and you know it."

"Can I tell you guys a secret?" she asked, her voice suddenly more serious than he was used to hearing from her.

Rafe nodded.

"I'm sick of the party scene. I want what Jess and Gianna have. And now Penny. You realize I've never had a long-term boyfriend, right? Think about it. My longest relationship was with Herbie Wilson my junior year of high school, and that lasted all of four months. I'm ready for something real."

Rafe hadn't put it together until she said it, but she was right. He'd never known a Keeley who wasn't perpetually single.

Not that his track record was much better.

Actually, he didn't even *have* a track record. He didn't date to change his relationship status. For him, dating *was* just about sex.

He hadn't grown up with a stellar role model when it came to love and marriage. Not that his mother didn't fall in love because she did. A lot. The problem was, she fell fast and hard and too impulsively.

Too many years of helping his mother pick up the pieces after her divorces had left Rafe trigger shy, wondering how the hell someone was supposed to know if it was really love or just a mirage, like the ones his mother chased. In the end, he'd decided the whole thing—love, and the inevitable pain associated with it —was not for him.

"Herbie was a putz," Gio grumbled.

"Yeah. He was," Keeley agreed. "But he was cute, with parents who didn't care if he threw a keg party in the basement every weekend. Underaged drinking and zero parental supervision—it was the equivalent of teenager Heaven. And for four brief, wonderful months, I was the queen bee at the parties."

"I'm surprised you gave all that up," Rafe joked. He'd never heard this story, and it appeared Gio hadn't either.

"So what happened?" Gio asked.

"I caught Megan, a bleached-blonde bitch and captain of the cheer squad, giving him a blow job in the bathroom at one of his parties. Herbie, the witless wonder, couldn't understand why I was pissed. He didn't consider blow jobs cheating. Claimed he hadn't laid a finger on her."

Gio rubbed his jaw, grinning widely. "How do you always find these idiots?"

"Hell if I know. But I'm not giving up. Onward and upward and all that crap. With any luck, tonight might just be the night I meet my forever guy."

Rafe wrapped his arm around her shoulder and tugged her close for a side hug, kicking himself for hoping tonight's date was a dud...because nothing could ever happen between him and Keeley. "Ever the optimist."

"That's me. Hey, tell Gio my idea about the inn tonight at dinner," she added, as Rafe attempted to stifle his wince.

With any luck, perhaps Gio hadn't heard her. Because he'd already crossed his arms and was hitting Keeley with his most fierce look. "Behave yourself."

She grinned shamelessly as she shoulder-bumped Gio on her way out. "Nope. Later, gator."

As was her new habit, Rafe heard her stop at the front door and call out, "Goodbye, Albert! Bye, Marta!"

Gio chuckled, then dropped down in Grandpa's recliner. "She's a piece of work."

"She is. It's been nice having her around this week. She's completely professional, a hard worker."

Gio observed, "Yeah. I can see that."

"She's been a godsend," Rafe continued. He leaned on the desk for a split second, then straightened up, still curious about why the thing had moved. "I mean, I always knew she was bright, but I don't think I realized just how creative she was. She's always thinking, always brainstorming ideas to improve each of the businesses, and her suggestions are good. *Really* good."

Gio looked around the office. "You guys cleared this room out quickly. I didn't realize it was this big."

"It was hard to tell with all those damn boxes. Felt like the walls were closing in."

Gio rose and walked around the room, running his finger along the dusty bookshelves that were newly revealed. "You know this house is incredible, right? I can't wait to see what else you uncover. Are you planning to live here, make it your home?"

Rafe had been trying to decide. He owned his own townhouse, but since Grandpa's passing, he'd stayed here to save himself commuting back and forth. It allowed him to work until late, or rise early when the overwhelming pressure of just how much there was to do kept him from sleeping.

With Keeley's help, he was feeling a bit less stressed about his never-ending to-do list. Plus, she'd yelled at him on Wednesday when she discovered he was up until midnight, going through boxes without her. She informed him he was "stealing her fun." So, now when he woke up in the dead of night, he forced himself to remain in bed and ride out the anxiety he felt until he could fall back to sleep.

"I can't decide if I want to stay here or not," Rafe said in response to Gio's question. "Right now, I feel like I'm living in a dusty old museum. The house isn't comfortable and some of the rooms aren't even livable. Besides, I'm not like you. I have absolutely no vision for the place and spent the better part of yesterday wondering if I'd be better off to raze the entire thing to the ground and just start over."

Gio scowled. "Erase that from your head right now. This house is over two hundred years old and demolishing it would be a tragedy."

Rafe raised his hands. "I know. I know. It's a cool old house, but it's too fucking big for just me. Shit, it's too big for a family of twelve."

"Yeah," Gio agreed, still strolling around the room, studying the ornate wainscoting of the chair rail.

"Plus, it needs a major overhaul. The hardwood floors need to be refinished; every room needs a fresh coat of paint. The kitchen looks like something right out of the nineteen seventies. It would be a huge undertaking and definitely not worth the effort or expense, considering it's just me living here."

"I get what you're saying, but the carpenter in me is itching to get my hands on this room, to show you just how amazing the whole house could look with a little bit of tender loving care."

Gio was part owner in a restorations business with his brothers, Tony, Luca, and Joey. The brothers were so good at what they did, they were hired for jobs not just in Philadelphia but all along the East Coast. After being featured on a couple of home renovation shows on HGTV, Joey had actually landed his own show, *ManPower*, and he was traveling the country currently filming the first season.

Rafe didn't doubt for a moment that Gio could bring this house back to life. And he'd certainly given it some thought ever since...

"What was Keeley saying about an inn?" Gio asked.

Fuck. He'd heard.

"It was just something she said Tuesday, and now, because it's Keeley, she's like a dog with a bone."

"What did she say?"

"She said this place would make an amazing inn."

Gio's eyes widened. "Damn. She's right. It would."

Rafe hadn't intended to have this conversation. "But I have zero time to take on a new project."

Gio, perhaps the only person as impulsive as Rafe's grandpa and mom, responded exactly the way he knew he would, which was why he hadn't mentioned the idea. "I have time."

"Seriously, Gio. While the bones of this house are good, it's fallen into disrepair. Like I said, it's too big a house for one man, so Grandpa closed off huge sections...for years. No, more like decades."

"The bones are the most important part. Everything else can be fixed. We rebuilt Pat's Pub in Baltimore and it was little more than a burned-out shell after the fire," Gio said, not bothering to mask his excitement. Not that he could if he wanted to. Rafe had learned a long time ago, if Gio felt *any* emotion—no matter what it was—everyone around him knew about it.

"What are you saying, Gio?"

Gio paused for a moment to think. But only for a moment. Then Rafe saw the gleam that was all too familiar. Because it was the same gleam his grandpa got when he saw a business he wanted to buy, or his mom got whenever she met a man she was certain was "the one."

"A partnership," Gio said. "Fifty-fifty. We get the house appraised, I come up with a quote of what I think it would take to renovate it from haunted mansion to haunted inn, and then we go from there." Gio began his trek around the room again. "I've been feeling stagnant lately, bored even. I mean, Moretti Brothers is doing well. Really well. But the business has grown to a place where we've got a lot of employees doing most of the heavy lifting. I've been saving up to buy my own house, but with the housing market the way it is...I definitely have enough to invest."

He was thinking aloud, so Rafe let him work through it on his own, aware he couldn't stem this tide if he wanted to.

"The idea of using that money for this, taking on a project that would be all my own, away from my brothers..."

"Gio," he started, but the man was on a roll.

"I'm being serious, Rafe. This house is full of character, history, and ghosts," he added, laughing. "We could build it into something really amazing."

"Do you know how much work you're talking about taking on?"

"It doesn't feel like work when it's yours and it's something you love, something you believe in," Gio countered.

Rafe considered that. He and Gio had been best friends for seventeen years, and Rafe could count on one hand—with fingers left over—the number of fights they'd had. While they were very different people, those differences were what seemed to make their friendship so strong. Even so, going into business together...

"We've never worked together," he pointed out.

Gio frowned and tilted his head. "You don't really think we can't work together, do you?"

In all honesty, no. Rafe suspected they'd make a really good team. "No. I don't think that. But...you think it could be a success?" Rafe asked, hating that Gio's enthusiasm was becoming contagious.

"A huge success. We build it, and then hire someone to run it for us. Didn't Gianna major in hotel and hospitality?"

Gio nodded.

"And we've got Keeley to do the marketing."

"Jesus," Rafe muttered. "You're already figuring out who can run the thing after it opens?"

Gio chuckled. "Say yes, Rafe. I can see it in your eyes. I know you want to."

Rafe sighed because Gio wasn't wrong. He loved the sound of bringing the old place back to life, now that he was talking to Gio.

No, that wasn't true. Keeley had been talking him into the idea since Tuesday, dropping some of her "plans" for the inn into countless conversations.

"Shit. Maybe I'm more like Grandpa Albert than I thought. He was always looking for the next big venture too, impulsively snatching up whatever businesses caught his eye. But this would be insane, considering I'm still struggling to figure out how to run Baros Corp. I don't have a grip on the businesses I already own."

"You're the smartest guy I know, Rafe. Stop beating yourself up and give yourself a little time. It's only been six weeks, for God's sake. You won't fail because you're the hardest worker I've ever met. You've got this," Gio said with a confidence that bolstered Rafe. "Besides, it's not like we'd be opening the place tomorrow. We're talking about a huge renovation project. By the time the inn is ready to open, you'll have the other shit so under control, you'll be bored."

Rafe looked around the office. "You really think you can bring this place back to life?"

"I know I can." Gio kept walking around the room as he spoke. "I mean, I still have my work with Moretti Brothers, but we can work on the house on evenings and weekends. You're good with a paintbrush, and it wouldn't hurt you to get away from the computer for a little while and do some manual labor. You're getting soft around the middle."

Rafe narrowed his eyes. "I'm as fit as I've ever been, and you know it."

Gio, the muscular, sporting-an-eight-pack bastard, ignored him. "We could start in this office, then move on to the bedrooms and the kitchen. That would give you and Keeley time to declutter the other rooms."

"That's a good plan. But..." Rafe figured if he was going in, he might as well go *all* in. "What if you moved in here while we worked on it? You'd have even more money to invest if you weren't renting another place. Like you said, the project will take some time, considering we'll both be working our full-time jobs as well. I'm not sure we're talking just months. Could be a year or even longer."

"You sure you don't just want me here to protect you from the ghosts?" Gio teased.

Rafe shrugged. "You joke about that now, but I gotta admit, there's a lot of shit that's hard to explain. The place creaks nonstop, stuff moves around, doors close on their own, and I swear to God, I've heard footsteps upstairs in rooms I know are empty. I go to bed every night wondering if this will be the night Jacob Marley starts rattling his chains."

"Is that your attempt at convincing me to live here? Because, dude, you're falling short."

"Be serious for a minute. Please," Rafe said, trying to decide if he was really about to commit to this. "Are we actually going to do this?"

"The inn—hell yeah. And if you really want me to move in here with you..."

"I do. It seems smart, considering you've just said you'd be here weekends and after work."

"Okay. So here's the next move. We crunch some numbers, get a lawyer, and if it all looks good and we agree, we sign some paperwork so it's legal, and then...you've got yourself a partner."

"And a roommate," Rafe added, Gio's excitement rubbing off on him. "I took my grandfather's room, but there are a couple of large guest suites that he kept nice for company. You could have your pick of one of those until we start making some headway on the renovations. Then, if you want, you can have one wing of the house, and I'll take the other until we finish the project. I know neither one of us is used to having a roommate, but this mausoleum is big enough that we could go frickin' days without running into each other."

Gio rubbed his hands together, and Rafe could practically see the wheels spinning.

"Some of the bedrooms are small. We could knock down walls to create larger suites. And I've already got a few ideas for this office. I think we could preserve the history and architecture of this place and still give it a more modern feel. I bet we could even incorporate some green construction, lower the house's carbon footprint and—" He paused mid-sentence. "Getting carried away, aren't I?" Gio asked.

"A little." Actually, a lot. Gio's grab-the-bull-by-the-horns approach to life was in direct counterpoint to the way Rafe lived. Rafe was much more conservative, a thinker by nature who took very few risks. If left to his own devices, Rafe would never get a damn thing done in this house because he'd spend way too much time simply trying to choose a paint color.

"Okay," Rafe said at last. "I'm in. Operation Haunted Inn is underway."

"Hot damn! We gotta work the ghosts into the name of the place."

Rafe grinned. "Keeley insisted that would be the biggest selling feature. The thing that would have folks lining up for a stay."

"She's not wrong," Gio said, reaching out to shake his hand. "Partner."

Rafe shook his hand, but when he started to pull back, Gio tightened his grip. "I know you're overwhelmed, Rafe. I can see you're stressed out, running on fumes. And I know this inn feels like one more obligation to you right now...but I really would like to do the heavy lifting on the project. At least until you get your sea legs under you on the rest."

Rafe was unaware of exactly how tense his shoulders had been until Gio found the right thing to say to loosen the muscles just a bit. "Maybe even after that. I trust your talent. I've seen your work. Thanks for saying that though. It helps. Hell, now *I'm* starting to get excited. You and Keeley are becoming a bad influence on me—getting me fired up about things that are ultimately more work," he joked.

Gio released him. "We're coming up with ways to make you richer, and you know it. Tony just bought this cool AR that I can use. It'll help draw up the designs, give you a chance to see what I've got in mind before we pull out the tools. Sound good?" Gio radiated enthusiasm, and Rafe suspected his best friend was only just barely restraining himself from grabbing a hammer out of his truck and starting work on the place tonight.

Rafe had always admired Gio's what-you-see-is-what-you-get attitude. No one ever questioned where Gio stood on an issue because he so readily expressed all the emotions—anger, joy, sadness—and when he wanted something, he went for it, all in with no reservations.

His personality was one of the main things that had drawn Rafe to him in high school. Gio, a sophomore at the time, was the first person to reach out to him, offer to help him find his locker and his classrooms. He'd confided that his family had just returned to Philadelphia the previous year, so he knew what it felt like to be the new kid.

Rafe's mom had moved them in with stepdad four, Douchebag, right after the wedding, and the change in address put Rafe in a different school district. So he started high school as the new kid, all his friends from elementary and middle school attending another school across the city.

Gio had been the first friend he'd ever confided in regarding his mother's relationship record. When he was younger, he'd been embarrassed by his mother's marriage and divorce routine, but Gio had helped him find a way to deal with it. Typically with humor.

Mom had surprisingly managed to move past her hurt over the will, and she'd texted him just this week to assure Rafe she wasn't mad. Because he was her only child, Mom tended to rely on him for pretty much everything, but only when she was single. Once she met a new man and made that trip down the aisle, he was relegated to white noise in the background until the next divorce.

She'd confided yesterday that stepdad number five, Rodney, was still pissed off about the will and talking to a lawyer. Rafe wasn't surprised, since Rodney was a lot like Douchebag. The two of them had only been married about a year. No doubt Rodney had learned she was the daughter of a wealthy, elderly, ailing man and had taken that trip down the aisle not with hearts in his eyes but dollar signs.

Grandpa's lawyer—now Rafe's—had assured him this morning that the will was airtight.

Mom was still hung up in the honeymoon phase, so she defended Rodney, certain he'd calm down soon enough. Then she mentioned that she'd booked a long weekend for the two of them in New York City because she was sure getting away for a little while would help. Rafe had been tempted to ask how she was paying for the trip, but he'd held his tongue, perfectly aware it was going on her credit card...and equally aware that at some point, he was going to have to decide if he would continue to bail her out the same way Grandpa always had.

Worrying about her and Rodney, the stepdick, was just one more thing adding to his stress, his sleepless nights, and his stiff neck.

Gio pulled him from those heavy thoughts, thrilled about their plans. "You know, if everything works out, I could move in pretty much immediately. I've lived in my apartment so long, I'm on a month-to-month lease. Once we sign on the dotted line, I'll give the landlord notice and start packing my stuff."

"That sounds great." In truth, it did. Gio, like Keeley, never failed to find joy in life. With Keeley here during the day to lighten his load and make him laugh, and Gio here on the weekends and evenings, Rafe hoped the loneliness that had settled over him since Grandpa's death would lift. "I hope this all works out," he said sincerely.

"Me too. Now let's go eat. I'm starving." Gio placed his hand on Rafe's shoulder, guiding him toward the door, when something obviously caught his eye. He turned his back to Rafe as he walked over to Keeley's workstation. "That's weird."

"What's weird?" Rafe asked.

"I swear to God I walked by this table three times and never saw this." Gio turned around, holding up Keeley's phone. "I can't believe she hasn't come back for it."

"She probably thinks it's in that gargantuan bag of hers."

"Yeah. You know...it seems to me a big decision like going into business together calls for a celebration, something fancier than a cheesesteak at Founding Fathers. What do you say we go celebrate our new living situation with a couple real steaks? Saloon's got good food."

Rafe tilted his head. "Keeley will kill us if we show up there."

"Maybe so, but you know she'd want this." Gio paused, then added, "And I want to check the guy out."

There was no way Rafe would argue with either reason for going. The idea of Keeley out on a date with a guy who was basically a stranger, without her phone, bothered him a lot.

"We're just dropping off the phone and leaving," Rafe stressed.

"We'll see," Gio said, more seriously than Rafe expected.

He sighed. "She's gonna kill us if we crash her date," he repeated.

Gio put a friendly hand on his shoulder, his grin firmly back in place. "Think Albert and Marta would share this house with us if she does?"

Rafe didn't reply, too many things fighting for dominance at the moment.

Somehow, the guy who'd never done an impulsive thing in his life had quit his job, taken over a company, hired his friend's little sister—a woman he was more attracted to than he cared to admit —moved into a haunted mansion he was now renovating into an inn, and acquired a roommate.

Those vast changes weren't coming anymore. They'd already arrived.

He wasn't sure, but for a moment, he could almost imagine he heard Grandpa Albert laughing.

Chapter Four

"What the hell are you guys doing here?" Keeley asked before she could stop herself.

She'd met Joel in the lobby of Saloon, and the two had engaged in some polite conversation while they waited for their table. She'd been very relieved when he'd arrived and looked exactly like his picture on Tinder.

She'd gone on dates with a couple guys who'd made liberal use of filters, and one idiot who'd flat-out photoshopped his head on some super-buff body. And, of course, her favorite was the guy who'd used a picture that had to have been him fifteen years earlier, insisting he hadn't lied about his age being twenty-seven.

Yeah, right. That asshole hadn't been a day younger than forty.

Gio held out his hand, revealing her cell phone. "You left this at the mansion."

"The mansion?" Joel asked, clearly surprised by the arrival of two men at their table.

"Joel," Keeley hastened to explain, "this is Gio and Rafe. Rafe's my boss. Apparently, I left my phone at work." She took her phone from Gio. "I didn't realize it wasn't in my purse until I got here. You guys didn't have to bring it to me. I could have swung by tomorrow and grabbed it."

"It was no problem," Rafe said. "We didn't think you should be in the city without it."

Though he was looking at *her*, Rafe's tone could be considered nothing less than a warning to Joel to toe the line.

"Well, I have it now. So…thanks." She hoped they would take the hint and get lost.

Gio was looking at Joel, who was starting to get visibly uncomfortable under the intense scrutiny. Keeley was no stranger to this tactic. God knew she'd watched her brother employ the same with every guy she'd dated during high school.

"Do I know you?" Joel asked Gio after a moment. "You look familiar."

Gio shook his head but didn't offer a verbal reply.

"I could swear…" Joel mused, not bothering to finish his statement.

"Okay." She waved her phone in front of them. "I'm good now. Goodbye," she said firmly, when neither man moved.

Gio's attention returned to her—and the second she saw his wicked grin, she knew she wasn't going to like what came next. "You two have a nice date."

Then he stopped a waitress who was walking by and pointed to the empty table next to hers and Joel's.

He wouldn't.

Shit!

Apparently, he would.

The waitress nodded, and he and Rafe claimed it.

Joel frowned. "That's your boss?" he asked quietly.

Keeley nodded, her blood boiling.

"And the other guy?"

"Just a friend," Keeley replied, glancing in Gio and Rafe's direction, trying to establish eye contact so they could see just how furious she was. Both men pointedly ignored her, looking at the menus, talking quietly.

She wondered if there would ever be a point in her life where her brother and his friends didn't treat her like some helpless child. She'd actually—foolishly—believed perhaps she had turned that corner with at least Gio and Rafe. After their night together in the storm, and this past week at work, she'd felt less like Kayden's kid sister and more like a friend in her own right.

Then there were those brief wonderful moments...

Gio's good-night kiss.

Rafe's near-miss kiss.

Both times, they had looked at her like she was a desirable woman. Those looks ensured her vibrator continued to get one hell of a workout every night. Her fantasies had been quite steamy of late, always starring either Rafe or Gio.

Even now, when she wanted to be totally pissed at them, she couldn't quite work up enough anger because it was overshadowed by the stupid feeling that it was sweet of them to go to such lengths to make sure she was okay.

If it was Kayden sitting at that table, she'd have already blown a gasket, so she wasn't sure why something that felt intrusive from her brother felt...possessively hot from Rafe and Gio.

Was possessively hot even a thing?

She forced her attention back to Joel, determined to ignore the sexy men at the next table.

"I'm sure I know that guy," Joel said again.

Keeley refused to discuss Gio, so she started with her standard get-to-know-you questions. The queen of first dates, she was a professional and had a long list of conversation starters on hand to keep things moving. The list also allowed her to get a pretty clear picture of the guy in just one night.

"So tell me about your job," she said.

Joel, mercifully, forgot about Gio and Rafe at the next table and began talking. He worked in the family business, running a flooring store downtown. It occurred to Keeley that was probably how he knew Gio, but she didn't bother to point it out.

Unlike a lot of her previous dates, Joel was very good at

keeping the conversation two-sided. He asked about her work, stealing a glance or two at the next table when she talked about Rafe hiring her to be his marketing director and how much she was enjoying it. She snuck a peek over as well, watching as Rafe and Gio received their drinks and placed their orders. They were obviously hunkered down for the duration of her date.

"I was really glad we were able to make a connection on Tinder," Joel admitted. "I took one look at your picture and knew I needed to meet you."

She tried to take that as a compliment, but she always hated it when guys confessed to asking her out because of the picture rather than mentioning the profile she'd put together. She was proud of her pros and cons list. If a guy started the date by discussing the list and laughing at the funny stuff she'd included, he got a point. If not...the first red flag.

This time, Keeley let the comment go because it was still early. She'd learned at least twelve dates ago to hand out those red flags judiciously.

From there, they discussed their families. Joel came from a pretty typical family of four, two parents, him, an older sister. His grandparents were still alive, but they lived in other states. She shared a little bit about her parents dying in the plane crash, and her brother stepping in to raise her. Her retelling of that part of her life was always kept simple and told with the same words. She found that helped her keep her emotions under control. She never dove any deeper than just those few facts. And Joel was appropriately compassionate about it.

She noticed that he'd downed three bourbons in the time she'd finished one glass of wine, so he was getting a lot more relaxed and talking more freely, laughing a little louder. She attributed the drinking to nerves and let it go.

By the time their meals arrived, Keeley was almost ready to call the date a success, despite the fact Gio and Rafe were sitting nearby. But there was one last big hurdle to leap.

So she guided them to the past relationships topic. He

managed to say all the right things, claiming he was tired of the dating game, and that he was looking for a woman long-term, with an eye toward marriage and kids.

And she believed him because Joel appeared to have better luck in the long-term relationship department, claiming three past girlfriends whom he'd dated for a year or longer. That was better than she'd done, and that information seemed to prove he wasn't just looking for online hookups.

But then she felt less good about him when he confessed that, ultimately, every single one of the girlfriends dumped him. "For no good reason," he claimed.

Which—fuck it, she was counting the first—was the second red flag.

She was old enough and wise enough that she knew not to tug on that thread...but she did anyway.

"No good reason?"

Joel shrugged. "They were dumb bitches, so no big loss."

This was what she got for tugging. Joel was slowly crossing the line from pleasant company to rude and inebriated the longer they talked. It wasn't a good look on him. At all.

"Yeah, well." She struggled for some way to recoup her losses, but nothing clever came. Instead, she changed the subject because, well, dammit, her steak looked really good, and she was starving. "The online dating game is tough," she threw out lamely, cutting a big bite of steak off and shoving it in her mouth.

"I guess." Joel laughed. "But you know, there are ways to make it easier."

She chewed and swallowed, and then against her better judgment said, "Oh yeah?"

Because karma hated her, Joel managed to screw it up once and for all with his next question.

"Have you ever considered having a boob job?"

"What?"

"My last couple of girlfriends got them and they looked great. Didn't feel fake at all."

"Riiiiight," she drawled, trying to decide if the steak tasted good enough to endure ten more minutes of this so she could shovel it all in. Then she studied the garlic mashed potatoes on her plate. She freaking loved garlic mashed potatoes. "I'm not interested in plastic surgery."

Joel shrugged, then sighed as his gaze drifted down to her tits, clearly unimpressed. "I'm just saying you should look into it. Maybe don't be so quick to dismiss it."

Aaaand now the date was over.

She was going to bed hungry tonight, but not before paying it forward for the next woman. Because Joel needed a little wake-up call.

"Here's a little dating tip for you, Joel. No woman is going to stay with you as long as you keep trying to make her into your ideal. That's a one-way ticket to becoming a skeezy, swaggering, lonely fifty-year-old man that no woman would touch with a ten-foot pole. If you seriously want to get married, get to know a woman and love her for who she is on the inside, not on the outside."

She reached for her purse and pulled out her wallet.

"What are you doing?" he asked.

"Date's over, hotshot. Because you just showed me your inside, and it's butt-fucking ugly."

"Oh God, you're one of those feminists, aren't you? Get pissed off whenever a guy offers a little constructive criticism on your looks."

"I have no idea what feminism has to do with criticism, constructive or otherwise, so let's just leave this with—you can go fuck yourself." Keeley tossed down enough cash to cover her meal. She'd wasted enough time on this dick.

She'd intended to storm out of the restaurant, but at the last second, she picked up her wine glass and carried it over to Rafe and Gio's table, where she sat down, certain there had to be steam coming out of her ears.

"Fucking bitch," she heard Joel mutter behind her, before yelling for the waitress to bring his check.

Gio and Rafe both started to stand, but she gripped their forearms tightly, pressing them flat against the table so they couldn't rise.

"Leave it alone," she murmured.

"If you think for one second—" Gio started angrily.

"Gio. Please," she whispered. Her anger was quickly giving way to depression, and she had to blink rapidly to beat back the angry/sad tears blurring her vision. She was so goddamn tired of this.

Gio settled down and remained in his chair. He plucked her hand from his arm, clasping it instead, and gave it a squeeze. "You okay?"

She nodded but didn't reply. Her throat was too tight. She hated confrontation, and the fact that Rafe and Gio had been there to witness one of her spectacular failures was embarrassing. She probably should have just walked out of the restaurant, gone home, and licked her wounds alone.

"I knew that date wouldn't last long," Gio confessed. "I know that guy from work. He's a grade-A douche and there was no way you weren't going to figure that out quick. It's why we stayed. We didn't want you to go home hungry."

She looked at him in surprise, then she saw an empty, extra plate on the table. He and Rafe both cut off the best pieces of their steaks and added them to the plate, along with two healthy dollops of—thank you, Jesus—garlic mashed potatoes.

Rafe grinned as he put the plate in front of her. "We bought the biggest steaks they had so we could all share."

"And added the garlic mashed potatoes after we heard you order them," Gio added.

Keeley laughed. Her anger and disappointment was gone in an instant. She was too touched by their sweet gesture to feel anything but gratitude. And God...attraction.

She glanced over her shoulder, relieved to see Joel had already paid and left. "He suggested I get a boob job."

Gio scowled, and for a second, she wondered if she should have given Joel a bigger head start. Because Gio looked ready to chase the asshole down.

"You gotta be kidding me!" Rafe said. "What the hell is wrong with that guy? Keeley, you're perfect exactly the way you are, you know that, right?"

She smiled. "Thanks. And believe me, I'm not upset because he said that. I'm more disappointed that, yet again, I managed to land a date with one of the biggest assholes in online dating. My record remains unbeaten. Keeley, zero. Tinder, four hundred and twelve. Why can't I just *once* find a nice guy?"

Rafe put his hand on her shoulder. "There's someone out there for you, Keeley. I really believe that."

Keeley looked from Rafe to Gio, wishing one of them would throw their hat in the ring. Or better yet, both of them.

Although, if they did that, she'd eventually have to make a decision, and there was no way in hell she could choose between Gio and Rafe. So ultimately, it was better that they all just remained friends.

Dammit.

"Yeah. I'd like to believe that, but..."

"Don't get too disheartened," Gio said. "It's a well-documented fact that dating sucks."

"Is that why you guys don't do it very often? I mean...when was the last time you went out with someone?" she asked, suddenly curious about why they were both still single. As an unattached woman in Philadelphia, she knew exactly how slim the pickings were, so it didn't make sense that these two were still flying around footloose and fancy-free.

"It's been a while for me," Rafe replied.

"For me too," Gio admitted.

Keeley considered that for a moment. "You guys are older

than I am. And I don't feel like you're looking at all. Don't you want to get married and settle down someday?"

"I definitely do," Gio said without hesitation. "And I go on dates. Not as many as you. And not with strangers I've talked to online. I prefer to meet women the natural way—in person. Which is a slower process."

"In person how? Because I'm so over Tinder."

Gio grinned at her confusion. "Sometimes I meet a woman at a bar and ask her to dance, or I've met a few women through work...contractors, designers...even clients, though that drives Tony crazy. If I'm attracted to a client, I usually wait until the job is finished before I ask her out, so big brother doesn't have a coronary."

"Seems to me you're missing out on a great opportunity. What are brothers for if not to drive them insane?" Keeley asked with a shameless wink.

"Poor Kayden." Gio accompanied those words with a quick tug of her hair. Her cheeks flushed pink, and for a second, she let herself envision him wrapping his fist around her hair and pulling it in a much more sexual way.

The vibrator wasn't cutting it anymore. She needed sex with a real person, preferably one of the men at the table with her.

"I've had quite a few long-term relationships," Gio added.

"What do you consider long-term?" Keeley asked.

Gio smirked, as if he'd just realized his previous comment was false. "Six to ten months."

"Nobody made it a year?"

Gio shrugged. "Maybe a couple girls when I was in my early to mid-twenties. No one has lasted that long lately. So I guess I'm in the same boat as you," Gio admitted. "I've watched Layla and Tony settle down with their partners, and it definitely looks nice. I wouldn't mind finding what they've got."

Keeley's eyes twinkled with mischief. "What they've both got are committed threesomes. Are you planning on going that route?"

Gio shrugged. "I wouldn't say it's off the table."

Keeley appeared to be the only person taken aback by that confession because Rafe didn't blink twice. "Really?"

"If the situation presented itself, sure. Why not?" Gio's gaze connected with Rafe's. Keeley felt like there was some sort of silent communication passing between them with that look, but she didn't have a clue what.

"I have to admit, what they have looks amazing," Keeley admitted wistfully. "But sweet Jesus," she added. "At this point, I'd be happy to find just one guy I'd like to go on a second date with."

"True," Gio agreed. "It's hard finding the person you want to spend forever with, but we're going to get there. I'm looking forward to finding a woman, settling down, having a pile of kids."

Keeley laughed. "What's a pile?"

"At least four, maybe five like my parents had."

Rafe shuddered and mumbled, "Jesus."

"So what about you?" Keeley asked him.

Rafe was slower to respond. "Marriage isn't in the cards for me."

"Seriously?" she asked, shocked by the utter assurance in Rafe's voice.

"Seriously," he replied.

"Why not?"

He rubbed his jaw as he considered his answer. Finally, he said, "I didn't grow up in the greatest environment."

Keeley held her breath, wondering if Rafe would go into more detail. Every time she thought he was getting close to opening up, he shut right back down again. His childhood was something Rafe rarely discussed. The night of the storm was the first glimpse he'd ever really given into his family life. He'd always played his cards close to his chest when it came to talking about himself.

"What do you mean?" Keeley pressed.

Rafe shrugged, and Keeley recognized the exact instant he regretted starting the subject at all.

"You know how it is. Sperm-donor dad wanted nothing to do with me, which led to a revolving door of men in my mom's life. She's married and divorced four so far. Husband number five is no prize, and I have a feeling that relationship is close to running its course as well. Watching my mom try to pick up the pieces after all those broken marriages has soured me on the institution."

Keeley leaned forward. "Just on marriage? What about love?"

Rafe shook his head. "No. It's turned me off the concept of love too."

"You mean you've *never* been in love?" she asked.

Rafe snorted. "Nope. Not interested. Love comes with too much fucking baggage."

"You don't really believe that," she argued.

"Of course I do. Look how many times my mom's fallen in love and been hurt. Her heart has the scars to show for it. I'm not interested in opening myself up to that kind of pain after the feeling fades. And believe me—it always fades."

"No, it doesn't," Keeley insisted.

"Yes. It does."

Keeley had long suspected Rafe's disinterest in relationships was driven by his mother's failed marriages, but she'd had no idea just how deep-seated his beliefs were.

Of all her brother's friends, Rafe was the one who dated the least. He was always too busy with work, or, as was the case this past year, spending time with his grandfather. Now he was trying to sort out his estate.

It made her sad to think that Rafe had closed himself down to the concept of love and marriage. "I hope you change your mind about that," Keeley said quietly.

"Why?" Rafe asked.

"Because love with the right person is amazing. No baggage at all."

Rafe was unconvinced. "How do you know that? You said yourself you've never been in a serious relationship."

"Because I saw what my mom and dad had. It was true love, plain and simple. And it was perfect."

Gio reached over and grasped Keeley's hand. "It *was* perfect."

She smiled. "Besides, I think you'd be an incredible husband and father, Rafe."

Rafe stared at Keeley, and she could almost see him trying to process her comment.

"I'm with Keeley on this," Gio added. "You would be."

"I appreciate the sentiment," Rafe said, after a few moments. "But that's a big *hell no* for me. Besides, I've got a lot on my plate right now. Miles to go with Grandpa's estate. I wouldn't have time for a relationship, even if I wanted one. Which...I don't," he reiterated.

There it was. The classic Rafe Baros side step. Her new boss was a master of excuses, always able to dodge a discussion about himself and his future by blaming his past and present.

And while Keeley was disconcerted to learn all of this about him, it ultimately didn't matter. Didn't help her beat down her growing feelings for him...feelings that were destined to remain unrequited because she was Kayden's little sister. And because Rafe didn't believe in love.

She let the subject drop, and the rest of the night passed with easy conversation as they discussed Gio and Rafe's plans to make her suggestion a reality by opening an inn. By the time they'd paid the bill and walked outside, Keeley had decided it was the best "date" she'd been on in ages.

If only it *had* been a date.

Now, like last week, Rafe and Gio walked her to her car. Rafe drew her into his warm embrace, giving her one of his signature amazing hugs. She pressed her cheeks to his chest and sucked in a deep breath, drawing in the smells she'd come to associate with him—sandalwood, bourbon, his Armani cologne.

When he released her, Gio was there.

She expected him to hug her as well, but instead, he gripped her shoulders and leaned in, his breath hot on her face. "I know you like good-night kisses. But you gotta remember, this doesn't mean anything," he whispered.

She was ready for him this time. He pressed his lips to hers, gently at first, then he added more force. Last week's kiss had been exploration and fondness. This one felt...different. Gio didn't seek as much as he claimed. It was like he'd gotten the lay of the land, and now he knew exactly where to go. She fought desperately to keep her hands by her side, aware that if she reached out to touch him, she'd never let go.

The crazy part was, as blown away as she felt by Gio's sexy kiss, she was constantly aware of Rafe's close presence, of the intense way he watched them, not even feigning to turn his attention elsewhere. In some ways, it felt like he was as much a part of the kiss as Gio.

Gio was the first to pull away, and she let herself pretend he looked reluctant to do so.

She dug deep for an easy, breezy smile, not wanting him to know the impact his kisses were having on her. Because she wanted more, and if all she had to do to get them was pretend they meant nothing, then that was a game she was willing to play, a price she was ready to pay.

"Good night," she said, cursing the breathlessness of her tone.

"Good night." Gio's voice was husky and deep.

Rafe reached out and ran the back of his knuckles along her cheek. "Drive home safely."

She nodded and got in her car, resisting the urge to turn back to look at them before driving away.

Now that Gio had planted the seed about wanting what his siblings Layla and Tony had, she wasn't looking at Rafe and Gio as separate crushes anymore.

There was no either-or in her mind.

From now on, her fantasies would include both of them.

At the same time.

Chapter Five

Gio took a swig of his beer, aware that the smile hadn't slid off his face pretty much since he and Rafe had decided to become roommates and business partners. They'd hashed out the particulars with a lawyer this morning and once the contract was written, they would sign. He'd been chomping at the bit to begin work, something Rafe had noticed. Since the deal was as good as made, they'd decided to just go ahead and get started. Gio had given his landlord notice.

He'd already spent the past two weeks sorting through his stuff—even though Rafe gave him shit for putting the horse before the cart. Since they were moving forward, now all he had to do was decide what to take to the mansion, what to pitch, what to sell, and what to move into storage.

"Everything ready for the move next weekend?" Rafe asked, absentmindedly petting Cricket, who was dozing on his lap.

"Yep. I've recruited the guys, who've all agreed to the standard arrangement. Beer, pizza, and strained muscles."

"Maybe we should make a full weekend of it, and they can help me clear some shit out my townhouse as well," Rafe said. "I'm trying to decide if I want to put it on the market or rent it out. No point in it sitting empty, since we'll be living in the haunted mansion for God only knows how long."

"You might sell it?"

Rafe shrugged. "I've gotten kind of used to living away from the hubbub of the city, and I'm not looking forward to dealing with my loud neighbors again. I swear to God I could hear every single one of their fights through the wall connecting our townhouses. I've gotten spoiled by the quiet of this place. There's a caretaker's cottage behind the mansion. I've been thinking that maybe I'll move in there once the inn is ready to open. Or fuck it, I might just buy a proper house with a bit of land. I've got some money to play with these days," he said with a wink.

"You've got a lot of money to play with, you rich bastard. And a new, practical-sized house sounds nice. Of course, we might have to spring for a few buckets of chicken too, if we try to talk the guys into moving two houses' worth of shit," Gio said.

Gio and Rafe had helped pretty much every other guy in their group of friends move into their current homes—always paid in beer and pizza—but they'd never done a two-fer. This house of Rafe's grandpa had been cold and dark for too long, and he was looking forward to bringing a little life to the place.

While he knew it was just a temporary living situation for both of them, Gio couldn't help but shake the idea that this change was just the start of many. He was pushing thirty-three, and lately, he'd been starting to feel like he had fuck-all to show for his life. He was committed to the family business and proud of all they'd accomplished, but there was a large part of him that still longed for something more, something that was his own. Taking on the mansion renovation project and investing in a new business fueled his creative juices and got his blood pumping.

But he was hoping to change more than just the professional front. His personal life needed a kick in the ass as well.

Keeley's comment about never having a long-term boyfriend had resonated with him. Probably because he hadn't broken her four-month streak by much. As he'd confessed, most of his relationships petered out somewhere between the six- to ten-month range, his last ending a few months ago.

He glanced to the other side of the couch and forced himself to acknowledge why the last few relationships had failed. It was because of Rafe.

Because of Gio's desire to find not only the perfect woman for himself but also the perfect one for *them*.

It was a fool's errand because the older they got, the more Gio had come to realize that Rafe was serious about never marrying. He'd watched Rafe walk away from too many women who'd wanted commitments over the years, his emotions never once engaged. Rafe had previously confessed that he didn't believe himself capable of feeling love, something Gio had dismissed at the time, but now he feared it might be true.

Maybe it was time for Gio to give up the dream and strike out on his own.

Rafe clicked the remote, scrolling for something to watch but finding nothing. They'd settled on the couch a half hour earlier with their beers and planned to order Chinese delivery later.

"What the hell is the deal in this room?" Gio asked. "It's colder than a witch's tit in here."

Rafe shrugged. "I have no idea. Sometimes it's hot, sometimes it's freezing. I've checked the windows and they're airtight. Nothing to explain the change in temperature."

"I'm surprised we can't see our breath."

"Blame Albert and Marta." Rafe tried to brush it off as a joke, but Gio suspected his friend now truly believed the house was inhabited by the spirits of his grandparents. Even Gio had to admit it was hard *not* to. He didn't even live here yet, but in the last couple weeks, he'd witnessed enough to convince him. Doors slamming, footsteps in empty rooms, the cold drafts in window-less areas.

The funny part was, the ghosts seemed most attracted to Keeley, though none of them could decide if it was a good or bad fascination. Regardless, it was *her* things constantly getting moved around. Pens and folders from her table kept finding their way to Rafe's desk. One day, the jacket she swore she'd hung up on the coatrack was discovered on the couch. And Keeley still insisted that her phone had been in her purse when she'd left for her date with Joel a couple weeks earlier.

They also seemed to get a kick out of pushing her—or so Keeley said. He and Rafe were still convinced she was just clumsy and tripping over the rugs, and Rafe had started teasing her that she needed to learn how to pick her feet up when she walked.

Gio rubbed his hands together, seeking warmth. "We're going to have to start leaving a stack of blankets in here if they insist on playing this way."

Rafe snorted but didn't disagree, turning his attention back to the TV in search of a hockey game or movie they could watch. Maybe they should consider going out. Gio wasn't in the mood to shiver all freaking evening.

They'd invited Keeley to stay in with them tonight, but she had yet another date courtesy of Tinder. Gio wished she would get off the damn dating apps once and for all.

Rafe had asked her where she was going, but unfortunately, this time she'd gotten wise to them, resolutely refusing to tell them where the guy was taking her.

"Think we should have insisted that she tell us where she was going? Doesn't seem safe for a young woman to go out with a man she doesn't know and not tell *someone* where she's going to be," Gio said.

"I said that to her," Rafe replied, not in the least surprised by Gio's abrupt topic change. "She assured me that Kayden had her location on Find My Friends, plus Liza and Gianna both know the guy's name and where she'll be. She's not reckless, Gio."

"Yeah," he grumped, not feeling much better. He knew Keeley was smart enough not to put herself in dangerous situations, but that still left him on the outside tonight, unable to step in if she needed him...and that was starting to rub against the grain in a way he couldn't quite explain.

"Besides, we already crashed one date. There's no way we'd get away with pulling that again."

"And you're okay with not knowing where she is or if she's safe."

"Truthfully? Not even a little bit. But I'm better at keeping my inner caveman under control." Rafe gave him a shit-eating grin. "Damn if she doesn't have a knack for picking the wrong guy though."

"Tell me about it. It took everything I had not to drag her out of Saloon when I saw her sitting with Joel. The guy is a total prick. I told Tony what he said to Keeley, and we've taken his family's store off our vendor list. They're not getting another penny from Moretti Restorations."

Rafe's grin widened. "I like the way you get revenge."

"Still would have preferred to teach the guy a lesson the old-fashioned way, but Keeley needed us with her more. I didn't like how sad she looked. Not used to seeing her without a smile on her face."

"Same. But at least our girl has enough self-esteem not to let his cruelty stick."

Gio nodded, though he wasn't agreeing with Rafe's assessment of Keeley, so much as the word *our*.

Unfortunately, Gio was sure Rafe wasn't using it the way he was starting to hope they could.

"Our girl?" he asked anyway.

Rafe looked over at him and sighed. "No," he corrected. "Not ours. Slip of the tongue. Don't go there."

Gio considered contradicting that statement, but he held his peace instead.

He hadn't meant to be quite so forthright with Keeley about his thoughts regarding a threesome relationship. His sex life— well, his and Rafe's sex life—was something they protected fiercely. No one in his family or in their circle of friends knew just how close he and Rafe *really* were.

Several years ago, his sister, Layla, had traveled from Baltimore to Philly with her new partners in tow. He and Rafe had gone to dinner with her, Miguel, and Finn. Afterwards, he and Rafe had gotten into a long, frank discussion about ménages. They both expressed an interest in participating in one. So...they did.

Jennifer Rodriguez, a woman from Rafe's workplace, had been putting out signals that she was attracted to him. He'd invited her to join him and Gio for happy hour, just to test the waters. Their desire for a ménage had come up after a few pitchers of beer, and they'd both been shocked when Jennifer agreed to try it with them.

It had been...incredible. Eye-opening. Life-changing for Gio.

They'd embarked on a month-long sex-fest, the three of them insatiable.

Things changed when Jennifer's interest drifted away from the "just sex" range. Gio had been ready to make the leap into a committed threesome. Rafe had not. So Rafe stepped away, and Gio and Jennifer had continued dating for six months before the bloom was off the rose and the relationship ended.

They'd repeated that same pattern two more times, always the same thing. The ménage sex would be awesome, but the moment the woman caught feelings, Rafe would back away, leaving Gio in the exclusive relationship. Rafe always insisted Gio needed to give the woman a chance at a true relationship—one not based merely on sex—since he was the one looking for a wife.

Their last shared affair had been with an ex-girlfriend of Gio's from high school, Jill Patrick. After Rafe bowed out, Gio had dated Jill for close to four months before remembering why they'd broken up back in high school. Since then, neither of them had dated anyone.

Gio had replayed the night with Keeley after her failed date with Joel countless times over the past two weeks, imagining himself and Rafe taking her out...taking her together. If it had been any other woman, he would have already made the suggestion to Rafe. But Gio wasn't sure he could put himself through another threesome if his friend was just going to walk away again, and—most importantly—it was Keeley. There was too much at stake if things went south, and he wasn't just thinking about his friendship with Kayden anymore. He was thinking about losing his friendship with *her*.

Although...the more time he spent with her, the more he realized she could be the perfect woman for him.

Maybe even for them.

He pushed that last thought away. Rafe had made his feelings regarding love and marriage very—VERY—clear. And he'd seen firsthand how quickly Rafe withdrew the moment women wanted more. He didn't want Keeley to suffer the same rejection if it came to that.

Rafe took another drink of beer, and Gio thought his friend had managed to let his concern for Keeley go. Until he said, "You know, if this was a month ago, we wouldn't even know Keeley was on a date."

Gio grimaced. "Are you trying to tell me ignorance is bliss?"

"Maybe."

Rafe had a point. Neither of them was used to spending so much time with Keeley or knowing so many intimate details about her life. Prior to her working with Rafe, they only saw each other at occasional social outings, always surrounded by a bunch of other people.

Since she'd returned home from college—boisterous, funny, beautiful—Gio had taken more notice of her than he cared to admit. But he'd always managed to keep the attraction at bay, simply by recalling Kayden was his friend. And while there was no actual bro-code—contrary to what Keeley thought—he still wasn't sure how his friend would feel about him asking her out.

In the past few weeks, Gio had seen her nearly every single day, and he'd become way too interested in her comings and goings. The possessiveness he'd felt the night of the storm had already tripled, making it hard for him to concentrate on anything that wasn't...her.

"We could ask Kayden to check her location on Find My

Friends for us. We'd have the information in one quick text," Gio mused.

"You're not going to let this go, are you?"

Gio snorted. "I think you know me well enough to answer that yourself."

The fact that Rafe sat up—Cricket grumpily jumping to the floor after being jostled—and grabbed his phone from the coffee table told Gio his friend wasn't as casual about Keeley's date as he pretended.

"What the hell am I supposed to say?" Rafe pondered after pulling up Kayden's contact info.

"Let's play on the last date's excuse. Tell him she left her wallet here, and we want to take it to her on our way out to grab some dinner."

"Sticking with a classic, I see," Rafe joked, even as he texted the request. Before hitting send, he asked, "What if he asks why we didn't just text her ourselves?"

Gio considered that. "Tell him we knew she would tell us she didn't need it, but we don't think she should be out without her ID and credit cards."

"Preying on her brother's insecurities. Nice."

Gio chuckled. "Just text him."

They waited a few seconds, and Kayden responded.

Founding Fathers. And thanks for looking out for her.

Gio rose. "You know, I've been craving those cheesesteaks ever since we talked about them. What do you say we move our happy hour over there? It's too cold here."

Rafe rose a bit reluctantly. "I still don't think this is a good idea."

"So noted." Gio didn't let that fact stop him, though, and mercifully, Rafe let him off the hook, offering to drive.

They walked to the car and Gio kicked back in the passenger seat.

When Rafe turned onto the highway, he broke the silence that had fallen between them. "You know, Keeley said if this date failed, she was coming off of Tinder for a while."

"Well, that's good, at least," Gio said.

Rafe shook his head. "Not really. I've seen one of the waiters from Eclectic chatting her up every time she spends the day working out of that office."

Gio scowled. "Who's the guy?"

Rafe shrugged, changing lanes. "Fuck if I know. I put everything on hold when Grandpa was dying, and since then, I've felt like a hamster in a wheel, spinning and spinning and getting nowhere. Of course, with Keeley's help, it's been getting a little bit better each day. I'm seeing some light at the end of the tunnel. But as far as learning the names and stories of all the employees...I got nothing," Rafe added after a brief pause.

"Maybe you should check him out."

Rafe turned to look at him, but he didn't call him out or question his intentions. Which was good because Gio didn't have a clue what he was doing in regard to Keeley.

He'd lost control of the narrative somewhere between the first and second kisses.

"You haven't dated anyone since Jill." And so it began. Rafe was going on a fishing expedition.

"You haven't either."

"I wasn't dating her," Rafe correcting. "She and I were just hooking up, exploring a kink together."

Gio nodded, uncertain where his friend was going with this. He decided to be patient and let it play out.

"I'm just kind of curious why you haven't been dating anyone," Rafe pressed.

"I haven't met anyone I'm interested in asking."

"You told Keeley you wanted a threesome relationship," Rafe pointed out.

"Not exactly," Gio corrected. "I said I wouldn't rule one out."

"You were skirting pretty close to something we've never shared with any of our friends before."

Gio wondered if Rafe was pissed off about that. "I didn't mention our affairs. Rafe, what we did...with Jennifer and Vanessa and Jill...I liked it. A lot."

"So did I. But, Gio, it was just sex for me. I'm not going to be a permanent part of any equation you cook up. I know you want what Tony and Layla have, but I'm not your guy. You know that, right?"

Gio sighed. Sadly, he did. So he decided, for Rafe's sake, to take the pressure off.

"I know that. And like I said, I'm not actively seeking a committed threesome. I know what we do is just sex. I'd be very happy to settle down in a monogamous marriage with the right woman."

He was glad Rafe had brought up this subject because some things had been rattling around in the back of his head since his breakup with Jill. With Rafe's grandpa dying, it had never felt like the right time to bring it up.

Now, well, Gio was about to prove that no one had ever accused him of being too bright.

Impulsive—yes.

The type to follow his gut over common sense—yes.

But bright—nope. Not once.

And he was about to demonstrate that again. "And I get what you're saying about not wanting a relationship. I know how you feel about love and marriage and that you're not going to change your mind. It's just that lately, I want...I want us to do it again. I haven't gotten my fill of," Gio forced himself to use Rafe's word for it, even though it felt wrong, "that kink yet."

Rafe fell silent, but Gio didn't press him for an answer. He never spoke without thinking, a skill Gio should probably try to learn from him.

"Did you have someone in mind?" he asked at last.

Gio rubbed his jaw, then looked at his best friend, debating whether or not it would be wise to let the desires he'd only managed to half hide come out completely. "Maybe I do."

"She's different, Gio," Rafe said—and he realized they were on the exact same page when it came to Keeley.

"I know that," he was quick to reply.

Rafe looked at him for a second. "I'm not sure you do."

Gio wasn't sure how to respond. Because he knew exactly how Keeley was different. She wasn't some woman they'd picked up at a bar. She was Kayden's sister and a friend in her own right. There was a hell of a lot more to lose if things didn't work out.

But if they did...Gio could see the future he'd always dreamed about, but never imagined finding, becoming a reality.

Rafe misinterpreted his silence, so he went on, trying to convince Gio. "When we share a woman...the sex is great, hot. The problem is when we *keep* doing it. There seems to be a natural progression in these affairs, and I can't take that next leap. Not even with Keeley. I'm not looking for a relationship. Love and commitment and all that shit just aren't in my genetic makeup. You know that."

"Bullshit," Gio said. "It's not that you *can't* take that next leap. It's that you've just never wanted to."

"Same difference."

Gio shook his head. "Not even close."

Rafe shrugged casually, which proved just how often they'd had this same fight. Every time Rafe pulled away from the women they shared, Gio fought to keep him in. Always to no avail.

After Jill, Gio started to believe the relationships he'd continued without his best friend were destined to fail because Gio wanted Rafe there...for the whole shebang. The sex, the love, the forever.

Which wouldn't bode well for either of their futures.

Keeley *was* different. Rafe was right about that. He just didn't understand how.

Because Gio's future wasn't looking quite as bleak or as lonely as it had a few weeks earlier.

If Rafe continued to push back against this idea, Gio would

go it alone, asking Keeley out and attempting to make a real, lasting relationship with her.

"We're here," Rafe said, dropping the conversation completely.

Gio considered continuing it, but he decided to leave it alone for now.

"What's our play?" Rafe asked as they got out of the car. "I'm sort of new to this date-crashers gig of ours."

Gio forced a laugh. "Let's wing it."

Rafe nodded but then gripped his arm, holding him back just before they reached the door. "Don't kiss Keeley again."

Gio thought he'd gotten a bye, but he'd been wrong. "What?"

"I don't think..." Rafe swallowed heavily. "I don't think it's smart."

Gio wanted to refute that fact, wanted to say it was starting to feel like the smartest thing he'd done in a long time, but there was something in Rafe's eyes that caused him to hold back.

"Because of Kayden?" Gio asked, though he was certain Keeley's brother had nothing to do with his friend's reticence.

"Just...don't do it again." Rafe walked on, while Gio stood there a moment longer, pondering what he'd just witnessed.

Rafe was usually very good at shielding his emotions, but not this time. Because Gio could plainly see he wasn't the only one suffering a bad case of desire for one Ms. Keeley Gallo.

However, while Gio was open to acting on his attraction, Rafe was fighting it with everything he had.

As soon as they entered the bar, they spotted Keeley, sitting alone at a table near the makeshift stage. The crowd around the bar was gearing up to watch tonight's hockey game on the big-screen TV.

They paused for a moment, unseen by her. Gio glanced around the bar.

"Think her date is in the restroom?" Rafe mused.

Gio looked back at the table and shook his head. "No. There's only one drink on the table. Come on. I don't like this."

They walked toward her, Keeley's eyes widening when she saw them. "Oh my God. What are you doing here? Is this going to become a thing?"

Gio pulled out a chair, sitting without an invitation. "Date over already?"

Keeley sighed. "It never started. Asshole stood me up."

Gio shook his head. "Keeley—"

She raised her hand. "Don't start. I already know what you're going to say."

Rafe reached over and placed his hand atop hers. "I'm sorry it didn't go the way you hoped. Did he text you at least, offer an explanation?"

She shook her head. "No. I've been here forty-five minutes. I texted him fifteen minutes ago. I can see that he's read the message, but he hasn't replied. He's ghosting me for some reason."

"Good riddance." Gio grinned, though he suspected that probably wasn't the right response. Regardless, there was no denying his mood had just gone from concerned over Keeley and annoyed at Rafe, to downright happy to be alone with the two of them in one-point-two seconds.

Something Rafe definitely took note of, given his pensive, somewhat anxious expression.

Keeley, thankfully, remained oblivious to the undercurrents at the table, finishing her glass of wine and not looking too terribly upset.

Gio sighed, wondering again if he was a fool for wanting this. Because there was too much to lose.

She was Keeley, Kayden's little sister, and a friend.

Rafe was his best friend, and soon-to-be business partner and roommate.

Adding anything else to either mix would be reckless and dangerous.

And even as that thought came, he knew if the opportunity

presented itself, he *was* going to be reckless and dangerous. He blamed his Moretti genes.

"To be honest," Keeley said, "it was probably one of my better dates. The conversation hasn't been awkward, he's obviously not hard to look at, and since you owe me for crashing another date, you're now buying my drink." She laughed at her own joke. "And food. How about a plate of wings?"

Rafe shook his head. "We came for cheesesteaks."

Keeley seemed to like that idea better. She raised her hand for the waiter. "Never mind on the check," she said. "We'd like to order food."

"Of course," the waiter said. "Let me grab you some menus. Would you like drinks?" he asked Rafe and Gio.

"A pitcher of Yuengling," Gio said, looking at Keeley's empty wineglass. "And three frosty mugs."

"You got it."

The waiter left to get their drinks and menus.

"You sure you're okay?" Rafe asked again.

"In case you guys haven't noticed, none of my dates end well. This is pretty much par for the course."

"I *have* noticed," Rafe said. "Maybe you should give Tinder a rest for a little while."

"Oh, totally," Keeley agreed. "I'm going to take a page from Gio's book."

Gio frowned. "What's that mean?"

Keeley leaned her elbows on the table, shifting closer to Rafe, giving him an adorable, playful grin. "How do you feel about dating amongst employees at Baros Corporation?"

Was Keeley coming on to Rafe?

Rafe was silent for a moment, no doubt letting her words sink in. Gio sat there, as dumbfounded as his friend, expecting some ugly emotion to appear.

Shouldn't he be jealous? Upset that she was expressing interest in Rafe?

Gio waited. And...nothing. It felt like all the common sense in the world wasn't going to help him stop his wayward, wicked thoughts. Because the truth was, he wanted Keeley, and he wanted Rafe there too, for as long as he was willing to stay.

Kayden was going to kick his ass.

Before Rafe could reply to her question, the waiter arrived with their beer and the menus, even though they all knew what they wanted.

"I'll take a Philly cheesesteak and fries," Rafe ordered, looking around the table.

Keeley and Gio both said, "Same," and the waiter left to place their order in the kitchen.

"What do you mean about employees dating?" Rafe finally asked.

"Chad asked me out," she confessed.

"Who the fuck is Chad?" Gio blurted out, louder than he'd intended.

Keeley leaned back, surprised by his outburst. "He's a waiter at Eclectic."

Gio had forgotten about the guy at the nightclub. He shot Rafe a glance, and he could see his friend grappling for an answer. Keeley had given him the perfect opportunity to put the kibosh on her dating Chad—he just had to say no company hanky-panky —but Rafe was too fucking nice to take it. More than that, he probably saw this as a way of keeping Gio, and maybe himself, away from her.

"Do you *want* to go out with him?" Rafe asked.

Keeley shrugged. "We've talked a few times, and he seems like a nice guy. At least I wouldn't be going into the date blind. We've met in person and he's cute. So...yeah, I guess."

Rafe nodded. "Okay. Fine. I don't see a problem with that." And while his friend's words seemed reasonable and calm, Gio couldn't help but get the sense Rafe wasn't as unaffected by Keeley's request as he was acting.

Gio was long overdue for a couple of heart-to-hearts—first with the man in the mirror, and then with Rafe. Because he could feel a shift not only in himself but in his friend as well. And Keeley was at the center of it.

He considered Kayden yet again and blew out a long, slow breath, trying to figure where the hell he was supposed to go from here. Because if he continued to pursue this, there was a chance it wouldn't be just one of Kayden's buddies taking his sister to bed. It would be two.

He put those thoughts away for now because they were a million miles from that possibility becoming a reality. Rafe wasn't on board...yet.

So tonight, they were just three friends hanging out.

"Hey, I've got an idea," Keeley started. "Now that you guys are going to be roommates and renovating the haunted mansion, I think it would be cool to film you working on it."

"Film it? Why?" Rafe asked.

"Think about it. I capture some video as you two are working, you can talk about the ghosts, the history of the mansion, the renovation work. It would be great marketing for the inn. Amazing promotion. I can almost guarantee if the videos take off, the inn would be booked out for months before it even opens." Then, because she was Keeley and too adorable for words, she added, "And if you take off your shirts when you're hot and sweaty, I can also guarantee women will be lining the block to spend a night or two with you...I mean, with your ghosts."

Gio scoffed. "I'll leave the TV star shit to Joey. He loves being the center of attention, mugging for the camera and all that crap."

"I'm being serious about this. I've given it some thought, and I really do think it would be a great way to promote the inn. I mean, you obviously want the business to be a success, right?"

"Of course we do," Rafe said, "But—"

"Don't say no yet. Just promise you'll think about it. Or better yet, I'll get some raw footage when you start working. I'll put it together, you can watch it, and you can make your decision then. After you see what I have in mind, you'll know I'm right."

One look at Keeley's face, and Gio knew they hadn't heard

the last about this. Regardless, he was determined to keep his answer a no.

But before he could say that, Rafe answered for them. "We'll think about it."

She smiled brightly. So brightly, Gio realized there was a good chance he'd get roped into this just because she wanted to do it so badly. Then he considered the perks. With her doing the recording, he'd get to spend even more time with her.

Gio sighed, then caught sight of someone approaching them in his peripheral vision. From the sudden resigned look on Rafe's face, he knew it wasn't someone he wanted to see.

"Hey, Gio, Rafe."

Gio pasted a fake smile on his face as he turned to greet Jill.

Jill was a pleasant enough woman, but once she got her hooks in a man, she was relentless. He'd had to block her number two weeks after their breakup because she kept blowing his phone up with calls and texts.

That had been his reason for dumping her in high school, which—like an idiot—he'd forgotten. He'd tried to console himself with the fact it *had* been fifteen years, and there'd been a chance she had changed. She hadn't. If anything, she'd gotten worse.

"Jill," Rafe said with a single nod.

"It's so great to see you both. I was sorry to hear about your grandpa," she said to Rafe.

He acknowledged the kind words. "Thank you."

"I haven't heard from you in a while." Jill was looking pointedly at Gio, who didn't have a clue why she thought she would. He'd told her the relationship was over, and when she suggested they be friends, he assured her the best thing was that they not see each other anymore.

"I told you that you wouldn't," Gio said, trying for gentle, but managing nothing better than an annoyed growl.

Then Jill finally noticed Keeley at the table. "Oh. I'm sorry. Are you guys on a date?"

Gio didn't respond because that question might lead to a conversation that revealed more than Keeley knew. Time to end the interaction now before Jill said anything more. "It was good to see you, Jill. Have a nice night," he said dismissively.

For once, she got the message, walking away without putting up a fuss.

Keeley's brow was creased in confusion. "You dated her, right?" she asked Gio.

He nodded.

"And you broke it off?"

"Yes," Gio replied. "A few months ago."

"Why would she think we were all on a date? Who goes on a date with their best friend?"

Gio tried to brush off the question. "Probably a slip of the tongue."

He should have known better than to try something that lame with Keeley. She was too smart. "I don't think it was," she mused.

"Leave it alone, Kiwi," Rafe warned, which was the equivalent to waving a red flag in front of her.

"Did *you* date her?" she asked Rafe.

He shook his head. Rafe wasn't lying. He hadn't dated her.

But...Keeley wasn't backing down. "Did you sleep with her?"

Rafe held her gaze for a long time, and Gio could see him debating his response. Finally, he gave her the truth. "Yes."

"At the same time as Gio." It wasn't a question.

Rafe sighed. "What part of 'leave it alone' are you struggling with?"

Keeley grinned, then turned her head, putting Gio on the hot seat. "Were you both sleeping with her *literally* at the same time?"

Gio nodded, despite the daggers Rafe's gaze lobbed in his direction.

"So that threesome thing you mentioned wanting wasn't hypothetical. You've actually gone there, done it."

"It was just sex," Rafe explained, jumping in quickly. His

friend clearly wanted to spin things his way. "The two of us were exploring a kink. It was nothing more than that."

"Is Jill the only woman you've ever shared?" she asked.

Gio shook his head, but Rafe had reached his limit on explanations.

"This conversation is over," he stressed.

Studying Rafe's face, Keeley finally nodded and let it go, clearly not willing to upset him.

But Gio knew she'd be back with more questions later. He could practically see them swarming in her mind.

The next two hours passed in laughter as they devoured their cheesesteaks, watching Elio play hockey on the big-screen TVs hanging from nearly every wall.

Once the game ended, they walked out together. Keeley had taken an Uber to the bar, so Rafe—their DD—offered to drive her home. They discussed the game the entire way to her place. Keeley was as avid a hockey fan as they were—maybe more.

Of course, that wasn't exactly surprising. All of his friends, brothers, and cousins were die-hard hockey fans, or more accurately, hard-core Philly fans. The sport didn't matter. Most of them played either high school hockey or football throughout their teens.

When Kayden moved back into his family home after his parents' deaths, he'd hosted a weekly hockey night for their big group of guys. Keeley was always there, sitting on the floor, yelling at the players, the goalies, the refs, and the coaches as much as they did. She'd grown up hanging out with them. Probably a lot more than most kid sisters. But that was to be expected.

After all, Kayden was overprotective to a fault, so she spent way too many of her teen years being dragged along to Eagles— let's go birds!—games and poker nights, so he could keep an eye on her. And he'd been right to do so.

Liza had once compared her to a preacher's kid, the type of teenager who constantly chomped at the bit. Keeley had a bit of a wild side, so she hadn't made things easy on her brother when she was in high school. She was a social butterfly at heart, something her parents had found easier to accept than Kayden, who'd enforced strict curfews. As such, she'd snuck out of the house at night to go to parties, and had invited boyfriends over when Kayden worked the night shift, even though he'd forbidden her to have boys in the house when he wasn't home.

Gio used to laugh whenever Kayden shared Keeley's crazy exploits, but now, he looked back on those stories and sympathized with her brother.

"Okay, here we are." Rafe pulled up to the curb and turned off the car.

"Well, I have to say my horoscope was right on today," she said before getting out.

"Oh yeah?" Gio prompted.

"It said, interesting news and stimulating conversations were coming my way. Nailed it."

Gio chuckled. Rafe did not.

Keeley climbed out of the back seat, surprised when he and Rafe got out as well. Rafe came around the car and stood next to Gio on the curb...making him curious. Rafe had warned him not to kiss Keeley again, so had he gotten out of the car as a way to reinforce his request?

"You don't have to walk in with me," she said. "There's a security code on the door to the building."

Gio knew that. Knew that was one of the requirements Kayden had laid down when his sister said she was moving out after college. It had taken Keeley a few months longer than she'd wanted, trying to find a place in a safe neighborhood that she could afford, that checked off all of Kayden's boxes.

Rafe leaned against the car. "We'll just watch until you get inside."

"Cool." However, Keeley didn't turn to leave. Instead, she just stood there.

"Is something wrong?" Rafe asked.

"Where's my good-night kiss?" she demanded.

"Did your horoscope predict that too?" Gio asked, hedging. He'd decided Rafe was smart to issue the warning, that he'd be wiser to hold back until he figured out how to proceed with Keeley. It was those first two kisses that now had his emotions in turmoil.

"Keeley," Rafe said, in the same tone he'd used a thousand times, whenever she flirted with them. It was the perfect blend of patience and exasperation, something only Rafe could pull off.

Keeley was a quick learner, so she hastened to say, "It's just a kiss. It doesn't mean anything."

Gio snorted. "You're getting spoiled."

She gave him a haughty look. "The kisses aren't *that* great, Gio," she teased.

He had to give it to her. She had his number. Wild horses couldn't have dragged him away from a challenge.

He reached for her shoulders, pulled her close, and made sure to give her the kind of kiss that would having her changing her tune—it was slow and hot and long.

Keeley's hands found their way to his waist, her fingers gripping his shirt tightly. It took everything he had not to pull her body flush against his, to let her feel the impact she was having on him.

He'd kissed countless women in his life, so he couldn't begin to understand why this kiss felt...different. Felt like so much more.

Maybe it was because he'd known Keeley for most of her life. He'd seen her at so many stages, watched her blossom into this beautiful, intelligent, funny woman.

It would be so easy to let himself get carried away, to push for more. But he wasn't sure Keeley was ready for what he wanted from her, and he *knew* Rafe wasn't.

So he slowly gentled the kiss, then backed away.

He expected this interlude would end as the previous two had. Rafe would hug her, they'd say good night, then he'd spend the rest of the night alone with his hand, as visions of Keeley danced in his head.

Keeley, apparently, had other plans. "Why don't you ever kiss me?" she asked Rafe.

He frowned. "That wouldn't be smart, Keeley."

"Why not?" she pressed.

"Because we're friends. Because you're Kayden's sister. Because you work for me now."

Keeley grinned, the look on her face pure minx. "You had that list ready to go, didn't you?"

Rafe opened his arms. "Behave yourself and come give me my hug."

Gio had become quite fond of Keeley's hugs as well, not even sure when those had started. They'd never touched much at all before, but somewhere during these past few weeks, in addition to simply saying goodbye after work, Keeley never failed to give both of them hugs.

Keeley crossed her arms. "No. I want a kiss instead."

Rafe looked at Gio. "See what you started?"

Gio shrugged, unapologetically. "Sometimes it's fun to act on impulse."

Rafe shook his head. "One of us in this little trio has to be levelheaded."

Gio wanted to respond to that, but he literally couldn't. He got too hung up on the word *trio*. He liked it. Too much.

So when he could speak again...he poked the bear. "Go on. Kiss her."

Rafe frowned.

"Yeah." Keeley added her own taunt to the game. "Unless you're afraid you're going to fall into the same category as all those other bad kissers in my past."

"I'm not Gio," Rafe said. "You're not going to taunt me into getting your way."

"Just one kiss?" she asked, in the most genuine, least-flirty voice he'd ever heard from her.

While Gio responded to teasing, apparently Rafe was a sucker for sincerity.

"Fuck," he muttered. "You were warned. Both of you were." That was all he said before he cupped Keeley's face in his hands and kissed her.

Gio's brows rose nearly to his hairline as Rafe took possession of Keeley's lips with a passion he had never witnessed in his friend. It was deep and sexy and hungry, almost desperate. Keeley gripped Rafe's forearms, but Gio didn't mistake her touch as part of the embrace. No. She was holding on for dear life.

Gio stood there, stock-still, watching. And that heart-to-heart he'd promised to have with himself transpired right there, right then.

This...God...

This was happening.

The kiss could have lasted for ten seconds or ten hours, but when Rafe released her, none of them moved. Hell, Gio wasn't sure any of them were breathing.

"Rafe," Keeley whispered at last, as she touched her kiss-swollen lips, her cheeks flushed bright red.

"Damn, man," Gio muttered.

That was when Gio suddenly realized Rafe had never kissed Jill or Jennifer or Vanessa. Not once. He had always left the kissing to Gio, just like he'd left the relationship part to him.

He had *never* seen his best friend kiss a woman. Not until this moment.

And he couldn't help but wonder what that meant.

Rafe should have looked victorious. Should have been as smug as hell, but instead...he looked lost. Especially when he said, "Keeley. When *I* kiss a woman, it means something."

With that, he turned around, heading back to the driver's side and climbing into the car, leaving Gio and Keeley standing side by side, speechless.

Chapter Six

"So what did he say then?" Liza asked.

Gianna sighed. "He accused me of being a control freak. Me! Can you believe it?"

Keeley and Liza exchanged a quick glance, but neither of them said a word. Because Gianna's picture was probably in the dictionary next to the words "control freak."

Gianna had texted them on a group thread this morning, upset about a fight she'd had with Sam before he'd left for work. A few weeks ago—just after Penny's birthday party—she, Liza, Jess, Gianna, and Penny had started a group text that Liza had dubbed "Sisters from Other Misters," and Keeley couldn't recall a single day that had gone by since without someone sending a message or meme to the thread.

After her parents' death, Keeley's life had become a bit—okay, a lot—guy heavy, as more often than not, her childhood home was filled with Kayden and his friends. Not in a frat house way, but more in a Kayden-is-in-over-his-head-and-we're-all-pitching-in-to-help-raise-the-girl-cub way.

She'd had a bunch of girlfriends in high school, but those friendships had faded, as they often do with distance, time, and a lack of anything in common other than Algebra II. Upon returning home after college, she'd turned acquaintances—Gianna and Liza—into real, true friends. And over the past year, they'd included Jess and Penny in their merry band.

"It sounds like it was a nasty fight," Keeley observed.

"They all are lately," Gianna replied sadly. Then she picked up her margarita. "But I don't want to talk about Sam tonight."

Liza lifted her glass in a toast. "Good for you. Tonight is girls' night out. We're going to get half-lit on margaritas, dance until our feet fall off, and man-bash with reckless abandon."

"Hear, hear," Gianna said, tapping her glass against Liza's.

Keeley followed suit, though she wasn't as on board with the man-bashing as much as she normally would have been. Before this month, she would have been leading the charge, declaring all men assholes and idiots, thanks to her shitty dating history. But tonight...she wasn't feeling it.

And it was all because of those kisses *last* night.

She'd gone to bed cursing herself for basically daring Rafe and Gio to kiss her good night. Part of her had actually expected them to put the kibosh on those kisses. After all, she'd flirted with them for years, and they'd never once taken the bait.

She'd brushed off Gio's first kiss as sympathy the night of the storm, chalking it up to a consolation prize after she'd gotten freaked out by the lightning, then bitched about her long list of failed dates. She knew Gio had a soft spot for her, especially since her parents died, and she assumed it was because he'd lost his mother when he was young as well. That compassion, combined with his charming bad boy, had prompted the kiss that night. She was certain of it.

The second kiss had been a little harder to brush off, but not really. Because once again, she'd been hurt by Joel. Gio and Rafe were born protectors, so her vulnerability had been the equivalent of her waving a red flag in their faces. Gio responded by giving her a kiss, and Rafe, one of his amazing, warm bear hugs.

But last night... Fuck...last night.

She didn't have a clue what to make of that. She could have

credited Gio's third kiss to the fact the two of them were a bit tipsy after splitting a couple pitchers of beer, though that felt like a weak excuse at best. And no matter how many times he told her the kisses didn't meaning anything, that didn't help her keep the crush she'd always harbored for him at bay.

God. She hated the word crush. It made her feel like a kid, when the truth was, what she felt for Gio—and Rafe—went far beyond that.

Especially now that she'd experienced Rafe's kiss.

Jesus. Christ.

Rafe...her quiet, somewhat repressed new boss...had a dark and delicious side. No man had ever kissed her with that much... raw masculinity. Her lips were *still* tingling.

She glanced across the room and spotted Rafe, Gio, and Luca at the bar, talking to the bartender, their backs to her. She'd purposely told them she was coming to Eclectic tonight because she wanted to see if they'd follow.

After an hour had passed and they hadn't shown up, she'd been relieved. Because it proved she'd been right. The kisses meant nothing.

Oh, fuck that. Who was she kidding?

She'd been disappointed as hell. Something she knew was completely unwise. Because despite the kisses, Rafe and Gio hadn't said a damn thing that indicated they didn't still see her as Kayden's little sister. The date-crashing was Moretti Protectiveness 101, and nothing she hadn't experienced before from her brother and other various males in the group.

Though usually, she could admit, it was just Kayden and Liza's brother, Aldo, leading that particular charge. The other guys just made an appearance if they happened to be out with her brother on whatever night he decided she was with the wrong man.

Now, she wasn't sure what to think. Because Rafe and Gio had arrived a few minutes earlier, each of them giving her a simple, single nod of the head, acknowledging they'd seen her, before heading straight to the bar. Her foolish heart had skipped twenty beats and was now racing at what had to be an unhealthy pace.

"Keeley," Liza said in a tone that told her it wasn't the first time her friend had called her name.

"Sorry. Daydreaming. What were you saying?" Keeley asked.

Liza's eyes narrowed. "I was going to see if you wanted to dance, but now I'd rather know what you're daydreaming about."

All the truth serum in the world wouldn't drag that information out of Keeley because she could already imagine the pitying looks and "oh Keeleys" she'd get from her friends if they found out she was interested in two men who would forever view her as Kayden's little sister and never as a woman they would date.

Keeley paused.

Because that was the moment she realized she'd stopped crushing on Gio *or* Rafe. When she thought of them now...she dreamed about both men, together, at the same time. They'd had a ménage before. That was the one piece of information she'd played over and over last night because...God...because she wanted that. With them. Desperately.

Damn Jess and her idyllic happily ever after with Tony and Rhys!

"I don't think you want to know," Keeley said, trying to buy time until she could come up with a lie.

Liza brightened up. "Of course I do."

Keeley glanced around the nightclub, the answer appearing just in the nick of time. "Work."

Liza scowled. "Work?"

"Yeah. This is my first time just hanging out at Eclectic as Marketing Director of Baros Corporation. I keep looking around thinking of different ways to promote it. What do you think of theme nights?"

Liza groaned. "No. No boyfriend talk. No work talk. When did the two of you forget how to have fun? Come on. We're dancing."

The three of them hopped up from the table, chiseling a spot for themselves on the dance floor. Keeley closed her eyes, shut down all the sexy fantasies that had been keeping her awake nights, and gave herself up to the music.

Rafe glanced at the dance floor, aware Gio's attention had been drawn there as well.

"You ready for the big move?" Luca asked them.

Rafe forced himself to stop staring at Keeley and focused his attention on Gio's twin brother. They hadn't intended to come out tonight at all. Gio had packing to do, and Rafe, despite his progress, was still buried in a mountain of paperwork. Those adulting reasons fell away the instant Keeley informed them it was girls' night out. She'd texted them the information, letting them know they could take the night off from date-crashing. Then she'd added the fact that she would be perfectly safe since they'd elected to come here...to Rafe's nightclub.

He wasn't sure why she'd thought that would set their minds at ease. There were still too many sharks circling their prey, something Keeley and her friends appeared to be oblivious to. Rafe had counted no less than eight men stealing glances at their table as they'd ordered yet another pitcher of margaritas. And right now —he peeked over at the dance floor again—there were three or four men jockeying for position, ready to break into the girls' circle.

Rafe scowled, then remembered Luca had asked a question. Problem was, he couldn't remember what he'd asked.

"We're ready. I'm nearly all packed. Just a few more things to box up," Gio replied, but unlike Rafe, he wasn't even attempting to pretend his interest was anywhere other than exactly where it was—honed in on Keeley, like she was a target in his sites.

"Worried about the girls?" Luca asked, his gaze following Gio's to the dance floor.

"I don't like the look of that guy in the black shirt trying to weasel his way closer."

Luca studied the man for a second, then shrugged. "He looks like every other guy out there. And you have to admit, if it wasn't Liza, Gianna, and Kiwi, *we'd* probably be out there, trying to score a dance with them as well. They look hot tonight."

Gio shrugged in response to Luca's comment but didn't look away from the women.

Nope. Scratch that. His best friend wasn't looking away from Keeley.

And leave it to Luca to call a spade a spade. Gio's twin was a straight shooter, someone who never minced words. He was right. Perhaps Rafe was biased, but he was certain Keeley and her two girlfriends were the most beautiful women in the nightclub. None of them wore overly provocative clothing, though Keeley's minidress was showing enough of her trim thighs that Rafe was doomed to sit here with a damn hard-on, like some teenaged boy with zero self-control.

Something had to give. Because he was getting in way over his head.

He'd kicked his own ass nonstop since last night.

What the fuck had he been thinking?

He didn't kiss. And he sure as shit didn't kiss—he forced himself to use the safer signifier—Kayden's sister.

Somewhere around three a.m., when he had given up all hope of sleeping, he'd decided to stop thinking of her as Keeley. If he could just put other descriptors at the forefront—Kayden's sister, his employee, his friend—maybe he wouldn't do any more stupid shit.

Like kiss her. Again.

He'd expected Gio to call him out for his actions last night, especially after Rafe had told him not to kiss her. But as soon as they got back in the car, Gio had gotten a call from Tony. There had been several break-in attempts at one of Moretti Brothers' warehouses. Copper piping was valuable, so thieves were on the prowl again last night. They'd installed a state-of-the-art alarm system, but Tony had still wanted Gio to meet him at the warehouse to talk to the cops and make sure nothing had been stolen. Rafe had dropped Gio off, and Tony had taken his brother home afterwards.

Rafe took a sip of his beer, his attention drawn back to the dance floor when he noticed Gio's dark scowl.

Looking over his shoulder, he saw that Gianna had left the floor and was back at their table, texting someone. Two men had joined Liza and Keeley, invading their personal space in a way that looked *way too* personal. The man in the black shirt had stepped behind Keeley, and he was trying to pull her back against him, his hands on her waist. Keeley continued to dance, but Rafe noticed her subtle attempts at putting more distance between them, something the asshole continued to ignore.

The guy dancing with Liza was more circumspect, the two of them facing each other in a way that indicated they were just having fun, sharing a dance.

It was Keeley's guy who kept crossing the line.

Gio stood up and cast a glance at Rafe, who nodded, albeit reluctantly, and rose as well.

"Where are you guys going?" Luca asked.

"Feel like dancing," was all Gio said in reply. Or at least that was all Rafe heard because his friend was already storming toward the dance floor.

Before Rafe could consider his next course of action, or what it meant, he followed, the two of them entering the space next to Liza and Keeley. Liza narrowed her eyes at their arrival, something entirely unsurprising. She was no stranger to overprotective brothers and male cousins.

However, Rafe witnessed her expression changing to something infinitely more dangerous when she realized Gio wasn't looking at her at all. Rather, his attention—and anger—was directed at the man dancing with Keeley.

Liza looked *intrigued.*

Something that was going to bite them in the ass later because Liza was like a dog with a bone whenever she sniffed out juicy gossip.

Gio reached out a hand to Keeley, who took it immediately, confirming Rafe's suspicions. She wasn't comfortable with the way the man was attempting to manhandle her.

The guy shot Gio a dirty look when Keeley danced away from him and into Gio's arms.

"Hey," the asshole bitched. "What the hell, man?"

Gio held her closely, possessively, as he shot daggers at the guy. The idiot was one more word away from Gio laying him out right there.

Rafe decided to step in before the confrontation ended in bloodshed. It *was* his nightclub after all.

"She's with us," he said, claiming the spot behind Keeley, his hands resting on her hips, just beneath Gio's, closing them into a tight, dirty circle of sexy bumping and grinding.

Keeley—a great dancer—never missed a beat, her body swaying between theirs. She flashed a grateful smile over her shoulder, one that might have made him grin at any other time. Right now, he was having a hard time concentrating on anything except how good Keeley felt, dancing between them. He leaned closer, taking a quick whiff of her hair. God, she always smelled so good. Lemons and roses.

He'd wanted to indulge in another threesome with Gio since the affair with Jill ended, but there hadn't been time, what with Grandpa's illness and passing and then the unexpected inheritance. Now that Gio had opened to the door to that possibility with Keeley—

Fuck. What was he thinking?

He needed to put the brakes on that, and quick.

Something that might have been easier if Keeley hadn't chosen that moment to grind her ass against him. Rafe tightened his grip on her hips, his intention to push her away...but instead, he held her there, not bothering to hide the impact she was having on him. His cock was rock hard and ready to roll.

A quick glance over her head proved Gio was just as overwhelmed by the dance, by the closeness of their bodies. Gio's hands were gliding up and down, stroking the sides of her breasts on every upswing. His leg split Keeley's, their closeness ensuring that his thigh brushed against her pussy.

Their bodies swayed in time to the beat, their motions mimicking too closely what it would be like if they gave into their need and took her to bed.

Rafe loosened his grip on her hips, forcing himself to recall they were on a crowded dance floor. To hold on to the knowledge that they weren't alone. There were too many people there, watching them, who were no doubt seeing all the things he and Gio weren't exactly working overtime to hide.

Yep. He was in over his head and going down fast. His previous shared affairs with Gio had been so simple. For him, it was just sex. He'd never once crossed the line between physical and emotional, never felt the tug to do so.

But Keeley was...

Fuck.

He couldn't finish that statement. Because he didn't want to, not even to himself in the privacy of his own thoughts.

This was going nowhere good, and he needed to stop it before someone got the wrong idea.

And not just Gio and Keeley.

Luca and Liza were observant as hell, and Rafe wondered— not for the first time—how Kayden would feel about what was happening here.

Nothing is happening here.

Rafe had zero experience with relationships or love, and he intended to keep it that way.

Gio was the one who wanted love and marriage and all that crap. It was glaringly obvious now that his emotions hadn't really been engaged with Jill, Jennifer, or Vanessa either. Sure, he stuck around longer, dating the women exclusively after Rafe bowed out, but those relationships had ultimately ended.

One glance at his best friend, at the way Gio was looking at Keeley as if she were made of pure diamonds, told him this time was different.

Which meant someone was going to get hurt if they didn't stop playing this game.

The song ended, another beginning, and mercifully—or unfortunately—Keeley stepped away from them, fanning herself.

"I need a drink," she said loudly, so that they could hear her over the music.

Liza pointed to the guy she was dancing with, signaling that she was going to keep dancing.

He and Gio led Keeley back to her table, where Gianna stood as if she'd been impatiently waiting on their return.

"I'm going to head out, Kee. Sam texted. He wants to talk. He's out front waiting for me."

Keeley nodded. "Okay. I hope you guys can work everything out. Call me later if you need to."

Gianna gave her a quick hug, then said goodbye to them. Rafe followed her progress toward the exit, sneaking a peek at the bar. Luca was engaged in a conversation with...shit...

Kayden and Aldo.

Fortunately, all three men had their backs to the dance floor, so maybe they'd gotten lucky, and none of them had noticed their sexy dance with Keeley.

Now that they'd gotten Keeley off the dance floor and away from the asshole, Rafe was breathing easier. Her face was flushed, but Rafe couldn't decide if that was due to the heat or a residual effect of the dance they'd all just shared.

"Thanks for the save," Keeley said when the three of them were alone. "I was this close," she pinched her pointer finger and thumb together, "to kicking that guy in the balls. I hate when assholes think they can cop a feel on the dance floor. Like, who tells these guys that there's any woman on the planet who enjoys some stranger coming up to her and grinding his tiny, limp dick against her ass?"

Rafe frowned—because he'd just done the same thing. Not that Keeley had pulled away. If anything, she'd shifted closer. "That happens to you a lot?"

Keeley shrugged casually. "Enough to be annoying. But it was under control."

Gio growled, "Didn't look like it was under control."

Keeley smirked. "I'd already given Liza the look, and we were a few seconds away from making our move."

Rafe was intrigued. "What move?"

"We dance toward each other and do a sexy girl shimmy. The offending asshole always takes a step back to watch the show. Then, in the midst of the girl-on-girl action, either Liza or I— whoever is closer—slam our heel down on the jerk's foot. Works every time. Liza's the best at it. I swear I think she's probably broken a few bones with her high heels." Keeley laughed, obviously amused by her own story.

"Is this the part where I thank you for not crippling me on the dance floor?" Rafe joked, aware Keeley's story had done nothing to cool Gio's jets. Rafe had seen his protective nature before, but it had never reached this level of...

No. Gio wasn't feeling protective. He was *jealous*.

Which proved Rafe wasn't the only one in over his head.

"You were in no danger of getting 'the heel,'" she air-quoted. "*That* dance?" She fanned herself. "God...*so* hot."

Rafe shook his head, fighting to restrain his cocky grin as she leaned her elbow on the table and shifted closer to him, her expression full flirt when she added, "So hard. And not tiny."

Gio laughed, and it appeared he'd managed to shake off the worst of his jealousy. "Behave, minx. You're gonna make Rafe blush."

Rafe narrowed his eyes. "I don't blush. Ever."

"So...what brings you guys here tonight? Thought you were both staying in," Keeley said, with a shit-eating grin that proved she'd sent that text earlier to provoke them into doing exactly what they'd done. Crashed her night out. *Again.*

Gio shrugged, aiming for casual and failing miserably. "We felt like a beer."

She laughed. "Sure you did."

Before they could reply to her taunt, a waiter approached their table. "Hey, Keeley."

"Hi, Chad."

The waiter glanced at Gio and then him. "Oh...hello, Mr. Baros."

So this was Chad.

"You can call me Rafe. Mr. Baros was my grandfather."

Chad smiled. "We still on for Tuesday night, Keeley? Thought we could go to Spruce Street Harbor Park. Grab some funnel cakes and ride the Ferris wheel."

Keeley grinned widely. "That sounds awesome."

"Cool. I'll text you later and we can figure out where to meet up."

"Perfect," she replied

"Gotta get back to work. You guys good on drinks?" Chad asked.

They all nodded, and Chad weaved his way back through the crowd.

Suddenly, Rafe was suffering from a bad case of what Gio had —and it scared him spitless. Because Rafe didn't do jealously any more than Gio did.

Then Keeley gave them a mischievous grin, one he couldn't help but return, even as he knew the joke was about to be on them.

"So...it sounds like we're all going to the park on Tuesday," Keeley teased. "What are you guys wearing? Maybe we could coordinate outfits."

* * *

Gio wanted to laugh at her joke. He really did, but his head was all over the fucking place tonight, and the only emotion he seemed capable of at the moment was jealousy. Which was not a comfortable feeling for him. He didn't have enough experience with it, so it was running rampant, and he had no way to get it under control.

"Your brother is here," Rafe pointed out. He said the words to Keeley, but Gio knew they were meant for him. He took a couple deep breaths, which helped him calm down, then he gave Rafe a subtle nod that he would be careful.

Keeley rolled her eyes. "Jesus H. Don't you guys have anything better to do than chase around after us?"

"You don't seem to mind the chase," Gio said with a smug grin.

Keeley considered his reply. "That's not entirely true. I wouldn't mind the chase if one of you guys would actually catch me at some point."

"Just one of us?" Gio asked.

Keeley leaned forward, and Gio realized he'd never understood the term "bedroom eyes" until that moment. "Is that an invitation for more?"

"Gio," Rafe said, shaking his head, his tone rife with warning. "That's enough. You're taking it too far."

Keeley glanced over at Rafe, took one look at his cold expression, and sighed sadly. "Guess not."

She wanted it too. She felt it, this pull between the three of them.

Gio was perilously close to laying down the gauntlet—with Keeley *and* with Rafe—but Liza returned to the table, picking up her margarita and taking a long drink. "Where's Gianna?"

"Sam texted. He just picked her up," Keeley replied.

Liza shook her head. "I'm afraid that's not going to end well."

Keeley nodded, and it looked like she was in agreement.

"So," Liza said, her wicked grin all the warning Gio needed.

"You three were really heating up the dance floor. Where did that come from?"

Gio narrowed his eyes. "That guy was getting way too close."

Liza shrugged. "And we were about to give him the heel. Though I have to admit, I enjoyed watching your method of cock-blocking him better."

"We weren't cock-blocking him," Rafe retorted.

"Of *course* you weren't," she replied sardonically. Liza, like Gio's sister Layla, was the youngest and only girl in her family. In Liza's case, it made her loud, bold, outspoken, and shamelessly honest. Gio figured it was either that or allow her brothers to run roughshod over her, something Liza had never allowed. And never would.

Though, now that he considered it, that bold-faced honesty thing ran through the entire Moretti line.

"What was the deal with the guy *you* were dancing with?" Keeley asked Liza, mercifully drawing the heat away from them.

Liza shrugged. "He was a good dancer, but not much personality. I tried to start at least three different conversations and got single-word responses in every case. Fuck that jazz. I need a man who can string at least two sentences together. Bonus points if he manages a whole paragraph."

Gio scowled when yet another man approached their table. Where the hell were all these guys coming from?

"Keeley?"

He started to tell the man to shove off—his jealousy already pushed to the brink too many times tonight—but Keeley's expression gave him pause.

She looked up at the guy and froze. It was just for a second, but Gio saw it...recognized her instant unease. Probably because it was something he'd never witnessed from her before. Confidence wasn't a trait Keeley lacked, but with this guy...it wavered.

"JT. Hey. What a surprise." Whatever had initially bothered her about him wasn't present in her tone or in her expression. Keeley had a good poker face.

"Yeah," JT said. "Long time no see. I've, uh..." He paused as he looked at Liza, Rafe, and Gio. "Liza," JT added, nodding at her somewhat nervously.

"Asshole." Apparently, Liza preferred another name for JT, not bothering to hide her disgust for the man. Gio had never loved his cousin more.

"Liza," Keeley chastised before gesturing toward them. "JT. These are my friends, Rafe and Gio."

He felt the inexplicable desire to change the word *friends* because he didn't like the way she was looking at this guy.

Keeley looked at him and Rafe. "JT and I went out for a hot minute about a year ago." She laughed as she said it, but there was something about the way she was holding herself that told him she wasn't as nonchalant about this guy as she'd been with all the others.

JT chuckled. Stupid prick. Anyone paying half attention could see through Keeley's act.

Liza's expression darkened, and Gio took his cues from her reaction to the man, not bothering to feign friendliness.

"You still working at the office supply store?" JT asked.

"No." Keeley shook her head. "Actually, I'm working for Rafe now. Marketing Director."

"Wow. Sounds like you got your dream job. That's cool. I've been thinking about you lately." He was apparently feeling confident about putting the moves on her, now that he knew she wasn't with one of them.

"Oh?" Keeley said softly, and Gio could almost see the wheels spinning in her head. Whatever happened between Keeley and JT appeared to fall into a different category than all her other failed dates. He racked his brain to remember if she or Kayden had ever mentioned a JT, but no memory surfaced.

Not that it was a shocker. He'd known precious little about her personal life before this month, only picking up the occasional tidbits from her or her brother or Liza. He'd listened with half an ear and hadn't asked questions because he'd been a stupid, blind fool, no better than apparently every other idiot male in Philadelphia. Because just like them, he'd failed to really see Keeley for just how special she was.

Now he was regretting not digging deeper for details.

"I was wondering," JT said, rubbing the back of his neck. He was uncomfortable, but apparently determined. "Would it be okay if I called you tomorrow? I was hoping to talk to you about some stuff."

"What about your girlfriend?" Liza asked, her question shining some light on the mystery of JT.

"We broke up. It would just be one phone call," JT hastily added when it became apparent Keeley was going to say no. "Then if you want, I'll lose your number. Promise."

"Or you could lose it now," Liza suggested.

Keeley shot her friend a warning glance. "Liza. Stop."

Regardless, she didn't answer JT immediately, and Gio's respect for Keeley rose. She was no one's fool, and nobody pushed her around.

"Fine," she said at last.

Liza shook her head, rolling her eyes, and Gio decided to pull her aside later to find out what the deal was with this guy. "I'm going to go talk to my brother. Not interested in watching this tragedy unfold."

She walked away, and JT visibly relaxed, grinning, as if Keeley's capitulation was the equivalent to getting the keys to the city. Which meant JT didn't understand Keeley at all. "Well, I'll let you get back to hanging with your friends. Talk to you tomorrow, Kee."

Gio gritted his teeth at the presumptuous bastard's nickname for her. Who the fuck did this guy think he was?

He looked across the table and caught Rafe's glower as well.

Once JT left, he and Rafe both turned to look at Keeley, who was studying her empty margarita glass with the intensity of someone trying to pick out which puppy they wanted to adopt.

"So," Gio said, when it was obvious she wasn't going to offer any insights on her own. "Who's JT?"

"I told you. A guy I went out with."

"And he had a girlfriend at the time?" Rafe asked.

Keeley raised her hands. "No, no. It was nothing like that. JT and I went out a year ago for a couple of months. He was super nice, and we had a blast. We talked on the phone for hours every night, and went out three or four times a week. I really thought... Well, we slept together and then..."

"And then..." Gio prodded.

"He called me the next day. Said he'd run into his ex-girl-friend, and they were getting back together. He was very apolo-getic, and I could tell he was genuinely sorry. They'd gone out for three years before he and I started dating. And she'd dumped *him*, not the other way around. Apparently, she'd had a change of heart, and he decided he still loved her. So that was that. I haven't seen or talked to him since then."

"He hurt you," Gio said, pressing for more.

She hesitated, then nodded. "Yeah. I guess he did. Liza caught the brunt of my tears, which is why she was so cold. It's just...JT was probably the first guy I ever dated that I thought might be the one, you know? We really had a good time together, always laugh-ing. Stuff that was hard work with other guys was easy with him. I could just be myself."

"Are you sure you want to talk to him tomorrow?" Rafe asked.

She lifted one shoulder. "Not sure what harm could come from it. It's just one phone call. We'll catch up on the last year and then...who knows?" She smiled at them.

Gio was tempted to lay his cards on the table, to tell her to kick JT to the curb and go out with him—with them.

But he hesitated.

Because of Rafe.

And because of Keeley.

Her mask was gone. And she looked happy—*really* happy.

Like a woman on the verge of getting a second chance at finding true love.

So he spent the rest of the evening kicking his own ass for being a fool because he wanted her, and not just in his bed but in his life.

Keeley was the woman for him.

For *them*.

He knew it with every fiber of his being.

And there was a very good chance their window of opportunity had just closed.

Chapter Seven

Rafe took a breather inside the front door, wondering what the hell he'd signed up for. He'd spent the last couple of months trying to clear his grandfather's house out. Now, in one day, he'd just helped Gio move all his shit in. And the piles that had been dwindling were replaced with new boxes. Not that he cared all that much. It would be nice to have someone to share this big-ass house with.

He was just feeling grumpy due to a lack of sleep. Every night since he'd kissed Keeley had been restless, alternating between dirty fantasies of him in bed with her and Gio, and anxiety over what the hell he was supposed to do now.

He wanted Keeley. Somewhere over the past seven days, it had become painfully obvious to him. Unfortunately, that insight had come too late.

He'd fucked up last week at Eclectic. Gio had started to lay it on the line, had opened the door with an invitation, and like a jackass, Rafe had slammed it shut, warning Gio off and allowing Keeley to believe he didn't want her. The worst part was, he hadn't just screwed up his own chances, but Gio's too, because now JT had entered the picture and...everything had gone off the rails after that.

Liza, Kayden, Aldo, and Luca had joined them at the table after JT walked away. They'd ordered more margaritas and partied the rest of the night, having a great time. Or at least, everyone except him—and Gio, who'd gone uncharacteristically quiet—had enjoyed themselves.

"Want this in the kitchen?" Kayden walked in with a box labeled *dishes*.

If Rafe was a better person, seeing Kayden today should have helped him put all thoughts of pursuing—seducing—Keeley to rest. However, they didn't.

He looked at his friend and shook his head. "No. You can put it there. The kitchen is already busting at the seams. We need to unpack and incorporate some boxes before dragging anything else in. Keeley, Liza, and Gianna are in there right now, tackling some of that."

Kayden put the box down on top of another, then wiped the sweat from his brow with the hem of his T-shirt. "How's it feel being your own boss these days?"

"I'm slowly getting used to it. Of course, it's gotten a thousand times better since Keeley came to work with me. That girl is a whirlwind."

Kayden grinned, pride written on every line in his face. "I appreciate you hiring her. We were perilously close to her having to move back in with me."

Rafe was torn between laughing and wincing. Because, while Kayden and Keeley loved each other tremendously, the two of them living in the same house would not have ended well. Keeley's free spirit and love for partying drove her straight-as-an-arrow, in-bed-by-ten-every-night cop brother out of his mind.

"I think we can all agree that would have been terrible."

"So things are starting to settle down? I know you've been working way too hard. Keeley's told me so." Kayden had been one of his closest friends since high school, and Rafe appreciated the concern in his voice.

"Slowly but surely," he muttered.

"Your stepdad still being a pain in the ass about the will?" Kayden asked.

Rafe gave his friend a curious look because the two of them hadn't talked in weeks.

Kayden grinned. "Gio told us about the scene at the lawyer's office at one of our weekly lunches."

"Ah," Rafe said. "Grandpa's lawyer assures me the will is airtight, but that hasn't stopped Rodney from trying to find a loophole. I suspect when he doesn't find one, he'll move on for good."

"For good? You mean leave your mom?"

Rafe sighed. "I think he married her because he believed she was Grandpa's heir. The guy's a prick. And as much as I can't stand him, I know it's going to kill my mother if he walks out."

"Poor woman. She can't catch a break in the love department, can she?"

"No. Not really. It doesn't help that she inherited Grandpa's impulsiveness. With him, it was businesses—find one you want and buy it. Meanwhile, Mom falls madly in love with every man she goes out with, without really getting to know them. And, predictably, in the end, it never lasts."

"I'm sorry to hear that. For her, but also for you. Because let's face it, you've been on that roller coaster with her your entire life, going through her highs of new love to the lows of her broken hearts. It couldn't have been easy for you growing up. To see someone you love constantly knocked down, especially by a person they cared for. Something like that had to have taken its toll on you."

Kayden was an astute guy, and empathetic. But he'd hit this nail a little *too* on the head. "Keeley told you my feelings about love and marriage."

Kayden gave him another guilty grin. "To be honest, you've never made much of a secret about your lack of interest in marriage, but yes, Keeley might have mentioned something about it on the phone this week. You gotta understand, Keeley told our mom everything when she was growing up. And I mean *every-thing*. I overheard Mom tell Dad once that she could stand to know a little less about Keeley's life. She was joking. Partly. After Mom died…well, Keeley's need to talk to someone about stuff didn't just go away. Over the years, she's figured out who to turn to based on the topic. Her girlfriends get the love life and sex stuff, thank God, but I get the rest."

Rafe nodded. "I don't mind that she told you. I know it bothered her to hear."

"It did. Probably because she couldn't possibly understand it."

"Yeah. And I have to admit, I've never really looked at my mom's failing relationships in quite the way you just described."

He hadn't. When he looked back at his childhood, in his mind, his mom's broken hearts had been her fault. Because she'd given her love too quickly, put her trust in the wrong men, set herself up for that pain. Mom always leapt without stealing a single glance beforehand.

It wasn't that he didn't put any of the blame on the men too. He hated them for what they'd put her through because he loved his mother. And when she hurt, he hurt. But ultimately, he'd always told himself she could save herself the tears if she would just harden her heart and shut her feelings down. Like he did.

Sooooo…great.

Now, he not only had a shit-ton of Grandpa's boxes to empty, but also a lifetime of fucked-up emotions and Mommy issues to unpack as well.

The hits just kept coming.

Kayden put a comforting hand on his shoulder. "Listen, I know life happens, man. But me and the guys were talking, and we think you should start making time for the Wednesday meetings again."

The *meetings* Kayden mentioned had nothing to do with work and everything to do with simply spending an hour or two each week with friends to chill and unwind over lunch.

"You need a break from work and some serious male bonding time. Nothing but bitching about the Eagles' shitty fucking defense this season, dirty locker room talk, making fun of Joey's new *ManPower* ad—because Jesus, how much gel did he have in his hair?—and which is the best craft beer on the market. You know, the shit that really matters."

Rafe laughed. "That sounds like exactly what I need. I'm sorry I've been absent the past few months."

Gio's brother, Tony, had started the weekly get-together at Paulie's Diner so many years ago, Rafe had lost count. Before his grandfather's illness and subsequent passing, Rafe had never missed a single "meeting," always looking forward to breaking free from his piece-of-crap, fluorescent-lighting-soaked, puce-green, postage-stamp-sized office at his old job.

Of course, now, he'd broken free from the place forever.

"I've been so buried. Grandpa's estate is—fuck me—a *lot*. I swear to God, he must have been the most impulsive businessman in history. In addition to the restaurant, there's the nightclub, a flower shop, a used bookstore, three apartment buildings, and this goddamned haunted mansion. How does any of that go together?"

Kayden winced. "I'm not sure it does."

"You're not sure?" Rafe asked incredulously, as Kayden laughed.

"Okay. It doesn't. But Keeley seems to think you're getting a good handle on things. She's excited about your plans to grow the businesses, and the way you're starting the inn with Gio."

Rafe chuckled. "She told you they were *my* plans?"

Kayden grinned. "Hers?"

"Hers. And they're brilliant."

They both looked up at the sound of Keeley's voice.

"Let me show you the office. You won't believe how different it looks without all the boxes. It's the first room Gio plans to reno-vate," Keeley said as she came out of the kitchen, Liza trailing behind. Keeley was carrying Cricket, who was bouncing excitedly in her arms. The dog had been a whirlwind of nervous energy all day, thanks to all the people and activity in the house. It was a far cry from the very quiet life the dog had led with Grandpa.

Both women smiled at them but kept walking past.

Rafe followed their progress down the hall and was about to return to his conversation with Kayden when he heard Liza ask, "So have you talked to JT again?"

Rafe frowned, suddenly pissed when they entered the office because he couldn't hear Keeley's response.

Keeley, who'd regaled him nonstop about her dating life prior to this week, hadn't mentioned the waiter, Chad, or any new online dates, or JT, since the night the man had walked over to their table.

He and Gio had discussed whether or not they should crash her date with Chad by treating themselves to a night at the fair, but that decision had become moot when Keeley canceled the date due to a headache. He knew it was legit because she'd made the phone call in front of him, and then left work an hour early to go home and lie down.

Now that he reflected on it, she'd been quieter, more subdued this week, sneaking her phone out to text when she thought he wasn't looking.

Rafe had been curious to know if JT had called, but he hadn't felt like it was his place to pry.

No. That wasn't the truth.

He hadn't thought he needed to *ask*. He assumed if the guy had called, Keeley would have told him. For God's sake, she'd been telling him everything since the day she started working for him.

Every dating horror story.

Minute-by-minute recounts of her clubbing adventures with her girlfriends.

Even a way-too-detailed synopsis of the latest season of *Big Brother*.

Keeley had been an open book about every aspect of her life

ever since accepting the job, the two of them sitting together for hours, going through box after box after box, while he listened to her stories.

So the fact she'd been silent about JT bothered him.

There was something about the guy he didn't trust, but he was hard-pressed to figure out what exactly it was. The man seemed nice enough, but...

He tried to brush it off as concern for Keeley—after all, the guy had hurt her—and not jealousy.

He sighed heavily.

Yeah, right.

Lately, Rafe had been getting damn good at avoiding conversations he should be having.

Like asking Keeley point-blank about her intentions regarding JT.

Like talking to Gio about where he saw this thing with Keeley going.

Though that discussion was going to be hard. There was no question he and his friend both wanted her, and sharing wouldn't be an issue because they'd done that before.

But what happened if Keeley wanted more from them?

Rafe didn't do commitment. So what happened if he walked away, and Gio stayed...for good?

Wait. *If* he walked away?

Shouldn't it be *when* he walked away?

Suddenly, his palms were sweating, his chest was tight, his heart was racing.

What the fuck?

He was actually on the verge of a goddamn panic attack. Over a relationship? He took several deep breaths. If he needed more proof that he wasn't cut out for commitment, this reaction solidified it for him.

He looked at Kayden, fighting hard to calm down, to harden his resolve.

"How are the plans for your trip coming along?" Rafe asked,

desperately seeking a distraction. For him *and* for Kayden. Because he wasn't about to let his friend see him freaking out.

The diversion helped, as he was able to control his breathing again after a few minutes.

Rafe listened with half an ear as Kayden detailed the upcoming hike he and Aldo were doing on the Appalachian Trail. The two men planned to hike the Long Trail portion of the AT in Vermont. And while he really was interested in his friend's trip, his thoughts—and gaze—kept returning to where Keeley had disappeared with Liza, wishing he could hear what they were talking about.

"So all in all," Kayden said, wrapping up, "we'll be gone three weeks. Leaving at the ass-crack of dawn tomorrow morning. Longest vacation I've ever taken in my life, and I've been living for it. Aldo and I have become experts on dehydrating shit. The other night we dehydrated hot sauce."

Rafe rolled his eyes. Kayden put Cholula on everything. And Rafe did mean *everything*, including pancakes, ice cream, and broccoli. "I'd like to say it sounds like a great time, but the only way I'd willingly trek through the woods for weeks on end was if I heard the banjo music growing louder in the distance."

They both laughed.

The rest of the guys who'd been helping with the move walked in.

"That's the last of it," Liza's brother, Elio, said.

Rafe had been surprised when Elio showed up early this morning, ready to help them lug boxes. Elio's visits to Philly were few and far between when hockey season was in full swing. A forward on Baltimore's team, Elio spent months on the road. However, his team was playing the Flyers tomorrow at home, and good friend that he was, he'd agreed to help with the move, claiming if it was the only way he could get some quality time with his buddies, he'd take it.

"I didn't realize I'd acquired so much crap over the years," Gio confessed.

"You've always been a packrat," his twin reminded him. "I told you it's easier to throw stuff away *before* the move."

"I thought I'd put a pretty good dent in it, but in the end, I ran out of time. We've been busting our asses all week to finish the Zinczenko project," Gio grumbled.

"Damn, I'm glad that job is done," Luca agreed.

"Tell me about it," Tony said, adding another box to the stack he and Kayden had just created in the foyer. "For the longest time, I couldn't decide if Mrs. Zinczenko was an exacting taskmaster or just fucking crazy. In the end, I didn't give a shit. Just wanted the project to be over."

"Anybody notice the way Rhys always gets out of helping us move?" Luca pointed out.

Tony grinned. "He always says the same thing. When people stop getting sick on the weekend, he'll be here."

Tony's roommate and partner, Rhys, was a general practitioner. A compassionate doctor, he was devoted to his patients, so he worked most weekends and took lots of late-night calls.

"He gets a bye," Rafe said. "Just means more beer and pizza for the rest of us."

Keeley and Liza walked out to join them, Cricket dancing around their feet. From the sound of dishes clattering in the kitchen, it appeared Gianna—God bless her—was still unpacking boxes and combining Gio's plates and utensils with Grandpa Albert's.

The kitchen, in direct opposition to the rest of the house, held very little. A simple man who entertained infrequently, Grandpa hadn't had more than four place settings, and very few appliances, apart from the standard stove, fridge, and microwave. He didn't even have a dishwasher, which was rocketing very close to the top of the renovations list. Rafe hated washing dishes by hand. With the addition of Gio's dishes, Rafe was looking forward to the larger stock because, while it would mean a bigger stack of dirties in the sink, it also meant more time between washing.

Unless he could foist that chore off on Gio, a previously unconsidered perk to having a roommate.

"I ordered the pizza twenty minutes ago," Keeley said. "So it should be here soon."

"Yes! Pizza. Manna from the Gods," Elio said, wrapping his large arm around Liza's shoulders and ruffling her hair playfully. She tried to shake him off, bitching the entire time, but Elio was strong and obviously didn't get enough time to terrorize his younger sister.

"Asshole," Liza said, finally pushing him away. Her grin proved her complaints weren't serious. "Go back out on the road."

"I'm afraid I'm not staying for pizza," Keeley said. "Got an appointment to get a manicure."

"A manicure?" Liza asked, drawing out her tone in a do-tell way.

Keeley's nonchalant, too-casual attitude sounded alarm bells in Rafe's mind. "Yeah. My nails look like shit. I called the place I like this morning, they had an opening, so I took it."

Liza narrowed her eyes in response but didn't question Keeley further.

"Then I need to head home. I have a mountain of laundry that refuses to do itself for some reason."

Rafe didn't have to be a rocket scientist to realize Liza wasn't buying Keeley's story—and that Rafe wasn't the only person Keeley had stopped sharing her life details with.

"Wanna go out for margaritas later?" Liza asked.

Keeley shook her head. "No. I've been going out too much lately. Really just need a night at home to relax. Rain check?"

"Okay. Sure." Liza looked as lost as he felt. Keeley wasn't one to ever turn down an opportunity to go out.

Kayden groaned. "Seriously, Kee? You're leaving? This is our last day together before I take off for the trail tomorrow."

Keeley kissed her brother's cheek. "So we'll say goodbye to each other now instead of two hours from now. Give me a hug."

Kayden wrapped her up in his embrace, squeezing her so tightly, she said, "I can't breathe!" The grin on her face said she didn't have a problem with that.

"I'm going to miss you, kiddo," he said, releasing her.

She patted her brother's chest, pure mischief on her face. "I'd like to say the same, but three weeks without you stalking me on Find My Friends...texting me all hours to ask me where I am and who I'm with...sorry, bro, but freedom is going to taste very sweet."

"You know there's Wi-Fi on the trail," he said. "I checked."

Aldo laughed, then got a dig in on his hiking partner. "Don't worry, Keeley. It's sporadic as fuck."

Kayden gave his best friend an exasperated look. "Why would you tell her that?"

"It's like you don't know me at all, man." Aldo and Kayden shared the same close friendship Rafe and Gio did, though Aldo was hell when it came to practical jokes and teasing. Rafe wasn't sure how Kayden, the eternal straight guy, put up with it as well as he did.

"Thanks for the info," Keeley said, digging the knife in deeper as she stepped over to Aldo, hugging him as well. "You take care of Kayden for me. Chase away all the bears and snakes and bugs. He's delicate."

Kayden muttered a few choice words as the rest of them laughed.

Aldo gave her a quick kiss on the top of the head. "You got it, Kiwi. I'm on the job. Nothing will hurt him while I'm around."

"You two realize I'm a grown-ass man, right?" Kayden muttered.

Keeley tapped her brother's cheek playfully. "And now you know how I feel. Have fun. Don't wipe your ass with poison ivy." She gave him one more big hug.

"Rafe, I'll see you and Gio on Monday." Keeley offered him a hug as well. He kept it short since her brother was watching.

She turned, and was nearly to Gio, when she suddenly stumbled forward. Gio was quick to catch her.

"Goddammit, Albert! Stop pushing me," Keeley said, laughing.

Gio gripped her upper arms, steadying her. "One of these days you're going to have to stop blaming Rafe's grandpa for your two left feet."

"I told you. I'm not tripping. He's shoving me. Tell them I'm not clumsy, Kayden."

Kayden hesitated, then said, "You called me delicate," in a tone that was pure payback-is-a-bitch.

"Sure, you're not clumsy," Gio teased, casting a glance at her brother and releasing her arms.

This wasn't the first time Rafe or Gio had been in a position to catch her. She'd tumbled into Rafe's arms twice since the inexplicable desk slide during her first week here.

Keeley, undeterred, hugged Gio. Rafe studied her in Gio's arms and felt the same stirring that was becoming too familiar. And uncomfortable. Because watching Keeley and Gio embrace never failed to send a rush of blood straight to his cock.

"Okay. Peace out," she said to the room at large, flipping them the peace sign.

"Pizza's here," Tony announced, glancing out the open front door. "I'll go get it."

"Cool," Aldo said. "Come on, Elio, we can grab some napkins and the beer from the fridge. Looks like we'll have to eat out on the porch. Every flat surface in the house is covered with boxes."

"I'll start moving some chairs out there," Liza said.

"I'll give you a hand," Luca said, following his cousin to the dining room to start dragging out seats for everyone.

Gio and Rafe started to follow, but Kayden stopped them.

"Can I talk to you guys for a second?" he asked.

Rafe had a brief moment of panic, wondering if perhaps they'd overplayed their hand, revealed their attraction to Keeley, and Kayden had noticed.

Kayden was a good friend, and Rafe never wanted to do anything to screw that up. But his desire for Keeley was definitely testing his restraint, his resolve.

"Sure. What's up?" Gio asked.

"I was hoping the two of you would keep an eye on Keeley for me while I'm gone. She wouldn't thank me for asking, but...this is the longest I've been away from her since our parents died, and it would set my mind at ease to know you were watching out for her."

"Of course we will," Gio replied quickly, placing a hand on Kayden's shoulder.

Rafe nodded his assent, guilt preventing him from speaking. He wanted to do way more than keep an eye on Keeley.

"Great. I can't tell you how happy I am that she's working for you, Rafe. That last boss of hers gave off creepy-ass vibes."

"Did he harass her?" Rafe asked.

"No, nothing like that," Kayden hastened to say. "I just didn't like the way he looked at her sometimes. Of course, that was probably just me being overly sensitive. Keeley's always drawn male attention."

"Because she's beautiful," Rafe said, the words slipping out before he could think better of them.

Kayden nodded. "I know, dammit. Not sure how I made it through her high school years. Always a bunch of immature idiots hovering around her."

"Doesn't sound like that's changed much," Gio said. "Some of her dating stories..."

Kayden groaned. "Tell me about it. She's a magnet for losers. It's the only way I can think to explain it. And it kills me too because she's grown up to be an amazing woman."

"She really has," Rafe agreed.

"She's going to make some lucky guy an incredible wife. I pray every night she'll meet a good man, someone who will love her for exactly who she is and make her happy. I keep telling her she'll find the right guy eventually, but after so many years on her own and looking, kissing all those damn frogs, as she calls them..." Kayden sighed. "She wants to fall in love, wants what our parents had, and I can't fault her for that because I want the same thing."

Kayden and Aldo had graduated from high school the same year as Tony, the three of them, plus Rhys, the oldest in their gang of friends. Kayden had put a few good dating years on hold when he became Keeley's guardian at the ripe old age of twenty-five, sacrificing a social life for his sister.

"You're both going to find what you're looking for," Gio said, squeezing his shoulder. "You just need to hang in there."

Kayden smiled, then walked out to the porch, the smell of pepperoni and cheese filling the air.

Gio started to follow, but Rafe held him back. "I think Keeley's been talking to that guy, JT."

"How do you know?" he asked, scowling.

"I overheard Liza asking about him."

Gio digested that information, then turned his attention back to Rafe. "You ready to admit it?"

Rafe nodded. But Gio wanted to hear the words.

"You want her too, don't you?" his friend pressed.

Rafe gave him a sad grin. "Yeah. I do. But, Gio, my feelings haven't changed about wanting a long-term relationship."

"I know, but..." Gio ran his hand through his hair. "If we pursue this, I don't see me walking away from Keeley...ever."

Rafe knew that was true. His friend was falling, and falling fast. "I know that, so maybe *we* don't pursue it. Only you do."

"You could do that? Walk away without ever knowing..." Gio frowned. "You're attracted to her too, even if you don't like admitting it. What if we leave the decision up to her?"

"I'm not sure that's a good idea."

Gio stared at him a long time, and he got the sense his friend could see more than he wanted him to. Because Gio was right. He wanted Keeley more than he'd ever wanted another woman.

Rafe schooled his features the best he could, hoping Gio didn't see any of the confusion—or desire—drowning him.

"Might be a moot point anyway," Gio said at last. "Do you think we waited too long to make a move?"

Rafe foolishly rejoiced over Gio's use of the word *we*, even though he knew that pronoun was wrong. Then, he shrugged and sighed heavily.

"I don't know. I really don't know."

Chapter Eight

A buzzing sound roused Gio from a deep sleep. He waved his hand in front of his face, thinking it was a fly. Then he realized it was his phone.

It was his first night in his new bedroom in the mansion, and he felt slightly disoriented.

Rolling toward the nightstand, he picked up his cell and looked at the number. It wasn't one he recognized. Ordinarily, he would have turned his phone off and gone back to sleep, but his sixth sense was telling him to answer.

Immediately, he thought about Luca, the twin bond between them a very real thing.

"Hello."

"Gio?"

Gio sat up at the sound of Keeley's voice, looking around the dark room, trying to get his bearings. It was darker and quieter here than it had been in his fifth-floor apartment in the city. No streetlights, no noise from the traffic below.

"Keeley? What time is it?"

"It's a little before two a.m. I'm sorry I'm calling you so late."

Gio's heart started to race. Her voice sounded...off.

"Are you okay? Where are you?"

She paused just long enough that he knew she *wasn't* okay.

"Keeley. Where are you?" As he asked the question, he rose from bed, reaching for the jeans he'd shucked before crawling beneath the sheets a couple hours earlier. When Keeley left today for her manicure, she'd said she was going home to do laundry and relax. He hadn't thought to worry about her because he'd taken her at her word.

From the sound of loud music in the background, it was clear she'd lied about her plans.

"The Dolphin."

Gio growled. The Dolphin was in South Philly, and nowhere he wanted her to be at this time of night. "Who's with you?"

She evaded his question. "I was wondering if you could come get me."

He pulled the phone away from his ear for the two seconds it took to pull a T-shirt over his head. "I can be there in fifteen minutes. You inside? Safe?"

"Yeah."

"Good. Stay there." Then he recalled the unrecognized number. "Whose phone is this?"

"I had to borrow one. Mine is broken."

"How did it get broken?"

Apparently, Keeley wasn't in the mood to give details because once again, she changed the subject. "Could you maybe not call Kayden? He's leaving in a few hours for his trip, and I don't want to ruin it for him."

Gio sighed. "I won't tell him. But, Keeley, when I get there, you're answering all my questions."

They hung up, and Gio quickly slipped on his shoes. He knocked on the door to Rafe's room, surprised when it opened instantly.

"Who were you talking to?" Rafe asked. Then he noticed Gio was dressed. "Where are you going?"

Gio had chosen the guest room right across the hall from

Rafe's, and he hadn't kept his voice down, his concern for Keeley overshadowing everything else.

"Get dressed. Keeley's at The Dolphin. She needs a ride," Gio explained quickly, not wanting to keep Keeley waiting a second longer than he had to.

Rafe didn't ask another question. Instead, he quickly threw on clothes as Gio attempted to find his keys.

"I thought she was staying in tonight," Rafe said as the two of them climbed into Gio's truck.

"Yeah. Me too. Apparently, she lied."

"Why would she do that?"

Gio pounded his palm against the steering wheel. "It's the middle of the night and she's in a nightclub in a not-great part of Philly with no phone," Gio said, unable to let his anger and concern go.

"She's an adult, Gio," Rafe replied calmly. Too fucking calmly.

"And yet she'll be lucky if I don't turn her over my knee and spank her ass after this," Gio said through gritted teeth.

Rafe sighed, shaking his head.

"Aren't you pissed?" he asked hotly.

"I'm not happy, but one of us needs to keep a cool head, and since you have out-of-control rage covered, it looks like that's me."

Gio took a couple of deep, steadying breaths, aware Rafe was right. Losing his shit wasn't going to help a thing.

"So much for keeping an eye on her," Rafe murmured. "Kayden hasn't even left town and we've already screwed that up."

"She lied," Gio repeated.

"Was she okay?" Rafe asked.

Gio threw his hands up briefly, releasing the steering wheel before quickly gripping it again. If Gio was talking, his hands were moving. That was true of all the men in his family. But...it was a problem when he was driving. "That's the thing that's really killing me. Because I don't think so. She sounded upset."

"Shit." Rafe turned and looked out the window, neither of them speaking again until they found a parking spot one block away from the nightclub.

The pressure that had been weighing on his chest since Keeley's call instantly lifted the second he saw her standing at the door with a bouncer.

"Those are my friends," she said to the man.

She walked over to meet them, and he instantly noticed she was limping slightly, something that, from the grimace on her face, she was working hard to hide from them.

The bouncer nodded at them. "You guys got her?"

Gio lifted his chin, appreciating the man's concern. "Yeah. She's with us."

"Cool. I'm gonna go finish closing up. I'll call you, Keeley, if we find your credit card."

"Thanks, Alec," Keeley said with a weak wave.

Gio wrapped his arm around her waist, while Rafe claimed her hand. He had to give it to her. She was working overtime to mask the obvious pain she was in. If the car hadn't been so close, he would have picked her up and carried her.

She pulled up short when she spotted Gio's truck. If he hadn't been out of his mind with worry, he would have told Rafe to drive. There wasn't a backseat in his old, beat-up Ford. Just a bench seat.

Rafe opened the passenger door and helped her climb inside, while Gio crossed to the driver's side. Once they were all in, Gio turned to look at her.

"How bad is your ankle?" he asked.

"What?"

"How bad, Keeley?" he repeated impatiently.

"It's fine. I just twisted it."

He studied her face, trying to decide if she was lying. "Do you need to go to the ER? Or we could swing by Tony's and ask Rhys to take a look at it."

She shook her head. "No, really. It's okay. I just need to get out of these heels and prop it up. It'll be better by morning."

"Where's your phone?" Rafe asked.

She pulled it out of the back pocket of her jeans. The screen was shattered and the case dented.

"What the hell happened to it?"

She blew out a long breath, exhaustion, and something else Gio couldn't put his finger on, etched in every line on her face. "I fell on the dance floor. My phone took the worst of it."

"You lost your credit card?" Rafe asked, doing a much better job at moderating his voice.

She nodded. "The credit card was in the same pocket as my phone. I guess it fell out when I pulled my phone out of my pocket to look at it, but I didn't notice at the time. My apartment key is...somewhere else. The dance floor was kind of crowded. The Dolphin closed a few minutes before you guys got here, and Alec, the bouncer, helped me look for the card, but it's long gone. I'm going to have to cancel it."

Gio started the truck. "This sounds like a long story. You can tell it to us when we get back to the house."

"No. My landlord has a spare key. I can go to my apartment."

Rafe took her hand in his. "You're staying with us."

Keeley dug in her heels, and Gio suspected it was because she didn't want to tell them about her night. "I'll be fine at my place."

Rafe shook his head. "You don't have a phone. It's not safe."

"I'll get a new phone first thing tomorrow morning," she said, continuing the argument.

Which was tough shit for her because Gio was driving, and he wasn't taking her to the apartment.

"Until you get a phone, you're staying with us," Gio said, making it clear the subject was not open for debate.

Normal Keeley would have put up one hell of a fight at that point, would have insisted and put her foot down, pitched a fit even.

This Keeley?

Well, Gio didn't know what to make of this Keeley. She was tired and sad and completely beaten down.

The anger that had been simmering since he'd discovered she was out alone faded, replaced with concern.

"Fine," she said softly after a moment.

The three of them rode in silence, and for a second or two, he thought perhaps Keeley had fallen asleep.

Glancing over, he saw that she'd rested her head on Rafe's shoulder, her eyes closed, as his friend held her hand, his thumb softly stroking her fingers.

It was her breathing that betrayed her, that told him she wasn't sleeping at all. She'd closed her eyes as another evasion tactic because her breathing wasn't the deep and easy rhythm of someone slumbering. It was shallow and shaky.

When they pulled up to the house, Gio put the truck in park and killed the engine. Rafe got out, then helped Keeley down as well. Keeley had complained once that his truck needed a damn stepladder to get in and out of.

She walked a bit steadier as they entered the house, and he realized that—at least as far as the ankle was concerned—she hadn't lied. She also seemed to have gotten her second wind somewhere between the nightclub and here.

She slipped off her shoes just inside the front door, closing her eyes in obvious relief. "I know where the guest room is. I can get there myself. Good night."

She started for the stairs to the second floor but turned back around when Gio chuckled humorlessly and said, "You don't really think that's going to work, do you?"

"I'm tired. Can we table this conversation until tomorrow?"

Rafe shook his head, walking toward her. "No. We can't." Putting his hand on her waist, he guided her to the living room couch, gently pressing on her shoulder until she sank down. Rafe sat next to her.

Cricket made her way into the room, yawning. They'd clearly woken the dog. She walked over to her doggie bed in the corner and lay down. Gio knew for a fact the dog typically slept in Rafe's room, something his friend pretended to be annoyed about, claiming his grandpa had spoiled the dog, letting her sleep with him. Despite Rafe's grumbling, it was obvious he cared about the tiny creature.

Gio followed them to the couch, claiming her other side.

Keeley leaned back, sinking farther down in the cushions, sighing heavily. "Okay. Let me have it."

"Have what?" Rafe asked.

"You're obviously pissed off at me, so just say it, give me the Kayden-like lecture, tell me I was stupid—which I know—and reckless and..." Keeley closed her eyes wearily.

"Keeley," Rafe said gently. "We're not your brother. And you need to understand, that's not what this is about."

Her eyes opened, and Gio could see his friend had surprised her with his calm, patient tone as well as his words.

"What happened tonight?" Gio asked.

"The same shit that always happens."

"Be more specific," Gio said. "And if you really are as tired as you say, you might want to just go ahead and give us all the details instead of making us drag them out of you one question at a time. Otherwise, we could be here awhile."

She frowned angrily, but it felt like an act. Like she wanted to give the appearance of being annoyed because she couldn't work up enough energy to feel the actual emotion. Finally, she just gave in. "You remember that guy at Eclectic?"

"There were three guys hovering around you at Eclectic," Rafe said. "Black shirt, Chad, and JT."

"JT," she specified.

Gio had known in his gut tonight's bullshit had included that guy.

"He called me last weekend, like he said he would. He was just as I remembered," she said, with a wistful smile that quickly faded. "He said he'd regretted going back with his ex five minutes after he'd broken things off with me, but they'd shared a long history, and she'd genuinely been trying to make things up to him. He said it took him eight months to get out of that mistake, and by the time he did...he figured too much time had gone by for him to call me."

None of that sounded bad, but given the way the night had ended, Gio could tell the asshole had found a way to knock her down again. Maybe literally, when he considered her broken phone.

"Anyway, we've been texting and talking on the phone, catching up on the last year, and it felt like we were right back where we'd left off. He called last night and invited me out for dinner tonight. Obviously, I said yes."

"Why the secrecy, Keeley?" Rafe asked. "Why not tell us, or Liza, or your brother you were going out with him tonight?"

"Liza and Kayden don't like JT. They're both still pissed about the way he dumped me, and they were upset when I told them he'd called me last weekend. I wasn't sure if it was going to go anywhere, so I just didn't tell them when he kept calling."

"And us?" Gio forced himself to ask.

"I was afraid you'd show up. It was okay with the other dates because I didn't know those guys, but I wanted a night alone with JT. Just to see if what I'd thought was there a year ago still was." She stopped talking, and neither he nor Rafe pushed her for more.

Gio *really* didn't want to know what she'd discovered.

Mercifully, she continued without prodding. "Dinner was awesome. We laughed and talked, and it was all so perfect. By the time it was over, neither of us wanted to say goodbye. So JT suggested we go dancing. I left my car at the restaurant, and he drove us to The Dolphin. I left my purse in his car, tucked the necessities—my credit card, ID, and phone in my back pocket— we paid the cover and went in."

"You didn't lose your ID?" Rafe asked.

She shook her head. "No. It was still in my pocket. Just lost the credit card. Which reminds me...can I use your computer? I really should cancel—"

"Later," Gio interjected. "Finish your story."

"We were dancing, and it was a lot of fun...until I discovered his ex was there with her new boyfriend."

"Did he know she was going to be there?" Rafe asked.

Keeley leaned forward, her elbows on her knees, her eyes cast down at the floor. The entire pose was so totally not her that Gio felt his anger toward that prick JT begin to rise again.

"Keeley." Gio put his hand on her upper back. "Sit up and look at us."

She took a steadying breath, then did as he asked. "I'm tired," she repeated, and he didn't think exhaustion was the cause for that. Instead, she looked like a woman who'd reached the end of the line and couldn't take one more step.

Gio nodded slowly. "I know you are. Just finish the story and you can go to bed."

"You're a bossy son of a bitch."

Gio laughed. "Yeah. Tell me something I don't know. It's probably the most annoying of the Moretti traits." He twisted so that his back rested on the arm of the couch. "Come here." Parting his legs, putting one up on the couch, he shifted Keeley until she was sitting with her back leaning against his chest.

Rafe picked up her feet, placing them on his lap, studying her ankle. From his position, Gio could see it was slightly swollen.

Rafe gently turned it, his eyes on Keeley's face. "You sure it's not sprained?"

"I'm sure," she said.

Rafe began to rub her feet, Keeley's sigh one of relief and relaxation.

Gio wrapped his arms around her, resting his hands on her stomach. It was an intimate position, but damn if it didn't feel right. "Tell us the rest, Keeley. Then you can go to bed, sleep it off, and put it all behind you."

"JT knew she was going to be there. She'd dumped him

again...not the other way around, like he told me. He took me there thinking it would make her jealous. It didn't. Of course, I didn't realize she was there or what he was doing until it was too late."

"What do you mean?" Gio asked.

"What had started as a happy buzz for him turned into a mean drunk really fast. We were out on the dance floor, and he was starting to get sloppy, staggering and shit. I suggested we leave. Told him I could drive him home and then get an Uber back to my place. He refused, tugged me closer. He told me we couldn't leave yet, that he wanted Cassie—that's his girlfriend—to see us. I stupidly said, 'She's here?' and he turned around to point her out. She and her new boyfriend were dancing and pushing the limits of public indecency big-time. JT saw it and flipped his lid. He grabbed the other guy's arm to pull him away from Cassie."

"Let me guess. They got into a fight," Rafe said.

Keeley nodded. "Both guys were wasted and out for blood. JT shoved the other guy really hard, and I was in the wrong place at the wrong time. I twisted my ankle and went down on my ass. My phone, as you saw, got smashed. I felt it crack and pulled it out to look at it. I think that's when the credit card fell out of my pocket. From there, the dominoes just kept falling. I heard police sirens outside, so I ran to the ladies' room."

"Why?" Gio asked.

Keeley twisted to give him a "seriously" look. "Because Kayden's on the force and there was no way one of the cops wouldn't recognize me and call him. I told you on the phone, Gio. He's leaving for Vermont at dawn, and I was afraid... Well, I was afraid he'd cancel his trip. This is the first time he's taken a break just for himself since Mom and Dad died. He deserves this vacation. More than that, he needs it. I would hate myself if I screwed it up."

"So you hid from the cops," Rafe said.

"Yes. When the coast was clear, I came out and heard the

bartender yell out for last call. JT and the other guy had obviously been carted off to the drunk tank, which meant there was no way I was getting my purse out of his car, which meant no apartment key. Which pisses me off because it's my favorite purse."

"The one that was your mother's?" Rafe asked.

"Yeah." Keeley was clearly surprised and touched that Rafe had remembered that fact. "I planned to get the bartender to call me a cab, since I couldn't use the Uber app on my defunct phone. That was when I discovered my credit card was missing. The bouncer saw me looking for it and helped. When I told him I was stranded, with no money, phone, or key, he let me use his phone so I could call for someone to pick me up."

"Why me? Not Liza?" Gio asked.

Keeley laughed softly, the first chuckle of the night, and Gio decided that making her talk about what happened was probably helping her. Because she was becoming more animated, more like herself as she continued. Keeley was a born storyteller, and as the emotions surrounding this evening faded, he suspected her retellings would become more entertaining as she embellished it.

"Liza got a new phone a few months ago with a new number. I put it in my contacts and that was it. Same with pretty much everyone's number. The only ones I have memorized are Kayden's and yours."

Gio chuckled. "Told you it was a great number."

Gio had landed an awesome phone number, and he'd bragged about the last four digits quite a lot after he first got it.

"Nineteen sixty-nine," Keeley muttered. "All I can remember is you saying, 'great year, great position.' Stupid number is stuck in my head."

"And it's a good thing too."

She lifted one shoulder. "I guess. I feel like an idiot. What's that saying? Fool me once, shame on you. Fool me twice? JT got me...twice."

"That's on him, little one," Gio said. "Not you."

"Yeah, well." Those two words were loaded with disappointment. Keeley was usually pretty good at shrugging off bad dates, but this one had gotten her down.

"I'm sorry. I know you liked him." Rafe pressed his thumbs into the bottom of her foot and Keeley moaned with pleasure. The sound went straight to Gio's cock, as he considered all the other ways they could make her moan...in bed.

Rafe had finally admitted to wanting her too. But as Rafe said —she *was* different from their previous affairs. Because Gio didn't intend to let Keeley go. He was pretty sure he'd found *the one*, and he was determined to hold on to her with both hands.

So why did he still feel this overwhelming need to share her with Rafe? Because Rafe said he didn't feel different, and he wasn't planning to stick around forever.

Then he realized the problem was...Gio didn't believe him. Rafe was lying to him. And to himself.

Speaking of lies...

"We're not happy about you lying to us," Gio said, because he couldn't completely shake free of the panic he'd felt when he had answered the phone and heard her voice earlier.

"It was just one bad night where everything went wrong. I'm a big girl. I'm going to be fine."

"Regardless, we need to know where you're going to be," Rafe stressed.

Keeley shook her head. "I don't tell Kayden where I'm going all the time."

"Kayden has you on that Find My Friends app," Rafe pointed out.

"He told you guys to babysit me, didn't he?" she asked, clearly annoyed.

Gio tightened his grip around her. "Doesn't matter if he did or didn't. We're always going to look out for you. And even you have to admit this wasn't a good situation for you to be in tonight. Alone in South Philly at two in the morning, with no money and no way to get home."

She blew out a long breath and Gio could see his words had

sunk in. "It wasn't good. I promise to tell you where I'm heading when I go out. But only until Kayden gets back."

She relaxed in his arms, and he realized if they remained here without talking, she'd be asleep within minutes.

"Keeley," Gio said.

"Yeah?" she asked drowsily, her eyes drifting closed.

He bent his head to her ear. "Open your eyes. We're not finished yet."

His close proximity took her by surprise, as did the soft kiss he placed on her cheek.

She turned to look at him, clearly exhausted. "You said if I told you everything I could—"

"I know what I said. But you need to understand something. We don't need the promise you just gave us. You don't have to tell us where you're going."

"Rafe said—"

He cut her off. "Because you owe us."

She frowned. "For the ride?"

Gio shook his head. "For not telling Kayden about tonight."

"Oh. What do you want?" she asked.

"A date."

Rafe shifted slightly, and Gio glanced his direction, could see his friend fighting to make a decision. *He'd better make it quick.*

Finally, Rafe gave him a subtle nod. He was on board.

"A date?" Keeley sat up, holding his gaze, waiting for him to continue.

Gio forged on. "With me and Rafe. Tomorrow night."

"With both of you?" She glanced from Gio to Rafe, as if to confirm that he was cool with the request.

Rafe ran his fingers along her cheek and gave her a smile. "We're tired of running off all those other guys. It's high time we staked our claim."

"But I didn't think you..." Keeley paused, and Gio got the sense she was confused by exactly what they were offering. He could understand that. However, rather than ask about their intentions, she changed gears. "You both slept with Jill."

Gio nodded. "Yeah. We told you that."

"And you said she wasn't the only one." She bit her lip, and Gio was amused by her uncharacteristic shyness.

Rafe shook his head. "There were two others."

Keeley's eyes widened as she digested that information. "Oh," was all she said.

Gio was glad to finally be able to admit it. He didn't want to hide this part of himself from her anymore. He remembered his shock the first time they'd gone to bed with Jennifer, how amazing it had been. He and Rafe worked well together in the bedroom, and he'd loved sharing. Probably because—as a twin—he'd shared pretty much everything in his life, starting with the womb.

And as incredible as that night with Jennifer had been, Gio knew with every fiber of his being that sharing Keeley would be a million times better. But there was a lot more to discuss, and tonight wasn't the time.

"I can see you're tired," Gio said. "Let's get you settled in a guest room. You can get some sleep and we'll continue this conversation tomorrow during our date."

It spoke to Keeley's level of exhaustion that she agreed to delay the discussion. After a good night's sleep, he suspected they would be subjected to no less than two hundred questions involving their past affairs.

"Okay." She rose from the couch, and they followed suit.

Gio held his hand out to her palm up, thrilled when she took it without a moment's hesitation. He clasped hers tightly, and he led her upstairs.

Rafe followed, the two of them walking her to the door of the guest room. It was right next to Gio's, also across from Rafe's. Gio went ahead and accepted that he wasn't going to get a second of sleep tonight, already hating the walls that would separate the three of them from each other.

After every single one of his good-night kisses with Keeley, he'd gone home, jacked off in the shower, then spent a restless night dreaming of all the things he wanted to do with her.

Tonight, he had a strong suspicion just one hand job wasn't going to cut it.

"Let us kiss you good night and then you can turn in," Gio said.

"Kiss?" she murmured, her sleepy brain struggling to keep up.

If Gio were a gentleman, he'd let her go straight to bed. She'd had a rough night, and there was no doubt they'd shocked her with their demand for a date.

But he couldn't stand how sad she'd looked earlier, how defeated. He wanted to erase some of the heaviness from her eyes, wanted to give her something other than that asshole JT to think about as she drifted off to sleep.

He closed the distance between them and pressed his lips against hers. Within seconds, he knew he'd made the right decision because Keeley kissed him back like she meant it, all traces of her previous grogginess gone. Her hands found their way to his neck, her fingers sliding through his hair.

She giggled breathlessly, and he pulled away for a second, giving her a curious look.

"Your beard tickles," she explained, before instigating the next kiss. It lingered, and despite the late hour, he suddenly felt as if he could stand here all night, sharing the same air with her.

However, he wasn't the only man who wanted her, and now that Rafe was on board, he intended to make sure his friend stayed there. For as long as possible.

It took every ounce of strength Gio possessed to break away from her, aware that he could go on kissing her for the rest of his life and never want for another thing. It was a powerful realization.

Keeley slowly opened her eyes as the kiss ended, and then Rafe was there, ready to take his place.

Rafe softly said her name, drawing her attention to him, then...

Gio had always thought himself a decent kisser, but it was clear he could learn a few things from his best friend.

As he had last time, Rafe cupped Keeley's face in his large hands, stared deeply into her eyes for a moment, just long enough to let her know what was coming. Then he lowered his head, his lips plundering, conquering. Their tongues touched, then Rafe nipped her lower lip, prompting a cute squeak of surprise and maybe even a spark of pain from Keeley. Her hands tightened on his shoulders as she tried to pull him closer.

Rafe didn't budge, didn't give an inch. With his actions, he made it clear he was in charge, and she was there for the ride.

Keeley moaned into his mouth, her body shifting in a way that told them she wanted—needed—more.

It took her a little longer to open her eyes after Rafe broke off this kiss, and she blinked several times as if seeking focus, clarity.

"Rafe," she whispered with such longing, Gio's already erect cock thickened even more.

Rafe drew his knuckles along one side of her face. "Take tonight. Think about what we want. Decide if you want it too. But *really* decide, Keeley. Because this attraction between us...it isn't going to be sated in just one night. Sleep well."

His words seemed to bring her to her senses. The spell broken, Keeley gave them an adorable little finger wave, then entered the guest room.

He and Rafe remained where they were, outside her closed bedroom door. Gio got the sense Rafe wanted to say something, but after a moment, he simply nodded his head once and returned to his bedroom.

Gio stood alone in the hallway for a minute more, silently sending up a prayer that this time, Rafe wouldn't walk away.

Chapter Nine

Once Keeley was in the privacy of the guest room, she closed the door and leaned against it, sucking in some much-needed air.

Her breathing was shaky as two emotions fought for dominance.

Arousal and shock.

They wanted to take her on a date.

Both of them.

Rafe had told her to take some time to think about what *she* wanted, but she'd be damned if she needed it.

She knew what she wanted, and it was them. The realization that they wanted her too was a dream come true, and there was no way in hell she was walking away from it.

If the JT thing had happened a couple months ago, perhaps she would have taken it a lot harder. She would have had her heart hurt by the stupid asshole again, but right now, she felt none of that. Because...it wasn't JT who'd been consuming her thoughts, her fantasies, her sleepless nights.

It was Gio and Rafe and those sensual, passionate, mind-blowing kisses of theirs. Years of flirting, of crushing on them, and nothing. Then, last week on the dance floor at Eclectic, she'd thought perhaps the bro-code had been officially kicked to the curb. Because there'd been no denying the chemistry between the three of them. Gio's hands brushing her breasts, Rafe's erection rubbing against her ass as they did the bump and grind.

She'd had to leave the floor after one dance because her arousal had reached dangerous peaks, and she wasn't sure she could keep the next dance from advancing to an X-rating.

When they'd returned to the table, she realized she'd obviously misread the sexy dance. Because once again, Gio had responded to her bold comments with his normal brand of harmless flirting, while Rafe brushed it off, his emotions locked down, the usual wall that told her nothing was going to happen between them back in place. She'd known in that instant she was still in the kid-sister box, doomed to only ever sleep with them in her fantasies.

She'd thought giving JT another chance would help her move past her unrequited desire for Rafe and Gio. It hadn't. JT hadn't hurt her feelings tonight. Not really. He'd just wounded her pride. And pissed her off. He'd used her, and she fucking *hated* being used.

But now, in the blink of an eye, everything had changed. All she could think was "be careful what you wish for," because while she'd dreamed about Gio and Rafe for years, she never—NEVER —thought they'd be interested in her, and she never—NEVER— imagined it would be the two of them together rather than separately.

She was surprised they'd pulled away from her after those good-night kisses a few minutes earlier. Because, holy fuck, if those weren't "let's get it on" kisses, then she clearly didn't understand kissing at all. But they'd stepped away and said good night. Which she was grateful for and annoyed about at the same time.

She sighed, the sound ridiculously happy.

How in the hell could it have gone from one of the worst nights of her life to one of the best in less than an hour?

They wanted her.

Her!

It was heady and wonderful...and overwhelming.

Rafe had been right to tell her to get some sleep. She needed some distance to consider what they were saying because right now, she was thinking with her libido. Rafe assured her it wouldn't be a one-night stand, which was awesome. But that also didn't really tell her what it *would be*...because he'd told her point-blank he wasn't looking for a committed relationship.

And it sounded like what he and Gio did together in the bedroom couldn't be classified as a relationship anyway. It sounded like it was just casual sex.

How had Rafe described it? Exploring a kink?

Keeley wasn't sure how she felt about that. She'd slept with men without love being part of the equation before, but she wasn't sure she would be able to keep her heart safe with Gio and Rafe. They'd been stealing little pieces of it here and there for a decade, starting with the night her parents had died.

She pushed away from the door and walked to the bed. Tonight had been...a lot. She was overtired and overwrought.

Of course, she was also overhorny—was that even a word?

"Enough. You're not doing anything else tonight except sleeping," she muttered to herself as she stripped out of her jeans and slid her bra off without removing her shirt. That and her panties were going to have to serve as her pajamas. She wished she'd thought to ask one of the guys for a clean T-shirt, and briefly considered using that as an excuse to seek them out again.

Down, girl.

Turning off the light, she climbed beneath the cool cotton sheets and glanced at the alarm clock on the nightstand. It was three a.m., and it had been one hell of a night.

She closed her eyes and willed sleep to come, willed her brain to shut down.

She wasn't exactly sure when she stopped tossing and turning, but apparently, she had for a little while. Because when she jerked awake nearly two hours later, she was bleary from a restless sleep.

She was also freezing.

Like, shoved-naked-into-the-Siberian-winter freezing.

She shivered violently, and her teeth honest-to-God chattered. She tried to burrow deeper beneath the sheets and the duvet, but it didn't help. Unfortunately, it was so cold in the room that the idea of peeking even one little finger from beneath the covers in search of another blanket—or twenty—or more clothes was unthinkable.

She lay there for a few minutes, caught between that half-awake, half-asleep state, aware of only one thing. She was going to freeze to death if she didn't do something.

The room was still dark. Pitch black, in fact. Rafe's haunted mansion was on the outskirts of the city on a fairly large parcel of private land. As such, there were no streetlights, and given the utter blackness from the window, the moonless sky wasn't going to provide any help either. In an hour, dawn would break, but for now, there was no reprieve from the unnatural darkness.

She pulled the duvet over her head, burying herself beneath it. Perhaps her trapped breath would provide some level of heat.

Her shivering grew worse, and she realized she was being stupid. There was no way she could fall back to sleep when she was this cold. She needed to find more blankets.

She took a deep breath and gave herself a pep talk. Then she threw back the covers, stood up, winced when she put weight on her still-sore ankle, and darted out of the room to the hallway—which felt like a sauna compared to her bedroom.

"What the hell?" she murmured, shocked by the extreme change in temperature.

She glanced back to the open door of her room, wondering if a window had been left open or something. Although, that shouldn't have mattered. It hadn't been cold outside. She hadn't even worn a jacket to dinner. Even though it was late September, the weather had been quite balmy for the past few days.

One moment, she was still looking through the open bedroom door, and the next, it slammed shut with a loud bang.

Keeley jerked, yelping loudly in surprise.

"Jesus!" she cried out, placing her hand on her suddenly racing heart.

Gio and Rafe emerged from their rooms quickly.

"What's wrong?" Gio asked.

"Are you alright?" Rafe stepped closer, grasping both of her hands. "Why are you so cold? Your hands are like ice." Then he looked at her more closely. "Jesus, your lips are blue."

"It was f-freezing," she said, her teeth still chattering. "I thought maybe a w-window was open or the AC was cranked down too low. I came out to look for more blankets. But then...I didn't slam that door. It just did it on its own."

Rafe looked over his shoulder at her closed bedroom door. "Tonight's not the first time random doors have slammed shut for no apparent reason."

"I know I said the haunted house thing would be a cool feature for the inn, but I think I changed my mind. I'm not going back in there. You can't make me."

"No one's making you go back in. Come on. Let's get you warmed up." Gio wrapped his arm around her waist, guiding her to his bedroom.

"I'm not taking your bed," she argued. "I can sleep on the couch. All I need is about thirty blankets in case it's cold in the living room too."

He ignored her, leading her to his bed. Rafe had followed them to the room, but he stopped before entering, leaning on the doorframe and watching them.

As Gio pulled back the duvet, she realized she was basically half naked. Her T-shirt just barely came to the top of her boy-cut panties.

"Get in," Gio said. "And slide to the middle."

She climbed in, doing as he asked.

Gio glanced toward the doorway, where Rafe remained. "Care to join us?"

Rafe gave Gio a look that could have been a warning or exasperation. She couldn't tell which.

"Us?" she asked, before Gio crawled into bed beside her and drew the duvet over them.

Then she felt the mattress give way on the other side, and Rafe slid in. He turned her onto her side, away from him, before slipping closer so that her back was pressed against his warm chest.

It was at that point that she realized both men were also half naked. Only they were baring their top halves, wearing nothing more than boxers in Gio's case and lounge pants in Rafe's.

"What are you doing?" she asked.

"Getting you warm," Gio replied, as if the three of them crawling into bed together was perfectly normal.

Rafe spooned her as Gio twisted onto his side to face her, grasping her still-cold hands, blowing his hot breath on her palms in an attempt to warm them.

"I'm sorry," Rafe said quietly, once she'd managed to stop shaking. It didn't take her long to warm up, not with two large male hot-water bottles flanking her. "I wouldn't have put you in that room if I'd known it was so cold. I've never noticed the temperature in there being drastically different. I'll get someone in tomorrow to check the AC."

"My room is clearly fine," Gio said. His and Keeley's rooms were right next door to each other, so it made no sense that hers would be unnaturally cold, while his stayed normal. "Looks like Marta and Albert were having some fun at your expense," he added.

"I don't know how to make them like me," she sighed, realizing the fact she felt hurt by two ghosts was a stupid reaction to have.

Gio grinned and shifted nearer, his face so close to hers on the pillow they shared that she could feel his breath on her face. "I'm pretty sure they *do* like you."

Rafe snorted. "And how did you come to that conclusion?"

Gio placed a soft kiss on her forehead, but he didn't stop there. His lips slid along her cheek until they were right beside her ear. "They knew she belonged in here with us. I think they were doing a little matchmaking. Which means you've got their blessing."

"Jesus," Rafe muttered. "You're as bad as Grandpa Albert was with the ghost stories."

Keeley shivered, but this time, it wasn't because she was cold. One of Rafe's hands had slipped beneath her shirt and was now sliding along her stomach...upwards.

Keeley lost the ability to breathe by the time his large palm cupped her breast, squeezing it firmly.

"Rafe," she whispered.

"Just helping you warm up."

"Is that what you're doing?" she asked with a breathy laugh.

His fingers found her nipple, pinching it with more force than she was used to, making her squirm against him. She'd learned through Rafe's kisses that he wouldn't be a gentle lover. And she'd read enough erotic romance to know the idea of dominance turned her on. Regardless, she had no experience with it. Her past lovers had been guys around her age, their skill levels about the same as hers. As such, she hadn't branched out much beyond missionary, doggie, sex in the shower, and sixty-nine.

Rafe and Gio were older, and she knew beyond a shadow of a doubt they could teach her a hell of a lot more.

Rafe pinched her nipple again, tight enough that she gasped.

"You went away there for a second," he murmured. "Care to tell us what you're thinking?"

"Or do we need to find more creative ways to keep your attention on what we're doing?" Gio asked.

She bucked slightly when he ran his fingers over the soft cotton of her panties.

"She's wet, so I'm going to go out on a limb and guess she was thinking about *this*...about what we're going to do to her." Gio backed up that pronouncement by slipping his fingers beneath her panties, sliding them along her slit until he found her clit. She'd never had a guy find it that fast. Hell, she'd had to draw a map to it for at least half her previous lovers.

Gio began to rub her clit, Rafe still playing with her breast, and she closed her eyes, sparks of electricity shimmering along her spine in response.

"Gio," she whispered, "Rafe."

"We promised you a night to think about this." Rafe, ever the sensible one, stopped pinching her nipple, though his palm still covered her breast possessively.

"I don't need time," she said.

"Keeley," he said, and it was clear he intended to stick to his guns. "There are some things we need to talk about before we—"

"No, we don't."

Gio, God bless him, was in the same boat as her—hot, horny, ready to roll. Which wasn't the least bit surprising. She and Gio were definitely kindred spirits, the impulsive, throw-caution-to-the-wind types, while Rafe never leapt without looking, measuring, analyzing, and then contemplating outcomes.

"How long has it been?" Gio asked, one finger sliding deeper, teasing her opening.

"A year or so," she admitted. "JT was the last."

Gio growled, and she wondered how such a threatening sound could be such a huge fucking turn-on. "We're going to make you forget about that asshole once and for all."

She gave him a mischievous grin. "You're welcome to try."

Gio had yet to resist one of her dares. Given that she was completely out of her depth with them in so many other ways, that one small bit of power felt like it gave her at least a chance to grab the upper hand from time to time.

Gio increased the pressure on her clit, and she trembled with need.

Yeah. So much for the upper hand.

"How many times do you want to come?" Rafe whispered in her ear, his hot breath reminding her she'd been freezing just a few minutes earlier. Lying here between them, the heat was so scorching, she was certain she'd never feel cold again.

"How many?" His question drove home exactly how out of their league she was. Because she was a one-and-done girl. Once a guy got her there, he typically saw that as the signal that it was his turn, and he could wrap things up. Not one lover in her past had ever made her come twice.

Her nonresponse was telling. Gio shook his head in disgust. "You've been sleeping with the wrong men."

She grinned. "I think, given the stories I've told you, that should be obvious."

Dawn was finally starting to break through the blackness of the night, the sky lightening to gray. They'd left the bedroom door open, light from the hallway streaming in, also helping to illuminate the room.

Gio glanced over her shoulder and exchanged a look with Rafe, one that seemed to be the equivalent to striking the bell at the beginning of a boxing round. He removed his hand from her panties.

Rafe released her breast, reaching for the hem of her shirt. He whisked it over her head, quickly, skillfully.

She felt herself blushing, something she rarely did. She wasn't shy, but there was something about the way Gio's eyes slid along her body that felt almost as sensual as if he was touching every inch.

He reached up, his fingers sliding along her side. "You've got a tattoo."

Rafe shifted away slightly and pulled the covers farther down, she suspected to get a better look.

"It's a Joshua tree," she said. "I got it after my parents died. I was sixteen, so I used an older friend's ID since I was underage. Managed to hide it from Kayden until the summer between my junior and senior year in high school. Forgot about it and wore a bikini to a pool party we were both going to. He lost his shit. But then...when he realized what it was..."

"Why a Joshua tree?" Rafe asked.

"My dad and I had this goal to camp in all the national parks. We had a book that we got stamped whenever we traveled to a new one. A few months before he died, we went to Joshua Tree, just the two of us. It was probably the best time we'd ever had camping. I remember roasting hot dogs and marshmallows over the fire. We sang songs where we'd always say the lyrics wrong." She broke into her Annie Lennox impersonation, singing, "Sweet Dreams are made of Cheese."

Rafe and Gio both chuckled.

"The night ended with him telling me about a million stupid dad jokes that had us laughing so hard, we were doubled over. I swear to God, I thought I was gonna pee my pants. He was..." Keeley stopped talking when she realized tears were flowing down her face.

This was why she never strayed from the parent script on first dates.

"Oh my God. I'm so sorry. Talk about killing the mood." She swiped at her cheeks, swallowing hard to dislodge the lump in her throat.

Rafe wrapped his arms around her once more, and Gio wiped the tears from her face with his thumbs before leaning closer to kiss the lingering wetness away.

"Don't apologize for something like that," Rafe said gruffly.

"We love hearing your stories, Keeley. Love listening to you talk and learning things about you that we never knew," Gio added.

"Although, I could have done without the rundown on *Big Brother*. That's two hours of my life I'll never get back," Rafe groused.

Keeley laughed, and she turned her head to kiss Rafe on the

cheek, grateful to him for finding a way to ease the sadness with humor.

"I love your tattoo," Gio said, running his fingers over the ink. "Love that you honored your father that way."

She smiled. "Yeah. Kayden was pissed at first, but he understood why I got it. Two weeks later, he got a tattoo to honor our parents too. Of course, that just started the ball rolling because now, he's as tatted up as you are," she said to Gio, running her hand up and down his muscular arm, covered with an elaborate entwined serpent and dog. And then, because she'd always wanted to, she bent toward him and ran her tongue along the black ink seductively.

Gio's eyes narrowed with a hunger that had her pussy clenching. "Slide your panties down. We're about to get serious, little one."

She'd never felt particularly little. At five foot eight, she was the tallest of her friends. But right now, with them, she felt almost tiny.

Gio overshadowed her with his too-broad, muscular shoulders, his tall frame, his chiseled-in-steel-chest. While Rafe was leaner—his desk job no comparison to the heavy manual labor Gio did day in and day out—he still had her by a few inches and probably thirty pounds.

She shimmied out of her panties, a tricky act, since neither man seemed willing to move away and give her some room.

She inhaled loudly when Gio's fingers immediately returned to the magic button. "Jesus, you're good at finding that."

He chuckled, but Keeley couldn't share the sentiment. Not when Gio started stroking it faster, harder. She gripped his upper arms as he drove her to the edge of climax within moments. She couldn't even get *herself* to this point so quickly, and she had some awesome toys.

"Gio," she cried out. "God!"

"Come for us, Keeley," Rafe murmured in her ear. "Let us see you fall apart."

Her back arched as lightning struck, but through it all, Gio kept stroking, kept up the pressure, drawing the orgasm out until she begged for mercy.

As she started to land, he gentled his strokes, then pulled his fingers away as she lay there between them, fighting for air.

"What. The. Fuck. Was. That?" she asked in awe.

"When you say stuff like that, I can't decide which track record is worse—your first dates or your lovers," Gio mused.

She struggled to regain her wits. "I never come that quick. Not even when I do it myself. And I know how to masturbate."

Rafe closed his eyes and shook his head at her confession. "Keeley, baby," he murmured, running his lips along her cheek as his hand sought her breast once more.

Joel's comment about her small breasts flashed through her mind, and because her brain still wasn't fully functioning, she said, "Not quite a handful, huh?"

Rafe pinched her nipple hard, and she squeaked with pain... or, well, it started as pain but ended as *whoa*.

"Say something else disparaging—and wrong—about yourself. I dare you." Obviously, Rafe hadn't intended the *whoa* part. His tone said he thought he was punishing her. More the fool him.

Keeley closed her mouth and tried not to grin because she didn't feel the slightest bit threatened. Actually, she was wondering what he'd say if she asked him to pinch the other nipple the same way.

"You might want to tread lightly," Gio warned. "My hand is still itching to spank your ass for lying to us about staying in tonight."

Well, hell. Now she really did have a dilemma. Keeley launched into a huge mental debate over what she could do to provoke that punishment. Because that sounded hot too.

"Shit." Gio chuckled.

"What's wrong?" Rafe asked.

"Roll onto your back, Keeley," Gio demanded. "Let Rafe see your expression."

She did as he asked, even as she said, "I would think it would be more useful if I flipped to my stomach."

That time, the curse came from Rafe. "Fuck."

"We're going to have to get creative with our punishments," Gio said to Rafe before looking at her. "We can see you want it—and believe me, I'm fucking tempted. But not tonight. Tonight, we're going to take things slow. It's been a long time for you, and you've never been with two men. Let us ease you into it."

She crinkled her nose. "Sounds boring." She meant her words as a dare, but this time, Gio didn't take the bait.

"Say that afterward." He shifted, his thighs straddling hers. Bending his elbows, he caged her beneath him, kissing her senseless.

How was he making her this hot, this horny, from just a kiss?

After what felt like several breathtaking days, he lifted his head, grinning at her like the cocky, sexy bastard he was.

She reached for his waist, drawing his boxers down until his dick sprang free. She wrapped her hand around it, fighting to keep her face impassive. But holy wow…

Gio was big *everywhere*.

He started to reach toward the side of the bed, then stopped. "Shit. I haven't unpacked much." He looked over at Rafe. "Condoms are still boxed up somewhere."

"I have some in my room." Rafe started to slide out of the bed.

He stopped when she said, "I'm on the pill."

Both men stilled but remained silent.

She gave a light shrug when their attention turned to her. "I'm just saying," she added. She'd never let any guy inside her without a condom, so she was trying to figure out why she really didn't want Gio to use one. Probably because…it was Gio.

"Keeley," Gio whispered, and she marveled at his almost reverent tone. And the intense, sexy way he was staring at her.

She'd noticed it a few times before. Lately, Gio was looking at her like...

Like she was special. And not in a snowflake way, like she was used to. But like a hung-the-moon way, which was she definitely *not* used to.

"We can use condoms if you want," Gio said, pushing his boxers completely off.

"I don't need them if you don't."

Gio kissed her again. "God, you're so beautiful."

She smiled, blushing again. Gio wasn't the first guy to tell her that, but he was the first to say it in such a way that made her think he meant it and wasn't just saying it to get in her pants. They shifted together, her legs parting as he knelt between them.

One second, he was poised just above her, and the next...he was inside.

Keeley released a long, slow breath once he was seated to the hilt. She'd dreamed of this night so many times, but none of those fantasies held a candle to this reality. It was a tight fit, maybe a little too tight, but all she could think was that it felt perfect. Like he was meant to be there.

Gio nuzzled her cheek affectionately. "Okay?" he asked, holding still.

She nodded. "This feels," she sighed, "*so* good."

Gio took her at her word because after that, it was on. And all she could do was hold on tight as he thrust inside her, gaining speed and strength, bending his knees slightly until he hit...

"Shit! There," she cried out. "Right there!"

"She's close, Gio," she heard Rafe say.

Her eyes flew open when she felt fingers on her clit, Rafe's touch turning her arousal up another ten decibels. He shifted closer, the warmth from his body mingling with hers and Gio's, until they'd created a heat wave that promised to singe everything in its path. He was looking at her the same way Gio had earlier, and it was too much.

"Come for us. Let me see it this time," Rafe demanded. "Do it now."

"Oh!" Keeley grunted, the sound completely unfeminine when an orgasm she hadn't seen coming hit her hard. "Shit!" she yelled, her fingernails clenching Gio's shoulders in a way that had to be painful. Not that he seemed to notice. He pumped faster.

"Jesus, Keeley," he said, his eyes closed tightly. "So fucking good!" His thrusts became harder but staggered, as if he was trying to make it last and losing the battle. "Goddammit. Too quick but—" He pushed in deep one last time and gave up the fight, coming inside her.

He dropped to his elbows, kissing every part of her face—her lips, her cheeks, her closed eyes, her brow. The whole time, Rafe whispered sweet, wonderful things in her ear, telling her she was beautiful, brilliant, brave.

She and Gio may have just had sex, but right now, it felt like both men were making love to her. She'd never experienced anything like it...and it made her want to cry. Not out of sadness but out of wonder and bliss and a happiness so huge, it took up every square inch of her body.

They took a few minutes more to catch their breath, then Gio withdrew from her body, shifted over, and dropped next to her on the bed.

Rafe still claimed the other side, but he made no move to take his turn, as she'd expected.

She looked over at him, lifting a limp arm to his dear face. "Rafe?"

He kissed her gently—too gently—and she knew what he was going to say before he said it.

"Not yet," Rafe murmured. "It's so late, it's morning. And none of us has had much sleep."

"But—" she started. But Rafe shook his head, and she knew anything she said would be wasted breath.

Keeley could tell his comment had taken Gio by surprise too.

She felt him stiffen slightly before he lifted up on his elbow so that he could look at Rafe.

She wondered if Gio would say something, would call him out, but she noticed—not for the first time—that the two of them had some sort of secret language, spoken through looks she couldn't begin to interpret.

In the end, Gio sighed and said, "Rafe's right. We need to get some sleep." And because he was strong, and she was still basically boneless, he twisted her until he could spoon her, his thick arm banded around her middle. Within seconds, Gio was breathing heavily, sleep claiming him quickly.

She wasn't going to be so lucky. Her exhaustion had apparently come out on the other side, so that now she felt wired and worried and confused.

Rafe lay on his side, facing her. He took one look at her expression and gave her a gentle smile. "You're reading too much into this," he whispered, not wanting to wake Gio.

"Did you not want—"

"Don't finish that question," Rafe growled. "I want you more than my next breath, Keeley. But you've had a hell of a night." He glanced toward the windows, where the sun was beginning to stream through a crack in the curtains. "And morning," he added with a grin. "Gio and I are taking you out on a date tonight. We can talk about what's going to happen between us. The decision will still be yours after that. That was the original plan after all. It just seems Grandpa and Marta had a different opinion."

She gave him a breathy laugh, trying to remain quiet so as not to disturb Gio. Then she realized everything Rafe was saying was completely in character. He was a thinker, and not the type to act on impulse...or because a couple ghosts drove her into their bed. Of *course* he would want to talk things out. It was just so Rafe.

"Okay. We'll talk later," she whispered.

He leaned toward her, giving her a sweet, soft kiss, his fingertips gliding along her face. "Gio was right. You're beautiful. So beautiful."

He shifted away, only a little, and closed his eyes. He didn't fall asleep as quickly as Gio, but he lay still and quiet. So she followed suit, shutting her eyes, waiting until her body gave up its fight to remain awake.

Her last cognizant thought was a simple—if powerful—realization. One she had waited for her entire life.

I did it.

I found what my parents had.

Chapter Ten

Rafe chuckled and shook his head at Gio, who merely grinned and kept whistling.

"Jesus, man," Rafe said. "You could at least try to tamp down some of that just-got-laid obnoxiousness."

Gio kicked back in the passenger seat and shrugged. "You could be feeling the same way, but you took the let's-think-it-to-death route."

"Nope. I chose to be a gentleman. The poor woman had been run through the ringer last night between that prick JT, the fight, the broken phone, the twisted ankle, the two of us blackmailing her for a date while breaking the news we wanted to share her in bed, and those damn ghosts. I think she deserved to have more than two hours of restless, freezing-cold sleep before we both jumped on her."

Gio's smile only grew wider. "You're not going to make me feel guilty. Because it was too fucking perfect."

Rafe rolled his eyes but didn't keep the debate going. Guilt hadn't been his intention anyway. He'd just been trying to explain his actions. The problem was, he wasn't sure if his justifications were for Gio or lies he was telling himself.

Nope. He knew the answer.

Lies.

They were lies.

He'd lain there with Keeley and Gio, in bed in the wee hours of morning, overwhelmed by a sense of belonging. It wasn't something he'd ever experienced—and it had freaked him out.

Rafe had grown up with a single mother who was always busy with her job and current husband, a workaholic grandfather, and a rotating door of stepfathers. He had a family, but he'd always felt a bit like an afterthought, like something there just hovering in the background. That love of family that Gio and Keeley always described wasn't something he'd ever really felt.

And while he'd been included in the greatest group of friends a man could ever have, Rafe had never been able to shake the feeling that he was the one who didn't truly fit. The Morettis, Rhys, Kayden—they were all confident, impulsive, fun-loving guys who'd never met a stranger or doubted themselves. They knew their place in the world, in their families, and they attacked life with energy, vigor, and joy.

In contrast, Rafe questioned every decision he made. He was quiet, slow to laugh, and, at the moment, terrified.

Because Keeley and Gio were making him feel things he had no experience with. Things he'd sworn he would never feel simply because he'd been so sure he *couldn't*.

He pulled up to the curb in front of Keeley's building, parallel parking before shutting off the engine. They'd driven Keeley to her car, still parked outside the restaurant where she'd started her date with JT a little after noon. None of them had stirred before midday, thanks to their sleepless night. They'd both kissed her goodbye, then promised to pick her up for their date at six.

Gio reached for the door handle, but Rafe reached out and gripped his forearm, holding him back.

Gio looked down at his hand and shook his head. "No more fighting this. No more excuses. The cat's out of the bag and we're not putting it back in."

"I know that. I just..." Rafe was perfectly aware that things were different with Keeley, but he and Gio hadn't really discussed exactly how. "You care about her," he said.

"Of course I do. I..." Gio gave him a lopsided grin, rubbing the back of his neck as if embarrassed to admit the next part. "I'm crazy about her, bro. Shit. More than that. I'm falling hard for her."

Rafe nodded. He knew that. Knew that Gio wouldn't walk away from Keeley even if—when—Rafe did. He'd thought hearing those words would help, knowing that Keeley wouldn't be left alone at the end of...

Fuck.

And there was the truth...the KO punch. The thing that had him putting on the brakes this morning despite the fact he'd been hard and hurting and so fucking desperate for her, he thought he'd lose his mind with it.

Because Rafe wasn't sure he could walk away from her. He only knew he *should*. For her, for Gio. He wasn't a good bet. Love was uncharted territory for him, and it should remain that way, if for nothing else than his own peace of mind.

His life had changed too fucking much in the past few months, and he had the chronic stiff neck to show for it. One more upheaval and he'd likely lose the ability to turn his head completely.

Rafe couldn't let this last domino fall. He'd help his mom pick up the pieces too many times, vowed he wouldn't go there, do that, open himself up to...fuck...desertion.

He released Gio's arm and got out of the car, desperate to escape before his friend saw the confusion on his face or—God forbid—asked him about his feelings.

Gio, too anxious to see their girl, joined him on the curb and slapped him on the back. "Nice to be here at the beginning of the date instead of having to crash midway through," he joked.

They hit the buzzer to Keeley's apartment, and she pressed the button to unlock the building's door. Then they climbed the three flights of stairs—Gio taking them two at a time—instead of bothering with the elevator.

Keeley was waiting for them with the door open, leaning on the jamb, and grinning as widely as Gio.

She looked gorgeous. They'd told her to dress up because they wanted to take her someplace nice to show her off. Keeley had taken them at their word. She wore a gray-and-white print dress that wrapped around and tied at the side. It showcased her breasts and her legs, the hem ending a few inches above her knees. Her hair hung loose with big, full waves and her makeup—as always—was minimal, natural looking. She was pretty enough to go without, so Rafe was glad she didn't go overboard.

Gio wolf-whistled his appreciation, and Keeley laughed with delight when he pulled a bouquet of flowers from behind his back. She wanted romance, and Gio was determined that was what she was going to get it.

"Come inside a minute. I'll put these in water and then I just need to switch handbags. I was running a little late."

They walked inside, but before they'd made it more than a few steps from the front door, Gio took the flowers and put them on the small table in her entryway. Then he closed the door and pushed her against it, kissing her hard.

Gio's hands slid down her sides until he reached her ass, neither of them breaking the kiss, consuming each other like people on the brink of starvation. Their tongues touched. It was hot and heady, and Rafe couldn't have looked away if his life depended on it.

Keeley's hands were everywhere, on Gio's chest, his shoulders, in his hair. She seemed to want it all, and at the same time. Finally, she closed her fist in his thick hair and deepened the kiss, a silent demand for more.

Gripping her ass, Gio lifted her, and Keeley followed his lead, wrapping her legs around his waist, grinding herself on his dick as her breath turned ragged.

Rafe had been sporting an erection since he'd seen her in the doorway in her short dress. Now the hem shifted upwards with their position, which meant there was nothing between them right now except Gio's pants and her panties.

Rafe knew his friend well enough to see that Gio was two seconds away from unzipping, pulling her panties aside, and giving in to his desire to fuck her. He was a passionate, insatiable lover, something Rafe had witnessed before. Just not...

Not anywhere near this level.

He reached out and put his hand on Gio's shoulder because if he didn't stop this now, they weren't going to stop at all.

Gio might have been out of his mind with arousal, but the simple touch worked. He slowly broke the kiss.

It took Keeley a few seconds longer to regain her wits, her eyes still closed, her face flush, her pelvis grinding against his friend in a way that told him just how much she wanted him.

She blinked a few times before she was able to focus. "You stopped," she whispered, the words an outright accusation.

Gio nodded as he released her ass and her legs dropped back down. He retained his grip on her until he was sure she was supporting her own weight.

"I'm not the only one here," he reminded her before taking a large step to the side.

Keeley followed his progress only until Rafe moved forward to take his place.

"Rafe," she breathed, smiling. "Missed you."

Rafe ran the back of his hand along her flushed cheek. "You look beautiful tonight, Keeley."

Her blush deepened.

"I'm going to kiss you," he said. "Just a kiss. Then the three of us are going on our date before we take this too far."

Keeley tilted her head playfully, her tone pure seduction when she said, "I'm okay with skipping the date and going too far."

Rafe shook his head. "No. That's not how tonight is going to play out. We still have things to discuss, remember?"

Keeley considered Rafe's words, then nodded her assent. "Okay."

He lowered his head to kiss her. The second his lips touched hers, every excuse, justification, every lie and every truth fell away until there was only her.

He was already laying his weapons down.

But only for tonight, he thought to himself.

He pushed her lips apart with his, plundering her mouth with his tongue, determined to steal every taste, every breath.

Keeley moaned, her fingers fisting in his button-down shirt, wrinkling it. He didn't give a shit.

Like Gio, he needed to feel more of her. His hands reached for her ass, but he didn't lift her. He had a different goal in mind.

He reached beneath her dress, his fingers sliding to the front, finding her damp panties.

She gasped. "But you said..." she whispered, her words falling away when he burrowed his fingers beneath her panties—a thong —and found her clit.

"We're not going all the way," he murmured, rubbing his lips against hers as he spoke. "But you *are* going to give us one of those sexy orgasms before we leave. Then you're going to sit with us at the restaurant with that gorgeous, just-climaxed flush on your cheeks, squirming in your chair in those wet panties, proof to every man who looks at you that you belong to us...tonight," he forced himself to add at the end. He had to keep the boundaries clear—for them and for himself.

"God," Keeley breathed, when Rafe backed up his words with action. He drove two fingers inside her, pumping them fast and hard—and he suddenly understood why Gio had been so annoyingly giddy all day. Keeley was hot, responsive, ready, and he went light-headed when he considered just how tightly her pussy was going to glove his cock.

He added his thumb to the game, stroking her clit, recalling her surprise that they not only knew how to find it, but how to use it to bring her pleasure so fast. He had to beat down his unexpected anger at every loser who'd taken her to bed and failed her. None of them had been worthy.

He wasn't either, but he sure as hell wasn't going to give her less than she deserved.

Keeley's head flew back against the door, her eyes closed tightly, bliss etched on her face.

Rafe might be doing all the work, but he didn't forget for a second that Gio was there, watching. Now, as always, the knowledge that he had an audience pushed Rafe higher. He loved watching, but there was something even more heady about putting on a show.

Gio stepped closer, right next to them, and Rafe felt his friend's gaze. He wasn't looking at just Keeley. He was looking at both of them.

The bastard had him on the ropes, knew exactly when and how to see the things Rafe worked overtime to hide. Because he wasn't able to shield a damn thing right now as Keeley's pussy clenched on his fingers. His name slid from between those plump pink lips of hers, lips that were going to be wrapped around his dick very, very soon.

"Fuck," he bellowed, when Keeley's hand found its way to his erection, firmly stroking him through his pants. The unexpected touch proved she wasn't the only one teetering at the brink. Unlike Gio, he hadn't found relief this morning, hadn't taken the edge off between her legs. So he'd suffered all day, despite the fact he'd jerked off not once but twice in the shower.

Regardless, he'd be damned if he came from an over-the-pants hand job like a damn thirteen-year-old boy.

"Gio," he said through gritted teeth, still finger-fucking Keeley, who was fighting her own orgasm, determined to give as good as she got.

God, he couldn't wait to tame this wildcat, to have her purring in his arms. He loved a challenge, loved a woman who knew how to draw out his hidden alpha, his demanding, take-no-prisoners conqueror.

Gio, mercifully, understood what he needed. His friend gripped Keeley's wrist and pulled her hand away from Rafe's dick, then caught the other before she could resume her grip. He lifted them both above her head, holding them with one large hand, pressing them against the door, then he cupped her breast with the other.

She made an annoyed sound that quickly morphed to a moan when Rafe added a third finger to the two inside her. It was the equivalent to pulling a trigger, and Keeley jerked roughly as she came, Gio's claim on her wrists and Rafe's weight pressing against her the only things keeping her from sliding to the floor.

Once the spasms in her pussy stopped, Rafe pulled his fingers out, eliciting one last, sexy tremor in her body.

True to his word, Keeley's cheeks were flushed bright red, something he couldn't resist pointing out. "Pretty in pink," he murmured in her ear, loving the way she narrowed her eyes at his cocky tone.

Her strength regained, she gave him a light shove, one that wouldn't have budged him if he didn't want it to. As it was, he took a step away, catching sight of Gio's pleased expression.

He was as big a voyeur as Rafe was. They'd had a long talk about their shared kink one night after Vanessa, the second lover they'd shared, had gone to sleep. Gio had admitted how hot he got just watching, and one quick glance at the front of his friend's pants proved he'd really enjoyed what he and Keeley had just done.

Of course, there was small comfort in the fact they were both sporting hard-ons now because—despite what he'd just done— Rafe was still determined to talk to Keeley about their desires. She was younger than their previous three lovers, less experienced, and, well...he felt protective of her. He didn't want her walking into their bedroom blind.

His kinks didn't end with voyeurism and sharing.

He pushed thoughts of that away for now. He had to, or he'd never get his erection under control.

Rafe had only been in Keeley's apartment one time before, when he and his buddies all helped her move in. He'd never seen it decorated, but as he looked around now, he was impressed. She had good taste, and either she'd cleaned up for them, or she was neat by nature. He tended to believe the latter, having watched her in the mansion the past few weeks, and the way her workspace was always cleared off and tidy by the end of every day.

He walked to the kitchen and quickly washed his hands before rejoining Keeley and Gio in the living room. She had a small clutch in her hand, and she was transferring things—lip gloss, her wallet, a phone—from her larger bag.

"New phone?" Gio asked.

She nodded. "My first stop after you dropped me off to get my car was the phone store. They transferred all my information over to this one, so the only harm done was to my monthly bill because I hadn't paid off the last one."

Rafe listened with half an ear, too hung up on something else. "What was your second stop?" he asked, unable to keep the anger out of his tone.

"What?" Keeley asked.

"Isn't that your favorite bag?" Rafe asked.

"Uh... Yeah."

Gio scowled when he realized what she was holding. He stepped next to her. "I thought you left that in JT's car."

"I did."

Gio crossed his arms. "Are we playing the twenty questions game again, or are you going to explain how you got the thing back?"

"I called him after I got my new phone. He *had* spent the night in the drunk tank, but he'd gotten out earlier this morning and retrieved his car from the bar. I drove by his place to get my bag. Met him in his parking lot because it was still in his car."

"Keeley," Rafe growled, displeased.

"It was no big deal."

"No big deal?!" Gio yelled.

Keeley wasn't the type to ever back down, and right now wasn't going to be the exception. "It was my mom's favorite purse. There was no way in hell I *wasn't* going back to get it."

Gio put his hands on his hips. "That's not the point and you know it. You should have told us you were going. We would have gone with you."

"Why? I was in no danger from the idiot. We were in public, in a parking lot. He was hungover and obviously regretting his actions."

"What did he say?" Rafe asked.

"It doesn't matter what *he* said. It only matters what *I* said after I got my purse. I informed him that he was a stupid asshole, right before I said I never wanted to hear from him again, and just after I told him to go fuck himself."

Gio relaxed, but only slightly. "That's all?"

She nodded. "That's all."

"Pack a bag," he said.

"What?"

While they hadn't discussed this, Rafe knew exactly where Gio was going with his demand, so he explained. "You're spending the night with us again."

Keeley, the little minx, tapped her chin as if there was some decision to be made. There wasn't. Even so, she feigned hesitance. "Oh, I don't know about that. I have work tomorrow and I can't be late. My boss is a real hard-ass."

Rafe wrapped one hand around the back of her neck while grasping one of Keeley's hands with the other. He drew it behind him, to his ass. "All I heard was 'my boss has a hard ass.' Now give it a squeeze, naughty girl, then go pack that bag like Gio said."

"Jesus, man," Gio said, chuckling. "And you call *me* the caveman."

Keeley squeezed his ass, winking at him as she did, then she walked down the hallway to her bedroom.

"Not sure how I'm going to make it through dinner," Gio

murmured. "Especially after watching you two just now." He paused, then tilted his head. "Little rough, weren't you?"

Rafe considered that. He *had* been rough with her. Rougher than with any of his previous lovers. He wasn't sure exactly why. Part of him could tell Keeley liked her pleasure with an edge of pain. But it was more than that. In the past, he'd held back, kept parts of himself hidden.

"I know you've got an alpha side," Gio continued. "I do too. I've just never seen you quite so..." He took a moment before adding what ultimately was the right word. "Aggressive."

Rafe blew out a long, slow breath, trying to figure out how he could explain in a way that didn't reveal too much. "Our past affairs have been with women we didn't know as well as Keeley. I wasn't sure how they'd react to my more forceful side. I know Keeley better. I can read her responses, can tell by the look on her face or the sound of her voice if she's enjoying something, if she needs more, or even if it hurts."

He hoped Gio didn't look too deeply into that, didn't realize how much Rafe had paid attention to Keeley not just in the past month but for years. He'd always watched her a little more than he'd let on, fascinated by her.

He'd chalked it up to amusement, but now he could see it had been attraction, plain and simple.

He'd also never felt the need to possess or claim his past lovers. But with Keeley...he could settle for nothing less.

Keeley saved him from having to say more when she returned with an overnight bag. "I have to say, you guys are awfully sure of yourselves. Even when past experience should have proven to you that my dates never end well."

Gio wrapped his arm around her shoulders, guiding her to the door. "We're about to break that unlucky streak. Show you how real men treat a woman on a date."

She smiled her thanks when Rafe took her bag to carry for her. It was light, so she obviously hadn't packed much more than a toothbrush and change of clothes. He was tempted to tell her to grab more. Because if she decided to go through with this, one night with her wasn't going to be enough.

"So where are we going?" Keeley asked once they were in the car.

She'd claimed the backseat, while he and Gio were in the front. Gio, as always, made his stupid joke about them "ridin' eye-talian," which Urban Dictionary had taught him meant men in the front seat, women in the back. Rafe had no idea why Gio found the phrase so funny, but he used it pretty much every single time the scenario fit.

"We made reservations at Alpen Rose," Rafe replied.

From the rearview mirror, he saw Keeley's eyes widen. "Wow. I've always wanted to eat there, but it's super expensive."

Gio chuckled. "Rafe's rich now, remember?"

"Is that your way of telling me I'm picking up the check?" he joked.

Gio, shameless as always, said, "Shit, I thought that was implied when we booked the table."

Keeley laughed. "You guys are crazy."

Rafe continued to sneak glances at her as he drove, noticing with some pleasure that the smile never left her face. Keeley was happy, and she didn't bother hiding that fact.

Once they parked, Rafe put his hand on her back as they walked into the restaurant. Gio gave their name to the maître d', who showed them to their table. They'd requested a booth, so Gio slid into one side as Keeley and Rafe claimed the other.

The intimate restaurant was perfect for their first date, as it only seated forty people. The dining room was cloaked in wood, and the lighting, provided by ornate chandeliers, was dim, which made it easy for them to pretend they were the only three people in the place.

Keeley ordered a glass of red wine, while he and Gio both opted for bourbon on the rocks. Once they'd placed their orders, conversation began to flow.

Keeley had remarked at Eclectic that she'd liked JT originally because talking to him had been easy. Rafe had to admit the same was true for the three of them. He couldn't recall the last time he'd felt comfortable enough to simply be himself.

"This place is incredible," Keeley observed, leaning closer to Rafe. He took advantage of the situation by resting his arm along the back of the booth, encouraging her to nuzzle in even more. He caught the scent of her citrus-y shampoo and marveled over how the smell of lemons had become an aphrodisiac for him lately.

"How's your ankle?" Gio asked.

"Better. Just a little twinge every now and then. And it's not swollen anymore."

Gio nodded, then said, "Even so, maybe you should keep it elevated. Slip off your shoe and lift your foot up." He gave her a wicked look that was one-hundred-percent dare.

"Are you suggesting we play footsie?" Keeley asked, though Rafe could tell from the way she shifted, she'd already lifted her foot.

Gio reached beneath the table. "Nope. I'm suggesting *you* play footsie."

"Gio," she whispered, glancing around. "Put it on the bench beside you. Not..."

"Where's the fun in that for me? No one can see," Gio assured her as he whipped his napkin open dramatically—for effect—then draped it over his lap.

Rafe couldn't see where Gio had positioned her foot, but he could definitely guess, especially when Gio groaned softly.

"Press a little harder."

"You two are incorrigible," Rafe said. "We've been here less than half an hour."

Keeley giggled, then lifted her face to give Rafe an affectionate kiss on the cheek. "You're the one who made us stop back at my place."

Rafe nodded, then took the opening Keeley had offered him.

"I did. Because I thought we should talk before we let things progress any further."

Gio sighed dramatically. "Talk, talk, talk. Rafe, man, sometimes it's okay to leap without looking."

Rafe shook his head. "That's actually never okay, and especially not right now." He turned his attention to Keeley. "Were you okay with everything that happened last n—" He paused and amended his timeline. "Early this morning."

"Yes," she said without a moment's hesitation. "I would have been even more okay with it if you and I..." She let him fill in the blanks.

He ran his finger along the back of her neck, loving the way that simple touch caused her to shiver with need. "We'll get there. So you're sure you're interested? In sleeping with both of us?"

"I am. Very much so."

He remembered Gio's comment at her place, and he felt the need to ask, "Did I hurt you earlier in your apartment?"

"No. I mean, it was intense. But..." Her voice had taken on a breathless quality. "I liked it. No one's ever..."

Rafe watched her face flush. He hadn't expected shyness from her, and while it wasn't there often, it did peek out from time to time. It was what told him that while she'd taken men to her bed, her experience was still limited.

"You like it rough," Rafe mused aloud.

She considered that, then nodded. "I think I do."

He was glad to have this opportunity to talk to her. "I don't want to hurt you, Keeley. I'll never take more than you're able or willing to give."

"I know you won't," she said with an assurance that hit him hard, blindsiding him. It told him that she trusted him. He never wanted to betray that, but God...he didn't see a way around it, now that they'd opened the door to this affair. "So, how did the two of you discover you liked sharing women?"

Gio reached across the table, holding his hand palm up. Keeley slipped hers into it. "Rafe and I went to dinner with Layla and her guys right after they got together. After they left, the two of us started talking, and we realized we both wanted to try it."

"How in the hell do you pick up women together?" she asked.

Gio chuckled. "Rafe knew our first lover, Jennifer, from work. He invited her to happy hour with us, and one thing led to another. We met our second lover, Vanessa, at Eclectic. We asked her to dance, and one thing led to another..." he repeated.

She laughed. "I'm sure it did. I've been a part of that bump and grind. It was why I had to walk off the dance floor after one song. So hot."

Rafe kissed the side of her head. He noticed neither he nor Gio seemed capable of being near her without touching her. "The last affair was with Jill. She and Gio dated in high school. We ran into her at a bar, and again..."

"One thing led to another," she finished. "I only ever heard about Gio dating Jill. From Liza and Jess. You..." she started, pausing for Rafe to fill in the blanks.

"I didn't date her," Rafe clarified. "Only Gio did."

"So you just..."

Rafe forced himself to nod. This conversation was going exactly where he'd intended it to, and yet he hated what he was about to confess. "For me, it was just sex. You know how I feel about relationships. Gio's the one looking for a woman to marry. And it was clear Jennifer, Vanessa, and Jill were all looking for the same thing. So I stepped aside after their feelings changed, and Gio..."

Keeley looked at Gio. "You dated them."

Gio nodded. His friend had been decidedly quiet throughout this part, letting Rafe do all the explaining.

"So...just sex?" she asked Rafe, repeating his words.

"Yes," he replied, though that answer felt wrong. "That's all."

Keeley picked up her wineglass and took a sip. She fell silent, and Rafe got a sense she was mulling over what he'd just told her.

Finally, she said, "I see." Then added, "And I understand."

Rafe wondered if she did. He hadn't come straight out and

said their affair would be the same. Had she assumed so? Or did she see what was happening between thc three of them as something different? Did *he*?

A wise man would stop screwing around with the subtleties and just state what he was thinking outright.

The problem was, his thoughts and feelings weren't in agreement at the moment.

His head still didn't believe in love. But his heart was starting to have some serious doubts.

So he held his tongue.

Dinner arrived, and the conversation changed, primarily to how delicious the food was. They were debating dessert when Gio growled.

Rafe looked at his friend, confused, until he realized Gio was looking at someone behind him.

He grinned. The Morettis had a special sound whenever a Russo was around, so Rafe had a pretty good idea what he was going to see when he turned around.

He glanced over his shoulder at the exact same time Penny spotted them. The maître d' was leading her, Gage, and Matt Russo to a table.

Penny detoured to their booth instead, while Gage and Matt reluctantly followed.

"Hey, you guys," she said cheerfully.

Rafe had grown very fond of Rhys's little sister over the years. She'd always been a quirky thing, but lately she seemed to have blossomed. Her fashion sense was still a bit out there, but she'd traded her too-big glasses for contacts and had started wearing her hair in an actual style, as opposed to pinning it up in braids or messy ponytails.

Keeley smiled at her friend's arrival. "Penny! Oh my God, I haven't seen you since your birthday. Where have you been hiding out?"

Penny shoulder-bumped Gage. "This guy keeps monopolizing all my time after work."

"Right. Just *after* work," Matt muttered grumpily, making it clear Gage and Penny were indulging in some office hijinks.

Rafe grinned briefly, then schooled his features when Gio frowned at him.

Gage obviously noticed as well, and Rafe's respect for the guy rose—despite his last name—when he decided to take himself out of the equation. He looked around and saw the maître d' waiting on them. "Stay here and talk to your friends, Penny. Take as long as you want. Matt and I will head to the table and order a bottle of champagne." He gave her a quick kiss on the cheek, then he and Matt walked away.

"I guess you don't want to hear me tell you that they really *are* good guys," Penny insisted.

Gio sighed. "Gage seems like a decent man, but Matt's an asshole."

Penny shrugged but wisely didn't try to plead the man's case any further.

"Champagne...?" Keeley asked, deftly changing the subject.

Penny's face erupted in a smile so big, Rafe wondered if it hurt her cheeks. Then she lifted her hand, revealing an emerald-cut diamond engagement ring. "Gage proposed!"

Keeley's eyes widened with glee as she looked at the ring. "Holy shit. That ring is gorgeous!"

"I know," Penny gushed. "I couldn't believe it when he asked me last night. I was going to text you and the girls to invite you to happy hour one day this week. I wanted to tell you in person."

Rafe frowned. "Didn't you just start dating the guy?"

Penny nodded. "Well, yeah. I guess officially we started dating at my birthday party, but before that, we..." She shrugged, making it clear she didn't intend to finish whatever she was about to say.

"And your birthday was only a month ago," Rafe pointed out. He'd never taken Penny as the impulsive type. Awkward and a little shy, sure, but never impetuous.

Penny shrugged. "Gage said we could have a long engagement.

Of course, two minutes later, he was talking about how awesome a winter wedding would be."

Penny and Keeley laughed.

"If he's moving that fast, you definitely need to set up that happy hour," Keeley said. "We have a wedding to plan."

"We do!" Penny grinned even bigger, something Rafe wouldn't have thought possible. Then she said, "I should get to my table. I'll text you later, Keeley. Bye."

"Wow," Keeley said after Penny walked away, clearly tickled for her friend. "That is so awesome."

"That is so *fast*," Rafe replied, recalling how his mother's marriages had all happened about five minutes after the first date. He hated to think of Penny making the same mistake.

Rafe expected Keeley, Miss Romantic Hearts, to argue with him, but he hadn't anticipated Gio beating her to the punch.

"Tony said it was the same with him and Rhys. Said they both knew within days that Jess was the woman for them. Took them a little longer to convince *her*, but I think when you know, you know."

"Yeah. I think so too," Keeley agreed.

Rafe wanted to debate that. After all, his mother "had known" that same thing five times in her life. But he didn't say that because he was too distracted by Keeley's face, by the way she was smiling at Gio. And the way he was smiling back.

They *knew*.

He could see it in their eyes.

And suddenly, he didn't want to tell them they were wrong.

Instead, he wanted her to look at *him* like that.

Chapter Eleven

Keeley considered pinching herself as she walked into Rafe's mansion for the second night in a row. Dinner had been absolutely perfect. Only Gio and Rafe could ensure a date was the perfect blend of romantic, fun, and naughty.

Gio had trapped her foot between his thighs the entire meal, encouraging her to play footsie with the hard-on tenting his dress slacks. Meanwhile, Rafe hadn't been able to keep his hands off her. He spent the entire night with his arm wrapped around her shoulder, or his hand cupping the back of her neck in a way that was strangely erotic, or with his fingers running through her hair. Gio reached for her hand whenever they weren't eating, and Rafe had placed no less than twenty kisses on her cheek or brow. The restaurant lighting was low and encouraged their sensual, nonstop touches.

The entire evening had been one long session of foreplay. Now her body was a live wire, and she was ready for the real fireworks to start.

Gio's arm was wrapped around her waist, and he started to guide her to the living room.

"Should we have a drink?" he asked.

Keeley dug her heels in. "No."

"Impatient much," Gio teased.

Rafe chuckled. "I think someone is finished being wooed. Ready to move this date to the bedroom, Keeley?"

She grinned. "You read my mind."

Rafe took her hand and the two of them headed for the stairs. Gio ran up behind them, then grasped Keeley's upper arm, spun her around, and tossed her over his shoulder. "You two are walking too slow."

"And I'm the impatient one?" She laughed as he sprinted up the steps. She'd never been with such a physically strong man. It took her breath away—figuratively and literally as her midsection bounced against his shoulder.

Rafe followed closely behind, though she couldn't really see his face, given her current upside-down position.

When they reached the top, Rafe said, "My room, Gio."

Gio headed that direction, the three of them entering together. Then he set her on her feet, holding onto her upper arms until she was steady.

"Caveman much?" she joked. "Why not just grab me by the hair and drag me?"

Gio reached up and closed his fist in her thick tresses. "Is that your way of asking me to pull your hair, little one?" He increased the pressure, using his grip to tilt her head back. She expected him to kiss her, but Gio missed her mouth, his lips finding her throat instead. He drew his tongue along the curve of it, the stroke so sexy, her insides began to quiver.

Her panties had been damp with arousal most of the night, and this wasn't helping that state. Her nipples tightened, and she was overwhelmed by the desire to strip off her bra, the lace suddenly constricting and annoying.

Gio released her when they heard a bark.

She turned around and smiled when she saw Cricket sacked out on the foot of Rafe's bed. Her bark hadn't been the manic, nonstop intruder kind. This one was a short, single yap that told them they were disturbing her beauty sleep.

Her amusement morphed to a laugh. "Oh my God. Are those steps?"

At the foot of Rafe's bed was a small staircase, three steps that allowed the tiny dog access to the tall bed.

Rafe sighed. "I didn't put them there. Grandpa Albert did. Cricket slept with him every night and I haven't figured out how to evict her from the bed yet."

Keeley walked over and wrapped her arms around his waist. "Liar. You haven't even tried, have you?"

Rafe narrowed his eyes, but it was all for show. Then he pointed to a dog bed in the corner. "I bought her that, but she's not interested."

Keeley flexed up on tiptoe to kiss Rafe on the cheek. "I think it's sweet that you let her sleep with you."

"Me too," Gio said, making it clear he was enjoying the information a little too much. Keeley could just imagine the teasing Rafe was about to suffer from the Morettis. She saw a lot of stuffed dogs, puppy treats, and squeaking toys in his future.

Gio reached for Cricket, picking her up. Now, as always, she showered him with an onslaught of affectionate licks. "But, Miss Cricket," he said to the dog, "the bed's going to be a little too crowded and the waves a lot too rough for the next hour or so for such a tiny dog." Gio placed her in the dog bed but, just as Rafe said, she wasn't impressed. She stepped out of it, and Gio pushed her back in, then raised one finger and pointed at her. "Stay," he said firmly.

Keeley doubted that was going to work—and was surprised when Cricket whined for only a second before laying down. She didn't close her eyes, though, her doggie gaze locked on Gio, who held it, letting her know he was serious.

Rafe, who'd been far too indulgent with the dog as far as Keeley had seen, stepped next to Gio. "Damn, man. You're going to have to teach me how to do that."

Gio placed his arm around Rafe's shoulders. "You've been treating her like you saw your grandpa treat her. He spoiled her rotten too."

Rafe shrugged, not bothering to deny it. "I know she misses him."

Keeley's heart panged, touched beyond measure by Rafe's sweet admission.

Confident the dog was going to stay put, Gio turned to look at her. "Now. There's something that's been driving me crazy all night," he said to her. "And I need an answer right now."

"What's that?" she asked, her tone pure flirt.

Gio crossed his arms. "Are you wearing a bra under that dress?"

She smiled widely. "What do you think?"

He shook his head. "I don't think you are."

Rafe chuckled. "I could have put you out of your misery before we'd even ordered the drinks at the restaurant. Slid my finger into her dress. No strap on her shoulder."

"You've never heard of strapless?" she teased.

Rafe smirked. "You don't give me enough credit for being observant. I had the better view in that booth. You reached for a piece of bread and your dress gaped a little. I got treated to a flash of one of your gorgeous tits."

"Next time, I get the seat beside her," Gio said, calling dibs.

"Who says there's going to be a next time?" She was having way too much fun with them. "This date isn't over yet. You've yet to stick the landing."

"Take off that dress," Rafe said, his tone taking on that demanding quality that never failed to turn her on.

Keeley reached for the ties on the side, slipping the knot free. Then she unfastened the two buttons there as well. It was a wrap dress, but because it dipped low in the front and the back, she couldn't wear a bra with it. Luckily, she wasn't so overly endowed that it was a problem.

With one flourish and a shrug of the shoulders, the dress slid off, leaving her standing before them in nothing but her thong.

"Keeley," Gio breathed, and again she was overwhelmed by the way they looked at her. Neither man shielded his…

God. *Appreciation.*

She crossed her arms, not to hide herself but to use them to her advantage, lifting her breasts and making them look fuller. "Am I the only one losing clothes in this scenario?"

Rafe shook his head, as if he wanted to chastise her, but couldn't after Gio took the bait.

Gio began unbuttoning his deep purple shirt. He'd paired it with black slacks that hugged his tight ass to perfection. Rafe, the more conservative and less flashy of the two, wore a simple pale blue button-down and khakis.

Keeley stepped in front of Gio when he shrugged off the shirt, her fingers itching to touch, to stroke, to feel. Gio's chest, unlike his bearded face, was smooth, his skin tanned dark, thanks to so much time in the sun and his Italian genes.

Bending forward, she ran her tongue over his brown nipple, then smiled wickedly before she sank her teeth into the tiny nub, her eyes locked with his as she did so.

Gio was passive for only a moment before his hands found her breasts. He cupped them, rubbing his thumbs over her taut nipples. Her breasts were super sensitive, and she moaned before she could stop the sound.

Gio gave her a charming smirk. He was a cocky lover—she'd discovered that this morning. Of course, he had every reason to be, so it wasn't like she could call him on it.

Rafe didn't seek to join them, but she didn't forget his presence. He shifted closer, his body mere inches away. He still hadn't taken off a single piece of clothing, and she started to panic that tonight—like this morning—he wouldn't go all the way.

"Rafe," she whispered.

"Unzip his pants, Keeley. Pull his cock out, fist it."

She did as he asked, though part of her was distracted by her concerns.

"I'm going to direct the show for a little while," Rafe said, easing her thoughts. "Going to show you how to bring Gio to his knees."

"Rafe," Gio said, his voice growly, laced with a promise of retribution. One he couldn't verbalize because Keeley had already gotten his pants unfastened, his rock-hard dick in her hand.

"And after that lesson," Rafe continued, unfazed by Gio's warning, "I'm going to bend you over that bed of mine and fuck you until you forget your own name."

"Ohhh," she breathed, certain she'd never heard anything hotter. She'd had a couple of lovers who liked to talk dirty in bed. Fool that she was, she'd thought it was hot. Now, everything those guys had said sounded like gibberish compared to Rafe's bedroom dialogue.

"Tighten your grip, Keeley. You can stroke him harder. He likes it that way."

Gio held still, remaining uncharacteristically quiet as Rafe gave her directions.

She clenched her fist, her gaze locked with Gio's. The sudden unsteadiness of his breathing proved Rafe was correct.

"Pull your fist along that thick cock," Rafe murmured, stepping closer, his lips scant inches from her ear. "Start out slow, ease him into it. *Tease* him into it."

She obeyed. Gio's tight jaw, the growing hunger in his gaze, her reward.

"That's it. God, you're perfect," Rafe praised. "So fucking perfect. Now pick up the pace, stroke him faster, but don't loosen your grip."

"Jesus, man," Gio muttered, but neither Rafe nor Keeley relented.

She increased her motions, Gio adding his own fuel to the flames, his hips thrusting toward her on each downstroke. He still held her breasts in his hands, squeezing them tightly. Every stroke, every squeeze drove them higher, both grasping, reaching, anxious for what came after.

Keeley pressed her legs together tightly. She needed more. So much more. She'd never been this hot, this bothered.

She felt something brush her feet and she glanced at the floor. Rafe had tossed a pillow between them.

"Get on your knees, beauty," he instructed.

She lowered herself down without thought, too hung up on his term of endearment.

Beauty.

Her gaze was now level with Gio's cock. She'd only opened his pants, but Gio took it further, shoving them down completely, toeing them and his shoes off.

His thighs were thick, muscular. He was built like a tree trunk, strong, unshakable. She still held his dick in her hand, so she directed the head of it to her mouth.

She'd just parted her lips when a firm fist found her hair, holding her back.

"Did I tell you to suck it?" Rafe asked.

Keeley closed her eyes, drawing in as much air as she could. She'd never...fuck...she'd *never* been this aroused.

"Please," she whispered.

"I like it when you beg, beauty."

Beauty. Again.

"You're going to do a lot more of that tonight," Rafe promised.

"Fuck, Rafe," Gio said, in a way that caught Keeley's attention. They'd shared women before...but Gio seemed as blown away by this dominant side of Rafe as she was.

"I didn't tell you to stop stroking him," Rafe said, as he stepped behind her and knelt, his fingers toying with the elastic waist of her thong. He didn't remove them, didn't do anything more than pull the elastic away from her skin. She was so hung up on what he was doing, she forgot to move her hand.

Until he released the elastic and it snapped against her, stinging.

She jerked with surprise, the pain turning inwards, the same way his pinch to her nipples had this morning.

"Move your hand," he commanded. "Like this."

He placed his hand over Keeley's, and it was Gio's turn to jerk in surprise as he watched, his furrowed brows telling Keeley they were in uncharted territory.

Rafe used his grip to move her hand, and together they began stroking Gio's cock.

Keeley wet her lips, wishing Rafe would give her the...what was she waiting for? An order? Permission?

She had never allowed anyone to call the shots in the bedroom. Hell, that wasn't something she'd ever really thought she wanted. Until now.

"Open your lips, Keeley," Rafe said at last, releasing his grip on her hand. "But don't take him inside. Gio's going to fuck your mouth."

Keeley thought maybe that should sound scary. She'd given blow jobs before, but she'd been in control of the situation, taking what she could, pulling away when it was too much.

But she wasn't scared. Because this was Rafe and Gio, and she trusted them. More than anyone she'd ever been with before.

Gio cupped her cheeks, lifting her face until she was looking up at him. He gave her one of his characteristically charming winks, though his expression was otherwise serious. "Rafe might be giving the orders, but you're still in control. You know that, right?"

She nodded. "I want you," she whispered.

"You've got me, Keeley. For as long as you want."

She could have played those words over and over a thousand times, but Gio didn't give her a chance. The head of his cock brushed her lips and she opened, allowing him to slide inside. He really was big, almost uncomfortably so.

"Grip the base of his dick like I just showed you," Rafe said.

"Close your hand around him nice and tight, then hold on." As he spoke, he rose, standing behind her.

No sooner had she done as he said, than Gio began thrusting in and out of her mouth and hand. He'd kept his grip on her head, holding her still, fucking her mouth just as Rafe said he would.

There was no mistaking this for a blow job. It wasn't that. It was something she'd never done, never experienced before. And she loved it.

Loved being surrounded by these two men, obeying their dirty demands, turned on by their rough, sensual touches.

Keeley had spent her entire adult life searching for this.

Now…

Her vision blurred with tears—the happy kind as well as the trying-to-catch-her-breath kind. Gio was pushing in deeper, and she had to fight against her gag reflex.

Through it all, she felt Gio's gaze on her face, knew he was watching her, keeping her safe, even as he took her mouth.

Rafe's hands rested on her shoulders, her back pressed firmly against his knees. He was also looking down. Both men seemed to derive a great deal of pleasure through the mere act of watching. She wanted to ask them about that.

And while neither was touching the other, they were clearly very comfortable in each other's space. Right now, they were only separated by her body, standing face-to-face.

"God," Gio gasped.

"He's close, beauty. I can't wait to feel those lips wrapped around my cock," Rafe growled, one of his hands leaving her shoulder, slipping around to rest at the base of her throat.

Fuck her. Rafe knew exactly how and where to touch her, what to say to make her body quake with need.

Gio's hands slid from her face to her hair, his thrusting growing faster, finesse slipping away as he approached his climax.

"Be ready," Rafe said.

Gio cursed, and she felt the first splash of come.

Rafe's hand completely cupped her throat. He wasn't applying pressure. Instead, she got the sense he wanted to feel her swallow.

So she did.

Gio thrust one last time, holding still within her mouth as he came.

After the last burst, he slipped free, staggering backward the two steps necessary so that he could drop down on the bed, as if his powerful legs couldn't hold him up anymore.

She'd done that. She'd brought Gio Moretti, the strongest man she knew, to his knees.

She smiled, and her too-pleased expression caught Gio's attention.

"I don't trust that look."

She laughed breathlessly.

Gio shook his head. "We're in trouble now, Rafe. Keeley just figured out she's holding the keys to the castle."

Gio's joke proved just how well he knew her. The past few weeks, they'd all grown closer, sharing secrets and stories. Rafe and Gio both listened to her. And not just to be polite, like most of her past dates, but because they were genuinely interested.

Rafe reached down to help her up from the floor. "She has them for the moment," he whispered in her ear. "Go bend over the side of the bed."

Keeley looked back at him but didn't move. She was in the mood to test a few boundaries, to have a few things confirmed. "Are you planning to undress anytime soon?"

Rafe's eyes narrowed the tiniest bit. If she hadn't been looking so closely at his face, she would have missed it entirely.

"What did I tell you to do, Keeley?"

"I have every intention of doing it. *After* you get undressed."

Gio whistled. "You sure you want to poke the bear like that, little one?"

Keeley looked at Gio. "So you guys are the only ones who get to make demands in the bedroom?"

"Now you're getting it," Rafe said, his hand gripping her elbow, guiding her to the bed.

"That wasn't what I was say—"

Before she could finish, Rafe placed a firm hand between her shoulder blades and pushed her facedown on the mattress. His bed was quite tall, and luxuriously soft.

She tried to push back against his grip, but Rafe was no slouch in the strength department himself.

"If you don't like something I do, or if it hurts, all you have to do is say stop," he said.

Keeley grinned at Rafe as she looked back at him. "Or I could just call you a son of a bitch."

His lips pursed, though she couldn't tell if he was amused or annoyed.

"Prefer motherfucker?" she asked.

Rafe, who all night had looked so sternly hot—she really needed to get a handle on her contradictory descriptions for these men—broke character and laughed. "Okay. Either one of those will work too."

She wasn't sure why his amusement pleased her so. Perhaps because Gio was easy to make laugh, but Rafe took a bit more work.

Then she held her breath as she waited for whatever came next. Gio had mentioned spanking her before, and she wanted it. Rafe, however, had promised to finally—*finally*—take her, and she wanted that too. She was a kid in the candy story, a fox in the henhouse, Veruca from *Charlie and the Chocolate Factory*. She wanted it all! Right now.

Gio remained sitting on the edge of the mattress, right next to her. Reaching over, he ran his hand over her ass gently. Over and over, he stroked her skin in such a soothing way, it worked a bit like a massage. Her eyes drifted closed, her body relaxing under his ministrations.

They flew open when his hand disappeared, and a much different touch took its place.

She jerked and tried to lift herself from the bed when Rafe spanked her. Three hard blows on each cheek, stinging hot. Her attempt to escape was fruitless, as Gio's hand had slid upwards and was now pressing down on her back, holding her firmly to the mattress.

Both men stilled for a moment, which confused her, until she realized they were waiting for her to say stop—or to call them a name. She considered it, that was for sure. The spanking had hurt at first. But now...

She glanced over her shoulder at them. "Finished so soon?" she taunted.

Gio shook his head, grinning widely. He loved her dares, and she knew it. Rafe, as always, was the harder one to read.

In the end, he didn't respond at all. Instead, he lifted his hand and smacked her ass again, harder, twice more, then his fingers slid along her slit. She knew exactly what he was going to find.

She'd been wet since the restaurant, their continual touches and kisses keeping her arousal on simmer for hours.

She groaned with pleasure when Rafe pushed two fingers inside her. Her pussy clenched, and it was then that she realized just how on edge, how close to the finish line she really was. Two or three more thrusts and she would be there.

Rafe seemed to realize the same thing because he withdrew his fingers instantly—the bastard.

"No!" she cried out, her complaint earning her two more smacks, harder than all the previous ones. Not that her body gave a shit about that. If he was trying to withhold her orgasm, he might not want to continue the spanking because she suspected the next blow would send her straight into orbit. She wiggled her ass, silently hoping he'd take the hint.

Rafe chuckled, then stepped away from the bed.

She opened her mouth to curse him all the way into next Thursday, but she realized he was undressing. So, for once, she wisely kept her mouth shut.

She was tempted to roll over and sit up. She hadn't seen Rafe completely naked yet, and she was curious.

Gio distracted her when he ran his finger along her cheek. "Okay?" he murmured.

She nodded. "I'm so happy," she admitted quietly.

Gio's grin was so carefree, so boyish, it took her breath away. Even more so when he said, "Me too."

He moved then, shifting onto the bed fully, laying on his side and propping himself up on his elbow like he was settling in for a show.

Once again, she marveled at Rafe and Gio's utter ease with each other in the bedroom. And then, maybe more surprising, she recognized her own lack of shyness with their outright voyeurism.

Keeley never could have imagined permitting, much less enjoying, someone watching her have sex with someone else.

But Gio's new position and his intense attention was heady. She lifted herself up on her own elbows so that her breasts were visible. Gio groaned, obviously appreciating her efforts.

Then Rafe was there, the front of his thighs brushing the backs of hers. He bent over her, his cock resting against her still-warm ass.

"Keeley," he said, his voice so deep, it sounded more like a growl than her name. She didn't have time to reply before he added, "Hold on."

And then, Rafe positioned his dick at her opening and slammed home.

He fucked her with a roughness that bordered on violent, with an unrestrained wildness that screamed of hunger and need, possession and control.

And her body responded instantly. She came on his second thrust.

But Rafe didn't stop, didn't even give any indication that he'd noticed. Instead, he kept pounding, drawing out her first orgasm until she thought she'd explode from the never-ending pleasure.

As it began to wane, she had a moment's reprieve. Long

enough to look up and realize Gio had sat up, that his cock was hard again and he was fisting it, jerking himself off, his rhythm matching that of Rafe's.

Keeley couldn't take her eyes away from him, from what he was doing. But soon, Rafe stole her attention away, digging his fingers underneath her body to find her clit. A few strokes later, her second orgasm began, and this one blew the first out of the water.

Throughout, Keeley cried out...curse words, prayers to God, Rafe's name, Gio's...an unending stream of bliss and passion and pain and wonder.

Her second orgasm passed more slowly, and Keeley went limp, certain one more of those would finish her off for good. She might have even said that aloud, though she was so light-headed, she wasn't sure she could tell the difference between speech and thoughts anymore.

Her confusion was answered when Rafe withdrew, flipping her over to face him.

"Just one more, beauty. Together. And don't worry, I won't let you die," he added with a sexy grin.

"Wait..." she said, recalling Gio. She shifted, with a lot less grace than she cared to admit. Her strength was depleted, but she knew what she wanted, how she wanted this night to end.

She moved so that she lay fully on the bed, so that Gio was next to her rather than above her. Reaching for Rafe, she guided him to come over her. Her legs parted, and Rafe slid back in, taking her much slower this time, with more care.

Glancing over at Gio, she looked at his hand, still rubbing up and down his erection, then gazed into his eyes. "Come with us," she asked.

He nodded, his serious expression one she would have expected to see on Rafe's face, not his.

"Yes," he said, "but you better be quick about it."

Rafe slid out until only the head of his impressive cock was buried inside her. "I don't think that's going to be a problem."

He'd only been teasing her with that gentle entry because her conqueror was back on the second return. Rafe took her hard, lifting her legs, the back of her knees resting in the crooks of his elbows. Within a dozen thrusts, she was there, coming loudly, *again*, and he was right there with her.

She heard Gio's climax but was unable to see it, blinded by a flash of bright white light.

She rode out the storm inside her, oblivious to everything else. For a few minutes, it felt like she was having an out-of-body experience as she was only vaguely aware of her surroundings, everything happening at a distance.

She was aware of Rafe pulling out of her, of Gio going to the bathroom to clean up, of Rafe gently lifting her to pull back the covers, of Gio urging her to the middle of the bed, of both men climbing in, flanking her.

Keeley closed her eyes, and when she opened them, she wasn't sure if she'd dozed for seconds or hours. All she knew was that she was curled on her stomach, surrounded by the heat of Rafe's and Gio's bodies, and she'd never in her life experienced anything so amazing.

It was so good, so overwhelming, she wasn't sure if she was looking forward to doing it again or afraid of it. She'd been completely out of control, and it had shaken her to the core.

Mercifully, Gio knew exactly how to set her at ease, the sound of his voice bringing her back to reality. A reality based on so many years of fantasy.

She was the luckiest woman on the planet.

"Bet you thought *I* was the bad boy," Gio joked, lifting his hand and slapping her ass just once.

"It's always the quiet ones," she retorted, laughing breathlessly.

"Ain't that the truth," Gio agreed.

Rafe mumbled something that sounded like "smart-asses," but he didn't open his eyes, didn't try to defend himself.

"Keeley," Gio said, drawing her attention to him. "Stay here with us while Kayden's out of town."

She frowned...and suddenly she remembered that her new reality wasn't all sunshine and roses. Not quite yet. "He'll be gone almost a month."

Gio nodded. "I know that. Just until he comes home. It's only three weeks."

It was on the tip of her tongue to ask where he saw this going, but she felt Rafe stirring behind her. He'd been dead to the world before Gio issued his invitation.

The coward in her was too afraid to look over her shoulder to see what he thought. Because she wanted what Gio was asking for. Desperately.

But did Rafe?

She recalled his comments about not looking for a relationship, not wanting love, commitment, kids.

Just sex.

And then he always walked away.

That was the one thing she'd played over and over since their conversation at the restaurant. The moment the woman expressed wanting more...Rafe walked away.

Three weeks.

Was that Gio's way of putting a time limit on the affair? Why did he think they needed one? Was he letting her know this wasn't forever? Or was he trying to protect their hearts—keep it short and sweet in hopes that no one got hurt in the end?

She didn't have it in her to tell him that ship had already sailed. She was definitely falling in love with both of them.

Then, she considered what they'd just done, and her body convinced her head and her heart that she did *not* give a fuck.

Three more weeks of that?

Hell yeah.

"Okay," she said quickly, keeping her gaze on Gio, and holding her breath as she waited for Rafe to rescind the invitation.

She didn't realize how tense she was until Rafe's arm snuck around her waist, and he spooned her against him.

"Cricket's not going to be happy about you stealing her spot in the bed," Rafe said drowsily.

Keeley laughed, though suddenly, her happiness felt just the tiniest bit dimmer.

Chapter Twelve

"Tell me again why we thought this was a good idea?" Rafe asked.

Gio chuckled but didn't respond. Primarily because Rafe had posed that same question at least a dozen times in the past week. "Just keep sanding."

"I fucking hate sanding," Rafe grumbled.

"Hello?" they heard Keeley call out from the front door.

"Back here," Rafe replied. "The office."

It had been one week since he and Rafe had taken Keeley on a date rather than just crashing her preexisting ones. Eight days since Gio had asked her to stay here with them, the three of them sharing Rafe's bed every night.

Well, actually it was the four of them, he thought, as he glanced across the room at Cricket, who was rolling around on her back beside Albert's old recliner. Keeley had been right when she said it looked like someone was petting the dog's belly.

Cricket typically started each night in her dog bed, simply because he, Rafe, and Keeley never went to bed with sleep on their minds. However, sometime after they all drifted away, she made her way up the doggie stairs and nestled in the middle of the bed with Keeley, the two of them even sharing a pillow.

190

The only time they'd parted during this last week was for work, though Gio wasn't sure they could count that because they sure as shit hadn't accomplished much. Rafe and Keeley hadn't left the mansion at all, Rafe running the businesses from here, while the two of them had begun to sort through the boxes in yet another room. So far, they'd cleared out the office and what they'd called Box Room One. Right now, they were halfway through Box Room Two, with another one to go.

They still hadn't found the boat or the combination to the safe, and Gio knew Rafe was beginning to give up hope of either.

Since Moretti Brothers Restorations had just recently completed a big on-site project, Gio had decided to treat himself to a few "work from home" days, which meant he'd converted one of the four outbuildings around the mansion into a workshop, where he'd moved a lot of his woodworking tools. The company's next job had him creating custom-made cabinets, which was something he was able to do in his shop.

Not that he'd scratched the surface on the job, something that was going to have to give soon. Tony had questioned his progress a couple of times, and he'd fudged the truth on how far he'd gotten. If he didn't buckle down, his brothers were going to kick his ass for slowing down the project.

The problem was, he'd been too distracted by Keeley, unable to stay away from her.

Oh, hell...from *them*.

For eight days, the three of them had christened far too many flat surfaces in the mansion, including his workbench, the floor in Box Room One, Rafe's desk in the office, the couch, the kitchen counter...the list went on and on. They would come together in a flurry of desire and passion. It was always hot and sweaty and, God, almost desperate, frantic. Then, when it was over and their arousal slaked, they'd drift back to work for a few hours before the need grew too great again, and they'd start all over.

It had been the best sex of Gio's life, and he never wanted it to end.

Today, Keeley had put her foot down, informing them she was working a full day in her office at Eclectic, away from them.

Rafe and Gio had reluctantly agreed with her decision, so after she left this morning, Rafe went to his office and Gio to his shop. By noon, Gio was chomping at the bit and ready to head to Eclectic. He'd suggested to Rafe that they surprise Keeley with lunch, but she'd put the kibosh on that when she texted to say she was having lunch with Jess, Penny, Gianna, and Liza to discuss Penny's wedding. Apparently, Penny wasn't interested in Gage's offer of a long engagement and the two had set a date in February.

Keeley walked into the office, frowning the instant she saw them. "You're working on the room without me?"

"You're late," Gio groused, putting his sander on the floor.

She glanced at her watch. "It's only quarter to six."

"You said you'd be home at five thirty."

"So, I'm fifteen minutes late," she said nonchalantly. "I didn't realize I needed gas in my car until I left Eclectic, and the light turned on. Had to stop to fill the tank. Let me change out of my work clothes really quick. Don't do anything video-worthy until I get back."

Rafe snorted. "I don't think that's going to be a problem."

Keeley had been trying—to no avail—to capture footage of them working on the inn that she could use for the videos she was determined to create. So far, he and Rafe had been less than entertaining, something they'd warned her about when she'd suggested the idea. Gio felt like an idiot trying to talk about what he was doing as he worked, and Rafe didn't like the work to begin with, so all he'd managed to do was bitch and moan.

Regardless, Keeley had remained undeterred, and she'd managed—somehow—to get enough material to make a surprisingly decent first episode, which she was ready to upload.

Keeley narrowed her eyes at Rafe. "You two need to figure out something to talk about before I get back because I'm not giving up on this. My goal is to put up a new video every three or four days, so get on board. This is happening."

Satisfied that she'd laid down the law, she started to walk out, but Gio stopped her. "Where do you think you're going?"

She turned and looked at him. "I just told you. I'm changing my clothes."

He shook his head and crossed his arms, looking at Rafe with exaggerated incredulity. "You believe this shit? We've been knocking ourselves out, giving this gorgeous girl the greatest good-night kisses she's ever had. And now? We can't even get one lousy hello kiss from her."

"Ridiculous," Rafe agreed.

Keeley laughed and crossed the room, acting like she was put out by the request. "Well, okay," she sighed. "But make it quick."

Gio grabbed her as soon as she was within arm's reach. "Nothing worth doing happens quickly. You gotta take your time with the important things."

He looked down at her but made no move to kiss her. This was *her* hello kiss after all. Keeley stared at him for a second before she realized what he was waiting for.

She lifted onto her tiptoes, but Gio leaned away. "By the way, little one, this is one of those important things."

Keeley gave him a mock salute. "So noted."

There were several attributes that Gio had always considered commonalities amongst the Morettis, like the fact they were all loud, that they talked with their hands, that they were honest. And now, as he looked into Keeley's dark brown eyes, he decided the Morettis also had a knack for knowing when they'd met "the one."

Tony had known Jess was the woman for him and Rhys. Layla had fallen for Finn and Miguel pretty much at the exact same time. And now that Gio had opened his eyes, had allowed himself to see Keeley for who she was instead of as Kayden's younger sister, he knew all the way to his bones, she was his future. His forever.

Their future, that annoying voice in the back of his head whispered. For his own sanity, Gio had tried to look ahead to his life as a couple with Keeley, though those attempts had been a complete bust. Because Rafe was a vital part of the equation, even if the stubborn fool wouldn't admit it.

Keeley's lips brushed against Gio's playfully. She still wasn't finished teasing him. Ordinarily, Gio would go along with the joke and give it right back to her. But she'd been gone for too long today, and any patience he'd had disappeared around ten o'clock this morning.

Gripping her hips, he dragged her closer, letting her feel for herself exactly how much he'd missed her. She hummed her assent, wrapped her hands tighter around his shoulders, and deepened the kiss.

Her lips parted and Gio took advantage, loving the way she tasted of cinnamon. She'd become addicted to the candy after finding Albert's seemingly endless bags of Red Hots stashed all over the mansion.

Keeley had paid attention to his demand that she take her time and do it right. The kiss lingered, neither of them willing to be the first to break the union of their lips. Now, as always, Gio felt Rafe's gaze on them, watching, waiting for his turn.

Finally, he released her, making her laugh as he placed one last quick kiss to the tip of her nose. "Rafe's been patient enough," he said, his voice huskier than before, aware that this interlude most likely wasn't going to end with mere kisses.

Keeley stepped over to Rafe, who lifted her up and placed her ass on the edge of his desk. He pushed her knees apart, stepped between them, then took over the hellos.

Keeley pulled back after a few seconds. "I thought I was the one giving the kisses."

Rafe smirked. "I think you should know me better than that by now." He lowered his head, his kiss rougher, hungrier than before, reiterating his point not only with words but actions. Keeley's fingers clenched the cotton of Rafe's T-shirt.

Rafe's tongue slid along her lower lip, then he pulled away. Not to end the kiss but to advance it to the next level.

He drew Keeley's shirt over her head, unfastening her bra with one hand—a skill they'd both mastered in the past few days, as neither he nor Rafe liked it when she covered her gorgeous tits.

Lowering his head, Rafe sucked one of her tight nipples into his mouth. Gio stepped next to the desk, closing the distance between them. As Rafe used his tongue and teeth to tease one breast, Gio claimed the other with his hand, pinching the turgid nipple, pulling on it, watching the impact their rough touches were having on her. Keeley reached back, holding herself up, her palms flat against the surface of the desk. Her eyes had drifted shut.

Rafe still stood between her legs, something she took advantage of by lifting her ankles and wrapping them around his waist, moving him even closer so she could gyrate against his pelvis.

"Please," she whispered breathlessly.

Gio had become accustomed to the sound of her pleas, to her sex squeaks and moans, and he knew what each and every one meant. This "please" meant she wanted them, which proved they hadn't been the only ones suffering through too many hours of abstinence.

"You're working from home tomorrow." Rafe was pulling the boss card. And it was cute that he thought it would work on Keeley.

She shook her head, even as she thrust her pelvis more firmly against Rafe's covered cock. "No. At some point, we have to learn how to control this."

They all knew what she meant by *this*, but Gio wasn't in the mood to control a damn thing.

Rafe, the king of fighting dirty, unbuttoned and unzipped her jeans, shoving his fingers inside her panties.

Keeley gasped when he found her clit, stroking it firmly.

"Fuck self-control," Rafe muttered. "You're staying home tomorrow. Keep fighting us on that, and I promise Gio and I will tie you to the bed if that's the only way to ensure we get our way."

Keeley's eyes darkened, not with anger or fear but with

arousal. She was by far the most adventurous lover he and Rafe had ever shared. And they'd yet to scratch the surface on all the ways they wanted to take her, all the things they wanted to do to her.

Keeley, their clever girl, had learned exactly how to get her way. She grasped Rafe's wrist, halting his movement, and said, "I'm going to work at Eclectic."

Rafe, rather than chastise her, chuckled darkly, shaking off her grip. "I was hoping you'd say that. I look forward to tomorrow."

Keeley laughed briefly, the sound cut short when Rafe resumed stroking her clit. "So. Do...ahh...I," she said between gasps, too overwhelmed to get the words out.

Gio continued to play with her breasts. They were sensitive and one of her favorite erogenous zones.

"Gio," she murmured, in her "stop fucking around and give me more" tone.

He lowered his head and took her nipple into his mouth.

She yelled out Rafe's name in a way that told Gio his friend had added more fuel to the fire, stoking the flames with his fingers inside her. Keeley came quickly, dropping from her hands to her back on the desk surface, her face flushed, her breathing erratic.

Rafe pulled his hand out of her pants, the two of them looking down at her. It took her a few moments to compose herself. When she opened her eyes, she gave them a cat-who-ate-the-canary grin. "I like the way you guys kiss hello."

Gio chuckled, then offered her a hand so she could sit up.

She gave them both a southern-regions glance, taking note of their obvious erections. So she was surprised when Rafe helped her stand, then took a step away.

"What about you two?" she asked.

Rafe sighed. "There's nothing I'd love more than to take you right here, right now, but we ordered Chinese food for dinner, and I suspect it will be here any minute."

"Shit," Gio muttered. He'd forgotten about that.

No sooner had he spoken, the doorbell rang.

"I'll grab the food," Rafe offered. "Go on and change, beauty, and we'll meet you in the kitchen. Then—dammit—we can record some more footage for your videos."

"Sounds good," she said as she grabbed her shirt and bra and darted upstairs topless. "Back in a flash."

An hour later, all three of them were back in the office, and Keeley was a lot less happy with them. Her phone was out, and she was waiting to hit record, as had become her habit whenever they were working on the house.

"Oh my God, guys. Are you going to give me something I can use or not?"

Gio glanced over his shoulder and winked at her. "I told you. Joey is the showboat in the family. That guy was born talking and he hasn't stopped yet. Of course, ninety percent of what he says is bullshit. Aunt Berta likes to say he's got diarrhea of the mouth and constipation of the brain."

Keeley laughed, then said, "So channel Joey."

Gio faked a shudder. "Hell no."

"What if you pretend you're just talking to me? Like, what are you doing right now?" she asked, hitting the record button.

"Sanding a chair rail." Gio kept his response short on purpose because pushing Keeley's buttons was quickly becoming one of his favorite pastimes. She was cute when she got fired up. Like right now, when she rolled her eyes so hard, she had to be staring at her brain.

"Let's attack this from a different angle," Keeley said, trying again. "So, Gio," she said, her tone short of patience. "What is the purpose of a chair rail?"

He grinned at her, then decided to give in a little. "Nowadays, most folks put chair rails in new homes as a decorative feature, but when this house was built, it served a more practical purpose. The rail kept the high backs of chairs from damaging the plaster walls."

Keeley brightened up, delighted he'd played along. She was convinced they would find a following with these videos and that it would be great marketing for the inn. Considering it was his business, and she was helping, he should probably stop giving her such a hard time.

Unfortunately, his mature side wasn't as strong as his immature, playful side.

"That's a great answer!" she praised. "And a terrific segue into some of the history of the house. Rafe, why don't you talk about when the house was built and—" Keeley stopped, looking at her phone as the ringtone "Boss of Me," by They Might Be Giants, started playing.

He and Rafe exchanged a glance, aware that song was her tone for Kayden. He hadn't called Keeley since he left for Vermont a week earlier.

None of them had mentioned Keeley's brother or how they were going to handle dropping the bomb about the status change in their friendship. Gio called it a relationship in his head, but didn't say it aloud because...

Fuck.

He was tiptoeing around Rafe and his commitment issues, and he hated himself for it, but Gio was desperate to keep this menage with Keeley going for as long as he could.

Because this was it. What he wanted for the rest of his life.

The three of them fit, even better than Gio had imagined they would.

Unfortunately, he knew where Rafe stood, and he feared that this would all be over the second Keeley asked for more.

He'd been a jackass for pursuing this, for drawing Rafe in. If he'd had a brain in his head, he would have asked Keeley out on his own, would have seduced her into his bed...alone. Would have protected her heart better.

Because Keeley wasn't hiding her feelings for them as well as she thought. And while his heart skipped a beat every time she looked at him like he was her Prince Charming, his chest tightened painfully when she looked at Rafe the same way…because he knew what was coming.

The longer he let this affair go, the harder it was going to be for both of them when Rafe walked away. When he'd asked her to stay with them, three weeks felt like a short enough time to keep any hurt feelings to a minimum. He could see now he'd been dead wrong about that.

There had never been a single thing Gio couldn't discuss with Rafe. While he and his brother, Luca, shared that twin bond thing, both experiencing a sixth sense when it came to the other, in many ways, he felt even closer to Rafe.

Yet he was hesitant to bring up the subject of the two of them making a real go of this thing with Keeley.

Too afraid of losing the best thing that had ever happened to him.

Keeley answered the phone. "Hey, Kay. What's up? How's the trip?"

Gio didn't even pretend to turn his attention back to the chair rail. Instead, he leaned against the wall and watched as Keeley listened to her brother talk about his hike, offering him the occasional "mmhmm" and "that sounds cool."

She glanced up when she realized both he and Rafe were eavesdropping on her conversation, but her poker face was in place. Gio didn't have a clue what she was thinking or what she was going to say.

Then she laughed at something her brother said. "I'm glad you were able to get showers." She pulled the phone away from her mouth and said to them, "Apparently, Aldo was starting to smell a little ripe, so they came off the trail today to get a hotel. They wanted beer, pizza, and showers, not necessarily in that order."

She listened once again. "Yeah. Sorry. I'm with Rafe and Gio. I was just telling them—" She stopped talking midsentence, frowning. "Why would you want to yell at Rafe?"

Gio had no intention of hiding anything from Kayden, but he

wanted to talk to his friend in person, to explain what was happening, to assure him his feelings were genuine.

Her question to Kayden took him aback. How the hell could he know anything about them? And why would he only be mad at Rafe?

Keeley snorted, the sound instantly setting his mind at ease. "He's not working me to death," she replied, exasperated. "Why the hell are you looking at me on Find My Friends? You're supposed to be on vacation."

That stupid app. None of them had considered the fact that Kayden could look up Keeley anytime he wanted and find her location.

"Yes, I know I'm over here all the time." Pause. "Yeah, I realize it's been late some nights, but that's because I'm recording Gio and Rafe working on the inn, and we're night owls. I told you, I'm posting videos about the project on Facebook and YouTube, showing the work at all stages. It's great promo for the business."

Wow. Keeley was one cool customer. Then Gio grimaced, recalling she'd had years of practice when it came to stretching the truth—or lying, actually—to her brother.

She fell silent again as Kayden spoke.

Gio wished he'd told her to put it on speakerphone. Then he realized he was following the conversation pretty well without hearing Kayden's side of it.

"Oh, believe me, it's been like pulling teeth. They're both doing this under duress."

Gio chuckled. Kayden was a good friend, and he knew them well. As such, her brother understood exactly how much they hated making these videos.

"Yeah. Gio said the same thing, but Joey's not exactly available. He's busy making his own show." She glared at them playfully. "And no doubt he'll be a huge success because at least he tries."

She was quiet again, and then she said, "Nope. No dates lately. I've..." She paused as she looked in their direction. "I've been too busy with the inn videos." Pause. "Okay, I will." Pause. "I'll tell them." Pause. "Love you too. Have a good time—and stay off Find My Friends or I swear to God I'll stop sharing my loc—" Keeley sighed heavily. She'd made that same threat a million times, so she should know exactly how much it panicked her overprotective, seen-some-terrible-shit cop brother. "You know I won't—" Keeley rolled her eyes. "He's right here." She handed the phone to Gio. "He wants to talk to you."

Gio took her cell. "Hey, Kayden. Sounds like you're having a great trip."

"Yeah, it's been incredible. I can't tell you how good it is to get away. I feel about a thousand pounds lighter. No stress, no work, no rushing from here to there," Kayden replied, sounding more relaxed than Gio had ever heard him.

"Good for you."

"Listen, I know you're probably hating every second of that video shit Keeley's making you do, but do you think you and Rafe could keep playing along with it for the next couple weeks? It seems to be keeping her off the dating apps. I can't tell you how relieved I am every time I pull up Find My Friends and see that she's with you guys."

"Sure, man. No problem," Gio reassured him. "We're not going to let anything happen to her."

Keeley closed her eyes and shook her head. "Jesus," she muttered.

"Thanks, Gio. Okay, Aldo's finally out of the shower. My turn. I've been dreaming of hot water for eight days, so the bastard better have left me some."

Gio chuckled.

"Say hello to Rafe and give Keeley a big hug from me, and tell her to behave."

"Will do. Talk to you soon, Kay," Gio said. He hung up and handed Keeley her phone back.

"What did he say?" she asked.

Gio looked at Rafe. "Kayden says hi."

Rafe nodded.

Then Gio walked over to Keeley. "He also told me to give you this." He wrapped her up in a big hug, loving the way Keeley's arms slid around his waist, holding him just as tightly as he held her. "And to tell you to behave."

"Of course he did," she replied, her voice muffled against his chest. He stole a quick kiss before letting her go, then grinned.

"He also wants us to 'play along'," Gio finger-quoted, "with the renovation videos until he gets home because it's keeping Keeley off the dating apps."

"Shit," she muttered. "On the one hand, I want to be annoyed as hell at that request. On the other, he's given me a great way to ensure you star in my videos. Because...my profile *is* still live on all the dating apps."

Gio narrowed his eyes. "Take it down. Get yourself off those things. You don't need them anymore."

Keeley studied him for a second, and he could see he'd gone too far with that declaration. Not that he had a problem with it. As far as he was concerned, she was spoken for and off the market. Forever, if he had his way.

It was just...Rafe was being too quiet.

"I'll hide my profile," Keeley said.

Hide, not delete. Gio noticed the difference. He wondered if Rafe did as well.

They were tromping through a minefield here, so Gio returned to his work. He expected Rafe to do the same, but he didn't.

"I noticed you didn't tell Kayden about us," Rafe observed.

"I..." Keeley paused, then apparently rethought what she wanted to say. "We haven't discussed it yet, haven't decided what we're telling people, or if we're telling them anything at all. In the past, you've kept these affairs a secret, right?"

"We have," Rafe answered simply.

"So the same is true for us?"

Gio held his breath, awaiting Rafe's response.

When it came, it offered absolutely none of the insight Gio was hoping for.

"It's only been a week. Why don't we let the dust settle?" Rafe said. "Kayden doesn't get home for a couple more weeks. We'll discuss what to tell people then. Who knows? Maybe you'll get sick of us before that and there won't be anything *to* tell."

"That—" Keeley started to say something but stopped almost immediately. That was when Gio realized he wasn't the only one tiptoeing. Rafe had made his feelings about love and commitment very clear. He'd also basically told her point-blank their menage would end the moment she decided she wanted more.

Keeley, the clever woman, knew better than to reveal her feelings.

Gio's jaw clenched with disappointment and a fair amount of anger that the two of them felt as if they couldn't be honest with Rafe. Though Gio knew that wasn't exactly fair.

Rafe hadn't lied about his feelings, nor was he acting out of character. His friend never jumped into anything without careful consideration. The problem was, Gio couldn't see a fucking thing here that needed to be thought about. The three of them were amazing together, a perfect fit, a slam dunk. They'd lived, eaten, worked, and slept together for eight days straight, and every single day was better than the one before.

And while he knew it was stupid to think it was always going to be smooth sailing, he knew these people. Rafe was the brother of his heart, and Keeley...

Well, he couldn't believe he'd been so blind. She'd been standing right in front of him all these years. She was funny, smart, independent, sarcastic, easygoing, and gorgeous. And while she was younger than them—six years younger than Rafe, seven younger than him—she didn't act like it. She was mature and confident, and she didn't defer to them.

Gio wanted a woman who knew her own mind, made her own decisions, charted her own course.

Keeley ticked every box.

"Fine," Keeley agreed. "We'll just stay the course until Kayden gets home. No problem."

While her tone was easy-breezy, something flashed in her eyes that told him she was disappointed too.

He and Keeley were on the exact same page.

The problem was going to be getting Rafe there as well.

$$Chapter\ Thirteen$$

L iza took a sip of her wine as Keeley perused the menu. For two weeks straight, she, Rafe, and Gio had basically locked themselves in the haunted mansion, existing exclusively on sex, takeout, sex, sleep, sex, and—occasionally— some work.

Gio had set up a workshop in one of the outbuildings behind the mansion. And while he spent a few hours there every day, he found countless excuses to come into the house to steal kisses from her. Not that she was complaining.

She'd broken away from the guys tonight, simply because she couldn't keep coming up with excuses not to go out with Liza, who was getting very suspicious. Prior to Keeley's new job with Baros Corporation, it wasn't unusual for her and Liza to get together two or three times a week, either for dinner—as they both lived alone and had no one to eat with—or to go clubbing.

Liza leaned back, not bothering to look at the menu. Instead, she was more intent on studying Keeley. "You've got a just-been-fucked glow."

Keeley laughed. "You can't tell that by looking at someone."

"Of course, you can. God, you practically reek of good sex. So let's have it."

"Liza."

Liza narrowed her eyes. "If it's JT, I swear to sweet Jesus—"

"It's not JT."

"Ah," Liza said, as if Keeley had fallen into her trap. "So there is somebody." She tapped her chin as if thinking, though Keeley could tell it was all for show. "Rafe or Gio. Which one?" Liza asked point-blank.

Keeley sighed. So much for being discreet. Liza had seen their dirty dance on the floor at Eclectic, and she knew Keeley was spending all her time with the guys, under the guise of "working late" on the inn project.

"You're being ridiculous," Keeley said. "Now are we going to order or not?"

"Gio seems to be the obvious answer," Liza continued, ignoring Keeley completely. "He's a shameless flirt, and I've noticed the way he looks at you."

Keeley stopped trying to play coy. "He looks at me?"

Liza nodded. "Oh yeah. You came back from college all grown up and hot. Gio noticed, but he pretended not to. Probably because of Kayden. So it could be Gio," she mused.

Keeley worked hard to school her features, determined not to give Liza the tiniest thread to tug.

"And while Rafe would normally be the wild card, with his Tin Man exterior, quiet and somber and repressed as fuck, the two of you *have* been spending a lot of time together. And I bet the guy is a serious freak in the bedroom."

Keeley mentally cursed as she felt her cheeks heat. She prayed she wasn't blushing because Liza would definitely notice. But damn if her friend hadn't hit the nail on the head.

Keeley picked up her wineglass and tried to hide behind it. "Are we finished with this game?" she asked, feigning boredom.

"We will be. As soon as you tell me which one." Liza wasn't going to let this go.

She probably should have asked the guys what she was supposed to say about them. So far, since that first and only date in public at Alpen Rose, the three of them had limited their time together to the mansion. She didn't think they'd done that on purpose, didn't think they were trying to hide what was going on. The truth was, none of them was willing to be too far away from a bed—or at the very least, a flat surface—in private.

Her mind drifted back to this morning, when Gio had tossed her onto the kitchen table, declaring to Rafe that breakfast was served, before going down on her. An hour later, hot and sweaty and basking in the afterglow of amazing sex, they plowed through a mountain of pancakes.

Liza's gaze narrowed and she leaned forward. "Ho. Ly. Shit. You're sleeping with *both* of them, aren't you?"

Liza didn't exactly possess an inside voice, and a few heads of people sitting near them twisted in their direction.

Keeley lowered her voice, murmuring, "A little louder, Liza. They didn't hear you in Jersey."

"Are you being for real right now?" Liza pressed, unrepentant but mercifully quieter.

"It just happened." Which was a lame explanation, but Keeley wasn't sure how else to describe it.

"It just happened," Liza repeated. "When? How?"

Keeley shrugged. "We got stuck at Divine the night of Penny's party. There was that big storm, remember?"

Liza nodded.

"We were talking, waiting for it to pass. When it did, they walked me to my car. I'd been bitching about the lack of *good* good-night kisses in my life."

"A valid complaint. I really think they should add kissing to the high school curriculum. Fuck new math. The world has bigger problems to solve."

Keeley grinned. This was why she loved Liza so much. She was funny and irreverent and always had her back. "Yeah, well, you know Gio. He took it as a challenge. So he gave me a kiss, and it was a *good* kiss. But he said it didn't mean anything."

"Apparently he lied."

Keeley wasn't sure if he had at that point. "Maybe, maybe not. After that, I started working for Rafe. Suddenly, he and Gio are learning more about me, about my life. And the next thing I know...they're crashing my dates."

Liza tilted her head. "I thought we found that annoying."

"Not the way Rafe and Gio do it. They sort of took over, claimed the dates, rather than just that shooting-intimidating-looks-from-afar tactic our brothers use. At the end of the first crashed date, Gio kissed me again. After the second, Rafe kissed me too."

Keeley had replayed that first kiss from Rafe over a million times, and the memory still had the power to make her blush.

"Wow," Liza said, staring at her too intently. "Must have been some *really* good kisses."

"Soooo fucking good," Keeley admitted. It was a relief to have someone to talk to about everything that had happened in the last month and a half.

"Get to the good part," Liza urged.

"The day we helped Gio move into the mansion...I had a date with JT."

Liza's eyes narrowed. "I knew you were lying. You don't get a manicure to do the laundry."

"Yeah, well. Let's just say...you were right about him. It ended badly, with me getting stranded at The Dolphin."

Liza gasped. "Alone? Not good."

"I know. I called Gio, and he and Rafe came to get me. They took me back to the mansion because my apartment key was locked in JT's car."

"Where was *he*?"

"Drunk tank."

"Jesus," Liza muttered. "Bet Gio was pissed."

"And then some. I took the guest room, but it was cold. Super cold. Gio blamed the ghosts."

Liza laughed but didn't interrupt.

"I went in search of blankets but ended up in Gio's bed. With him. And Rafe."

"That feels like the SparkNotes version, but we're to the good part finally, so I will allow it." They'd bought a bottle of wine, so Liza lifted it out of the chiller and refilled both their glasses.

"I only had sex with Gio that night."

"But Rafe was there?"

Keeley nodded. "They both like to watch. Anyway, the next night, they took me out on a real date. God, it was so romantic, and after that..." Keeley didn't bother to fight her flushed cheeks. She couldn't if she wanted to.

"So you've been shacking up with my cousin and his best friend for two weeks and this is the first I'm hearing of it?"

Keeley glanced at her nails, diva-style. "I've been busy," she said shamelessly. "Very busy. And then tired. So, so tired."

"Bitch." Liza broke a chunk off her breadstick and threw it at Keeley, who just barely dodged it with a laugh.

They both took another sip of wine, and Keeley could see her friend trying to process everything she'd just learned. She'd accepted Liza's invitation to dinner this morning, then spent the entire afternoon trying to come up with an excuse to get out of it. Simply because she hadn't wanted to leave the guys. Which just proved she was in way too deep.

In the end, Rafe had convinced her to go, telling her a few hours apart wouldn't kill them. Then Gio—the irreverent, hilarious asshole —had piled on, adding his dick was sore and he needed a break.

Finally, Liza said, "What the fuck is it with Baltimore?"

Keeley frowned, completely confused by the question. "What?"

"Uncle Frank moves his family to Baltimore, then comes back to Philly a few years later after Aunt Moira died. Now all his kids are threesome people. That shit had to happen in Baltimore."

Keeley laughed, until she realized Liza wasn't.

"I'm being serious. Think about it," Liza continued. "First,

Layla hooks up with Finn and Miguel. Then, Tony and Rhys are moving Jess in with them, becoming an instant family with her and Jasper. Now Gio. All of them. Threesomes."

"It's not quite all of them. I mean, Luca and Joey are still single. But I have to admit, I hadn't really thought about that," Keeley replied, but Liza was on a roll.

"Then Aunt Rose and Uncle Tommy's youngest, my cousin Erin, moves to Baltimore. Boom. She's living down there with two guys, Oliver and Gavin. It's gotta be Baltimore because nobody in *my* branch of the family is doing that. We're straight-up Philly. Bruno's married to one wife. Elio sleeps with his rink bunnies, one chick at a time."

"What about Aldo?" Keeley asked.

"He's a workaholic who practically lives at the fire station. Who knows what his deal is."

"You don't think you'd be interested in trying a menage?" Keeley asked.

Liza scowled. "Hell no. I don't want two of those things coming at me at the same time," she admitted, gesturing in such a way that made it clear she was talking about dicks, not men.

Keeley laughed. "Don't knock it until you try it."

Liza rolled her eyes, grinning. "I'll take your word for it." Then she added, "So I'll repeat again. What the fuck is going on in Baltimore?"

Keeley shrugged, enjoying this conversation and time with her friend more than she expected. "I have no idea. But I'm thinking I might like to visit there one day."

Liza shuddered. "You're taking that trip alone."

The waiter returned to take their orders.

"Have you talked to Gianna today?" Liza asked her after the server walked away.

"No. Just a bit of texting after she dropped the bomb," Keeley replied. Gianna had sent a text to their Sisters from Other Misters group late last night, telling them Sam had broken up with her and moved out of the apartment they shared. "I meant to call her today, but…" Keeley blushed, not wanting to confess what had kept her from calling.

Liza snorted, prompting Keeley to say, "I'm a terrible friend."

"Nope. Just a well-fucked one. I called to invite her out tonight with us, but she said she was going to reorganize her bedroom, now that she has so much more space."

Keeley frowned. "She said that? I mean, I kind of got from the texts that she wasn't in a fetal position in the corner, crying her heart out, but…for pity's sake, she dated the guy for almost eleven years. He was her first love, her first time, her first *everything*."

"I know," Liza said. "I'm worried about her. You know Gianna. Wound up tighter than a spring. I'm sort of afraid that when reality hits, she's going to crash hard."

"And if—when—that happens, we'll be there for her," Keeley said.

Liza smiled, and they tapped their wineglasses together to cement that promise.

The waiter returned with their salads, and they thanked him.

"In other news," Liza began. "I got the job."

Keeley's eyes widened. "And I'm only just now hearing about it? You should have said that the second we sat down."

Liza laughed and waved away her complaint. "Your sex life gossip was way more interesting."

"I'm so happy for you."

Liza had a dual major in English and Nonprofit Management, and she'd spent the last eight years since graduating from college working her way up the ranks of the Philadelphia Initiative—a foundation that worked to increase philanthropic donations in the community—first as a grant writer, and now as…

"What's your official title again?" Keeley asked.

"Executive director," Liza replied. "It's seriously my dream job…except for one little thing."

"What?"

"You know the Initiative has a board that it answers to. They just held an election for new leadership. Matt Russo is now the chair." Liza crinkled her nose in distaste when she said the man's name.

"Ugh. Sorry."

"That guy just…I don't know. He gets under my skin, rubs me the wrong way. I mean, I know there's no love lost between our families, but it seems like he's taken an extra-special kind of dislike to me."

Keeley couldn't debate that, as she'd witnessed it herself. They'd only run into Matt out in public a few times, but every time they did, the man's attention—and scowl—was zeroed in and focused solely on Liza.

The waiter returned with their food and they both dug in. Liza had opted for the eggplant parmesan, while Keeley chose the lasagna. Anytime she went out to an Italian restaurant, she went for the lasagna because it was her favorite, and her mother had always made it for her.

For ten years, she'd been searching for a lasagna all over the city that could rival her mom's. So far, no luck, and tonight was no different. Though, the older Keeley got, the more she realized she was probably searching for something that didn't exist. What she wanted—plain and simple—was her *mom's* lasagna.

"So, back to our original topic," Liza started after they'd put a major dent in their meals. It was clear Liza hadn't covered all the ground she wanted to yet about Keeley's newfound love life. "What's the deal with you, Rafe, and Gio? Is this just a hookup that's running into overtime or…" Liza paused so Keeley could fill in the blank.

She blew out a slow breath, considering how to respond. In the end, she went with the truth because the fact was, she needed advice.

"I don't really know."

Liza frowned. "Doesn't that feel like something you *should* know?"

"Yes. I mean…" Keeley closed her eyes and shook her head

briefly. "After the first date, we went back to the mansion and..." Keeley waved her hands rather than saying the words.

"Fucked like a bunch of rabbits," Liza filled in.

"Anyway, afterwards, just before we went to sleep, Gio asked me to stay with them while Kayden was out of town."

"You've been staying with them?"

Keeley nodded.

"Every single night?"

She nodded again.

"What the hell does that mean?"

Keeley grimaced. "I probably should have asked him that, but I didn't."

"Why not?" Liza was getting more confused by the minute, and Keeley decided she needed to give her friend more information.

"I'm not the first woman Gio and Rafe have shared in bed."

Liza's brows rose. "Wow. How did they manage to keep that a secret in our group of friends?"

Keeley shrugged one shoulder. "I probably shouldn't have told you that, but—"

"I don't betray confidences," Liza interjected, holding one hand up.

Keeley knew that, knew Liza would take anything she told her to the grave. She'd played Rafe's confession at Alpen Rose about his dating—no, it was hooking up—history over and over in her mind these past two weeks. "With each woman, the relationship began as a sexual affair between the three of them. But whenever the woman expressed feelings, Rafe excused himself and Gio remained. He dated the women because he's looking for love and marriage. Rafe isn't."

"So when Gio asked you to stay with them for three weeks, he was putting a time limit on the sexual affair with Rafe?"

"I don't know. He just asked me to stay with them while Kayden was away. You know my brother. He asked the guys to look after me."

Liza scoffed. "They could have kept an eye on you if you were in your apartment too. So that doesn't wash." And because Liza was like a prosecutor trying to bring a serial killer to justice, she reworded the question, determined to get down to the truth. "Was Gio telling you that this threesome thing you've got going on ends completely once Kayden gets home?"

Keeley shrugged, as she considered the last two weeks. "Kayden called last week, and Rafe said something about us reevaluating where we were when my brother got home. He didn't really close the door, so I guess there's a chance that this could continue even after Kayden's back in Philly."

Or at least that was what Keeley liked to pretend. Because she could see the writing on the wall. Rafe didn't talk about the future like Gio did, didn't give her the slightest indication that his attitude toward relationships had changed.

At some point, the hourglass was going to run out of sand.

"So Rafe is the flight risk. You know he's leaving, or at least, that's what he's done in the past. But what does Gio want?" Liza asked.

While Rafe had continued to keep an emotional distance from her, Gio acted like a guy who was all in. She couldn't begin to count the number of times he'd discussed future dates they would take. Trips to the shore. Holidays with the Morettis. Restaurants he wanted them to try if they ever managed to make it out of bed.

He painted beautiful pictures of the life he wanted them to lead. And while Rafe was there for those conversations, he never joined in, never gave Keeley any indication that he would be a part of that future. The last few times, he'd even gone one step further and walked out of the room. "I'm pretty sure Gio wants what Tony and Layla have."

"A committed threesome," Liza said.

"Yeah. And he wants it with Rafe. So when Rafe walks away from the threesome—"

"It falls apart. Gio and the woman inevitably break up and the cycle starts again."

Keeley nodded.

"And you think that's going to happen here?"

"No. I don't. I think...I *hope*..." Keeley couldn't finish that thought. She started to tell Liza that she thought Gio planned to stick around for the long haul. And while a huge part of her genuinely hoped that was true, that wasn't all she longed for. Because ultimately, she wanted what Gio wanted.

What Tony and Layla had.

She wanted Gio *and* Rafe.

Liza toyed with the stem on her wineglass, though her gaze remained on Keeley's face. "You're in love with both of them."

"So much it hurts."

"But you haven't told them."

"How can I?" Keeley asked. "I say those words and Rafe definitely walks away. What if...what if we *can* have more than three weeks? What if I just don't say the words? Because—God—I'm scared. I don't know if Gio and I can really make a go of it if it's just the two of us. His past relationships haven't survived without Rafe."

"Wait. Keeley. Hold up. How can you *not* say it?" Liza pressed, refusing to let Keeley get away without acknowledging her feelings.

Keeley hadn't really expected Liza to come to the same conclusion she had. Hadn't expected her best friend to actually advise her that if she wanted to keep this wonderful, magical, amazing thing she shared with Gio and Rafe, she would have to remain silent about her feelings.

Because that was a crazy, stupid, insane, impossible thing to do.

Liza leaned back in her chair, staring her down. She was waiting for a response, but Keeley didn't have one.

Because Liza was right. Too many times in the past week or so, the words "I love you" had been right there, so ready to be spoken. She'd managed to hold them back, but she couldn't do that forever. One night, they would slip out.

And then...

What if Rafe left her? Left *them*?

She knew Gio cared about her. Hell, she was pretty sure he loved her too. But would that be enough? Or would their relationship eventually end like all his others?

The idea of losing Rafe was unbearable, but the thought of losing both of them?

That was terrifying.

"So what's your plan?" Liza pressed.

Keeley shrugged hopelessly. "I wish I knew."

Chapter Fourteen

Rafe rubbed his eyes wearily, fighting to focus on the computer. He'd logged on a half hour earlier to tackle his email after arriving home from Eclectic with Keeley. It had been a long night at the end of a long week.

When he'd said he was going to do a little work in the office, Keeley, the eternal night owl—who should have been as tired as he was—had gone to unpack a box or two before turning in. Now it was almost midnight on Friday, and he was fucking beat.

He, Gio, and Keeley were three weeks into their whirlwind romance, and so far, it showed no signs of slowing down. Which was a problem.

Typically by this point in his shared affairs with Gio, Rafe was starting to feel stifled, ready to move on. And the sexual encounters with Jill, Vanessa, and Jennifer hadn't progressed to anywhere near this level, as he, Gio, and the other women only met up once or twice a week for a bit of fun between the sheets.

He'd spent twenty solid nights—as well as a shit ton of mornings and afternoons—in carnal bliss with Gio and Keeley.

Twenty nights.

Kayden came home tomorrow, and Rafe was no closer to

217

figuring out what came next than he'd been after the first night. He wasn't sure why he saw Kayden's return as the end of this affair. None of them had specifically said that. At least not in those words. Gio had asked her to stay with them while Kayden was out of town, and he'd suggested they reevaluate the affair at that time. So, it didn't make sense that he saw tomorrow as D-Day.

All he knew was…fuck…it should be.

The longer he remained, the harder it would be to leave.

Their sexual escapades had died down a little this past week, but that wasn't because of a lack of desire. Nope. It was because shit had hit the proverbial fan Monday on the work front.

Tony had stopped by to check on Gio's progress…and realized he hadn't made any. Since then, Gio had been hunkered down in his workshop, determined to make up for all the lost time. He'd come in after a fifteen-hour day just a few minutes earlier, announcing he was going to take a shower.

As for himself, on Monday afternoon, Rafe had uncovered undeniable proof that Rick, the manager at Eclectic, was indeed skimming money from the business. He'd fired the man on the spot, which meant until he hired someone new, he was managing the club, something he had no fucking clue how to do. Keeley had offered to help him as much as she could, so between the two of them, they'd come up with a work schedule, placed the orders for food and alcohol, and dealt with the seemingly countless issues that cropped up every other minute.

He rubbed his neck. The stiffness he hadn't felt the past few weeks had returned with a vengeance. He needed to find a chiropractor.

"I found it!"

Rafe looked up as Keeley dashed in excitedly.

"What did you find?" Gio asked, following her into the room. His hair was wet from his shower, and he was shirtless, wearing nothing but a clean pair of lounge pants.

Keeley was momentarily distracted by Gio's bare chest, something that would have amused Rafe if he wasn't so tired. Their girl was insatiable, and Rafe was here for it.

"The boat!" she said, waving several pieces of paper in the air. "It's at Pier 3 Marina. Your grandpa kept it there in an annual slip. It's paid for through December."

"I wonder if he ever got to go out on it," Rafe pondered. Upon studying the title, he discovered his grandpa had bought the boat a month before he found out he had cancer. He assumed the boat was going to be part of Grandpa's retirement plan, something he'd only begun discussing at their Monday dinners a few weeks before his terminal diagnosis.

"We need to plan a trip to the shore before the weather turns too cold," Gio said excitedly.

Rafe grinned. "Yeah. I guess we should. Still no safe combination?"

Keeley shook her head. "Not yet. But we've long since figured out there's no rhyme or reason to what's in the boxes, so I'm sure we'll find it." Rafe and Keeley had originally expected the paperwork to be in some sort of chronological order date-wise, thinking it made sense for the older stuff to be buried deeper in each box room. That had not been the case. If there was some plan or pattern to the boxes, how and where they were stored, they'd yet to figure it out.

At this point, he'd accepted there was no organizational schematic. It was merely random. Either that, or Marta and Grandpa Albert were moving the boxes in their spare ghost time, just to fuck with him.

"So..." Gio wiggled his eyebrows. "Are you two finished with work?" He was clearly ready to move this conversation to the bedroom.

Rafe, who'd been weary to the bone, found his second wind in an instant.

Keeley grinned as she walked toward the hall. The moment she reached the door, she called out, "Race ya!"

She was at the foot of the stairs by the time Rafe emerged from the office, but Gio was hot on her heels.

She laughed loudly when Gio caught her by the waistband of her pants, slowing her down as he attempted to pass her.

"You're cheating," she cried out, trying to break free of his grip.

Rafe didn't even bother to enter the competition, happy enough to watch their antics. Gio and Keeley were far more playful than he was. He'd wondered on more than a few occasions if that was because they'd both grown up with siblings, while Rafe was an only child. He'd had far less opportunity to wrestle and roughhouse as a kid.

There were a lot of similarities between Gio and Keeley, things that made them a natural couple. They both had a cutting wit and seemingly endless energy. They loved the same crappy reality TV shows, a genre Rafe would never get into. Whenever *The Circle* came on, he excused himself to his office to do some work. They also enjoyed cooking competitions, which Rafe was at least willing to sit through, though *Is it Cake?* was starting to get on his nerves. He never guessed right.

Rafe had sat beside them on the couch for two hours last night as they'd all watched a J. Lo movie. It had been Keeley's night to pick, and he was pretty sure she did research to find the movie most likely to drive him and Gio nuts, just for shits and giggles. He'd been humming the stupid "Marry Me" earworm all fucking day, something Keeley had taken great delight in pointing out to him every time it happened.

As they'd watched the movie, Keeley curled between them, her head on Gio's lap, Rafe had realized...they'd done it.

Found her.

The perfect woman.

And she'd been standing right in front of them for years.

Rafe tried to correct the pronoun in his head, tried to tell himself that *Gio* had found the perfect woman, but it was harder than he liked.

Keeley squealed as Gio got by her. She wrapped her arms around his waist but couldn't get a good grip, so she just slid down his body. Gio dragged her along awkwardly, struggling to walk with her clinging to his thighs.

"Just concede," he taunted.

"Never!" she yelled, very nearly tripping him when she lost hold again and made a last-ditch dive for his ankles at the top of the stairs.

Rafe smiled lightly, but he was struggling to let go of the heavier thoughts tonight.

He couldn't shake the feeling that Gio expected him to walk away tomorrow. After all, he'd basically put a time limit on the affair by asking her to stay with them just until Kayden returned home. Whether it had been intentional or not, he'd given them... God...an end date.

A reevaluation date. A D-Day.

Rafe was making himself insane worrying about tomorrow. Why couldn't he be more like them? Why couldn't he stop thinking, stop panicking, stop questioning every goddamn thing?

His genetic makeup was fucked.

What was he supposed to do anyway? Tell Keeley he loved her? How the hell did he even know if that's what this was? He'd never been in love. Not once. What if this was something else— like a blend of lust and friendship and that overprotectiveness he'd always felt for her? He'd never mixed those things together, so he could be completely misreading the emotion.

What happened if he said the words and then a few months down the road, he realized he'd made a terrible mistake? He'd promised not to hurt her, and he meant it.

Of course, there was another concern as well. What if Gio didn't want more than the shared sexual experience? What if he saw a future with Keeley that didn't include Rafe?

Rafe shook his head and blew out a long, slow breath.

Put it away. Put it all away.

That was easy to do when he entered his bedroom just in time to see Gio playfully pick up Keeley and toss her onto the mattress. His friend followed her down, caging her beneath him, kissing her senseless.

"Concede," Gio taunted.

"Nope," Keeley said, laughing when Gio began to tickle her.

Fuck it.

Tomorrow was coming. There was no stopping it.

Tonight...he was going to be here, with them, living in the moment.

He leaned against the doorjamb for a few minutes, watching them kiss and play. They were beautiful together. The two of them would make adorable babies.

Rafe frowned, the idea of them making a family without him cutting like a knife.

Put it away.

Keeley looked in his direction after a few minutes. "Why are you all the way over there?"

Rafe pushed away from the doorframe, pulling off his shirt as he walked into the room. Stopping next to the mattress, he toed off his shoes and shed his pants as well.

Gio and Keeley lay next to each other, watching.

"That's better," she said, coming up on her hands and knees to crawl to the edge of the bed to meet him. Kneeling, she wrapped her arms around his shoulders and kissed him.

Rafe had never been a kisser. Period.

Kissing felt intimate, and that wasn't something he was interested in.

Sex without strings. Sex without accessories.

None of that was true with Keeley. With her, he wanted everything and more.

Reaching for the hem of her shirt, he drew it over her head. Gio was two seconds behind him, unfastening her bra and tugging it away as well. Then, they both took a moment to admire what they'd uncovered.

She laughed. "You guys act like you've never seen my boobs before."

Rafe reached out and pinched one of her nipples, then the other, loving the way they tightened. She had gorgeous nipples.

"Very suckable," Gio murmured, shifting to her side so he could take one into his mouth, while Rafe cupped the other, playing with it. They'd learned early on that the quickest way to get Keeley's motor revving was to play with her breasts. Or her clit. She wasn't fussy.

Keeley's head fell back, her eyes closing with delight. She gave them one of her cute little moans. "You guys are way too good at that."

"We're bachelors in our thirties," Gio joked. "We've had plenty of opportunities to practice."

Keeley opened her eyes, gaze zeroing in on Gio. "I don't want to hear about past practice."

Gio chuckled. "What's this I'm seeing? Did you know our Keeley had a jealous streak, Rafe?"

He shook his head. To be honest, he didn't. Keeley seemed to take everything in stride, and she'd never seemed to mind hearing about their past liaisons with Jill, Vanessa, and Jennifer. In fact, she was typically the one who brought them up. Keeley wasn't shy about asking stuff she wanted to know.

"Stand up and take off your jeans," Gio demanded, as he took off his own clothes.

Rafe took a step back so Keeley could rise. She slid her jeans and panties down together. She was barefoot already, and he assumed she'd shucked her sandals at the door. Keeley seemed to have an aversion to shoes, always taking hers off the second she got home. It was why there'd been a stack of no less than five pairs of shoes in his front foyer these past few weeks.

Once she was naked, he expected her to climb back onto the bed, but she held her ground.

"Can I ask you guys something?"

He and Gio both nodded.

"I know I just said I didn't want to hear about your past practice, but…" She bit her lower lip, and he caught sight of that uncharacteristic shyness that crept out from time to time.

"But what, beauty?" Rafe prompted.

"Is what we do together…is it like what you did with the other women?"

Rafe tilted his head, unsure of her meaning.

"Be more specific," Gio said, patting the mattress next to him, encouraging her to sit.

She took a seat, then forged on. "I mean…you guys just take turns. We've never…" Keeley threw her hands up, shaking her head. "Forget it."

"No," Rafe said. "We're not forgetting it. Keeley, you were new to menage sex—" he started.

"So were the other women," she interjected.

"Yes," Rafe replied, "but they were also older, more…" He paused and looked at Gio, uncertain how to finish that thought, who nodded, encouraging him to go on. "They weren't you," Rafe finally said. "We've been taking things slower because we care about you. We don't want to hurt you."

"So it *was* different with them," she pressed.

Gio considered that, then shrugged. "Truthfully? No. Not a lot different. We still took turns most of the time, but on occasion…we'd take a woman at the same time, one of us in her mouth, the other in her pussy."

Keeley nodded. "Oh. Okay." She looked disappointed.

Rafe rubbed his jaw and tried to hide his growing grin. "Keeley, are you trying to ask us about anal sex?"

She flushed bright scarlet, but he had to hand it to her. She looked him in the eye and held it. "Yes. I kind of thought…"

"Wait. Have you been watching porn? Group-sex porn?" Gio asked, laughing with pure glee.

Keeley narrowed her eyes. "So what if I have been?"

Gio grinned shamelessly. "I'm pissed that you watched it without us. Talk about a missed opportunity."

Rafe rolled his eyes. "If you had questions about what we were doing, or if there was something you wanted to try, why didn't you just ask us?"

"Because I wasn't sure if it *was* something I want to try. Thought I'd better scope it out first."

"Jesus," Rafe said, amused. "So, what do you think now?"

She shrugged and crinkled her nose. "I think it would hurt. A lot."

Gio shifted on the bed, fluffing the pillows up against the headboard before sliding over to what had become "his" spot. "I think this conversation is going to take a few minutes. Why don't we get comfortable?"

Keeley moved into the middle, and Rafe claimed his place after her.

Gio wrapped his arm around her shoulder and placed a soft kiss on the top of her head. "I guess the first question is...have you experimented with anal at all before?"

Keeley shook her head. "No. I've never had a long-term boyfriend, and butt stuff isn't something I'd want to do with someone I didn't trust completely."

Rafe laughed. "Butt stuff," he murmured, shaking his head.

"God." Keeley covered her cheeks. "This is a lot more embarrassing than I thought it would be. I mean...we've seen each other naked more than dressed the last few weeks."

Gio tapped under her chin, encouraging her to look at him. "You don't have to be embarrassed, but I get it. We've been friends for years, and now suddenly, we're more. In some ways, it's hard to move beyond the way we've always been with each other because that part of our relationship lasted years, while this part is still very new."

"Yeah," Keeley said. "That feels true."

"Do you want to try anal?" Rafe asked. He wasn't sure how

he'd respond if she actually said yes. He'd walked into this bedroom viewing tonight as possibly the end. Now, Keeley was asking them to take it up a few notches.

"I don't know. What if it *does* hurt?"

"Keeley," Rafe said, taking her hand in his. "I told you the first night we were together, we're never going to do anything that hurts you. I meant that."

"So the two of you haven't..." She waved her hands around, letting that motion fill in the blanks.

"We've never taken a woman that way at the same time," Gio replied.

"But you *have* had..." More hand-waving. Too much more of this and Keeley was going to take flight.

"Yes, Keeley," Rafe responded. "I've had anal sex with past lovers."

"Me too," Gio added.

"Only with women?" she asked.

Rafe was stunned for a moment. "Where did that question come from?"

She lifted one shoulder casually. "The night of our first date... you put your hand over mine. Helped me give Gio a hand job."

Rafe recalled that very well because he'd asked himself a million times since then what had compelled him to do so. He and Gio had never touched each other intimately before that. Hell, they hadn't touched each other since. Still...that night, Gio didn't pull away from his touch, even though Rafe knew he'd shocked the shit out of his friend.

"I've never..." Rafe started, his words falling away. He kept his gaze locked on Keeley's face, too worried about what he'd see if he looked at Gio.

"We've never touched each other sexually before that night," Gio responded. "But I'm not gonna lie—it was hot."

"It was," Keeley agreed.

Gio gave Rafe a look that he struggled to interpret. In the past, he never had any trouble figuring out what was on his friend's mind, but this time...Rafe didn't have a clue what Gio was thinking.

Mercifully, he deftly changed the subject, drawing Rafe out of the line of fire in case Keeley decided to ask him why he'd touched Gio that particular night.

"And if you decide you want to try the 'butt stuff,'" Gio finger-quoted, "we'll revisit it another night. For tonight, kinky girl, do you think we could keep it fairly simple?"

She cupped Gio's cheek and gave him a quick kiss. "I guess," she sighed, grinning wickedly. "If we have to."

Rafe's body always reacted to stress before his head could catch up. So his chest was tight before his brain engaged enough to leave him wondering if he was going to be a part of that future plan they'd just agreed to.

Put it away, the little voice inside whispered.

Gio expanded on Keeley's quick kiss, giving her one that rang the bell and signaled it was time for the next round. The good round.

Keeley moaned into his mouth. "Want you," she whispered. "Want you both so much."

Gio broke the kiss and twisted, lying on his back. "Crawl on top of me."

Keeley threw one of her legs over his waist, her hair a curtain around their faces as they began to kiss again. Rafe sat and watched, let the beauty of their kisses ease away all his anxiety.

Keeley lifted briefly, grasping Gio's cock and guiding it to her pussy. She slid down slowly, sneaking a peek at Rafe as she did so.

The sexy/sweet grin she gave him took his breath away.

She moaned softly once Gio was seated fully, then she held still, giving herself those few necessary seconds to adjust. She'd confided one night that both of them were bigger than her previous lovers.

Gio remained still beneath her, his hands on her hips. He stared at her like she hung the moon, completely under her spell.

Rafe had never seen Gio so in love.

Gio had professed having feelings for Jennifer and Vanessa, though not Jill. But it was clear his heart hadn't been fully engaged with either of those women. Not like it was now. With Keeley.

Keeley lifted up, then lowered back down, faster this time, a bit harder. She bounced on Gio's dick a dozen times before bending forward to steal another kiss. Gio lifted his hips, thrusting his pelvis so that he was still fucking her, shallowly, from his position below.

Rafe was overwhelmed by the desire to join them. Perhaps Keeley had planted the seed with her questions, but right now, it simply wasn't in him to wait his turn. Not this time.

He sat up, then crawled toward them, his actions drawing their attention. He knelt directly behind Keeley. While she was straddling Gio's hips, Rafe chiseled himself a spot between his friend's parted legs.

Neither of them had an issue with proximity, or with glancing brushes of hands or legs. It was sex, they were naked, and body parts were going to touch. However, this was a more intimate position, and he could see the furrow in Gio's brow. His friend wasn't annoyed, but he was definitely curious about Rafe's intentions—especially when Rafe reached down and briefly, just briefly, cupped Gio's balls.

Gio grunted, his eyes closing with pleasure for just a moment, before opening once more, his gaze locking with Rafe's. Gio, the impulsive fucker, raised one eyebrow and quirked a grin as if to say, "So it's like that now?"

Rafe wanted to laugh, but damn if he wasn't in over his fucking head. Because he couldn't understand this sudden desire to touch Gio too.

Were his feelings for these two getting mixed up? He'd always shared a tight bond with Gio, their relationship solid, reliable... platonic. But now, with Keeley there—making him feel shit he had zero experience with—it suddenly felt like there could be more between him and Gio. Like something had already been there, buried beneath the surface all this time, unseen because Rafe had always refused to dig deeper.

He was spiraling out of control, spinning wildly, with no way to stop himself from crashing into the brick wall looming large and impenetrable right in front of him.

Keeley, unaware of the exchange between him and Gio, started to lift up on her knees once more, but Rafe placed his hand in the middle of her back.

"Stay down. Like that. Fuck her the way you were, Gio."

Gio tilted his hips, and Keeley, who seemed physically incapable of remaining still during sex, added her own force to the motion, sliding up and down the length of Gio's body.

On one upward swing, Rafe used his grip on her back to push her even higher, until Gio's cock slipped out of her pussy, just as Rafe had intended. He was ready.

Gripping his dick, he guided himself inside her, loving Keeley's adorable little squeak of surprise.

"Oh!" she gasped, as Rafe began fucking her. He pounded inside her fifteen, twenty times—then he pulled out.

Gio caught on quickly, taking Rafe's place, fucking her from below.

Over and over, they pounded, then retreated, allowing the other man a turn.

"We're sharing you," Rafe said, placing a kiss on Keeley's bare shoulder. It wasn't what she'd meant earlier, but fuck if it wasn't the most moving sexual experience of his life.

Keeley cried out, "Yes," but Rafe had no idea if she was agreeing or if she was simply close to the end.

On his next retreat, Rafe wrapped his hand around his dick as Gio slid back inside. "Make her come," he demanded. "Then we're coming too."

Gio nodded, just once, and Rafe suspected that was all he was capable of. Like Keeley, he was teetering on the edge.

Gio's fingers slid to her clit, his touch doing the trick.

Keeley cried out, her back arching as she came. Gio went down with her, drawing her body down on his, his fingers grasping her upper arms tightly.

"God, Keeley," he grunted as he climaxed.

Rafe placed his hand on her upper back once more, holding her down as he tightened his grip and increased his speed, jacking off with a fury. A dozen strokes later, he was there, coming so hard his bones rattled, painting her bare back with his release.

"Fuck. Yes! Jesus," Rafe cried out. "Beauty."

The three of them remained there, close together, until Rafe forced himself to rise.

"Stay there, Keeley. Don't move. I need to clean you off." He walked to the bathroom and dampened a washcloth.

Neither Gio nor Keeley had stirred, and he wondered if they'd fallen asleep like that, with Gio's soft cock still nestled inside her.

Keeley's eyes drifted open when Rafe gently washed her back clean. She gave him a drowsy smile of thanks. Then she rolled over, flopping onto her back in the middle of the bed, lifeless.

Gio grunted when she moved but didn't bother to open his eyes. The heavy way his chest rose and fell told Rafe if he wasn't asleep, he would be in mere seconds.

Rafe washed himself up, tossed the washcloth in the laundry bucket, then joined them in bed. He lay on his back for several minutes, listening to their soft breathing.

Keeley slipped under the covers once she'd cooled off and shifted into her usual position, stomach down. They'd slept together enough nights that their sleep routines were familiar, comfortable.

He let their soft breathing lull him right to the threshold of sleep. A second more and he would have been there.

But he heard Keeley whisper. She'd rolled over to face Gio while his friend still lay on his back, on his side of the bed.

"Gio," she whispered, so low Rafe had to strain to hear her, and he was right beside her. Her words were more breath than whisper.

"Yeah," Gio murmured back quietly.

"I love you," she said.

Rafe couldn't see either of their faces in the dark, but he could hear the smile in Gio's voice when he whispered back, "I love you too, little one. So much."

"I just needed to tell you," she breathed back.

And that was it. All they said. Then Keeley nestled closer to Gio, who wrapped her up in his embrace. The two of them were asleep within seconds.

Rafe lay there in the silence that followed, his heart thudding so loud, he felt certain it would wake them. Then he recalled Keeley reading his horoscope to him this morning. The words had bothered him all day.

It's scary to do anything risky for fear of failure. Perhaps you've tried to become invisible in situations so you can avoid being noticed. These defense mechanisms won't get you where you need to go.

For three weeks, Rafe had felt like he belonged here, with them...but he'd resisted it heavily, tried to deny it by hiding his feelings. Apparently, he'd made himself *too* invisible.

Had Keeley waited until she thought he was asleep to say those words to Gio?

Why? Because she thought he didn't want to hear them?

Or worse, because she didn't want to *say* them to Rafe?

Gio had made no bones about his feelings. He was in love with her, and he'd found ways to show Keeley every single day they'd been together. He wanted to marry her, wanted to be with her. Forever.

Meanwhile, Rafe had purposely put himself on the outside, had told her—told both of them—that all he wanted was sex.

Now he was here.

Alone.

Exactly in the place he'd put himself because he'd been too afraid to open himself up to the possibility of love.

She loved Gio.

Rafe played her confession over and over in his head, into the wee hours, until he thought he'd go mad.

Ultimately, the clock had run out...and now it was time for him to do as he promised.

It was time for him to walk away.

Chapter Fifteen

Keeley walked around the house, searching the living room and kitchen for Rafe before heading to his office. She and Gio had been surprised when they'd woken up to discover him gone. The three of them were sleepy starters ordinarily, usually dozing for a few minutes past the alarm before waking each other up in such a manner that they didn't get out of bed until waaaay past the alarm.

Gio had frowned when he realized Rafe wasn't there, but he'd covered up his concern quickly, coming up with a bunch of lame reasons why Rafe had probably risen early.

Keeley hadn't been fooled by any of them. She knew what today was. The date had been circled in red in her brain ever since Gio had asked her to stay with them until Kayden returned from Vermont.

The day Rafe said they would decide where they all stood.

So many times last night, she'd opened her mouth to tell them both she loved them. The feeling simply wouldn't be contained anymore. Mercifully—and just barely—she managed to wait until Rafe fell asleep so that she could at least, *finally*, say the words to Gio. And he'd said them back.

But as magical and wonderful as that had felt, she'd still wanted to tell Rafe the same thing. Fear of losing him for good had held her back.

Given his absence in the bed this morning, it didn't seem to matter if she'd said them or not.

"There you are," she said, forcing a cheerful tone. She walked around his desk and gave him a kiss on the cheek. Rafe made no move to return the kiss with a hotter one. Instead, he gave her a wan smile—and just like that, she knew.

It was over.

Keeley was instantly reminded of the night her parents died. Kayden had walked in. She'd taken one look at his face and known they were gone. He didn't have to say a word.

The same was true now. One glimpse into Rafe's eyes and she could see what was coming.

Rafe's gaze traveled to the door.

"Gio's taking a shower," she replied to his unspoken question. She wondered if he would wait until Gio was here to do this or if he preferred to say it to her in private.

Rafe nodded, but he remained quiet.

Keeley took a deep breath, fighting for composure as she tried to figure out the best way to handle this. If she remained in this room too long, the pressure would break her, and she'd fall apart.

She was going to fall apart regardless, but she didn't want to do it in front of Rafe.

He'd never promised her forever, never alluded to the future.

Nope. He'd told her at Aspen Rose that for him, what they shared would only be sex. She walked into this with her eyes wide open, so she couldn't be mad, couldn't yell or scream or call him names, even if that was exactly what she wanted to do.

Because he'd never lied about what this was. Not once.

Her anger…God…her *sorrow* over him breaking this off was her fault because she'd let herself hope, let herself dream that he'd change his mind.

Ugh. She cursed herself. A wise woman wouldn't have started this damn affair to begin with. Especially not with her boss.

What the fuck had she been thinking? She wasn't a robot. Maybe Rafe could keep his emotions under lock and key, turn his feelings off like a light switch, but she wasn't that person, wasn't capable of the same.

"I'm going to work from my office at Eclectic today. Actually, the whole week," she said, hoping he couldn't detect the tightness in her voice. Her throat was constricted, closing fast.

He nodded. "Okay. I'll come by later this afternoon if I have time. I'd already decided to spend this week stopping by all the other Baros Corp. properties. Just to make sure things are running smoothly."

"Great. I, um..." Keeley felt like Gio should be here for this part, but if he was...

There was no way she could keep it together if he was there too.

"Kayden comes home today."

"I know," Rafe said.

She was tired of tiptoeing around him. It was time she forced him to show his hand. Not knowing how he felt killed her.

"So I'm going to pack up my stuff and head back to my place for tonight."

She held her breath, waiting for Rafe's response. As always, the bastard took his time. Damn him and his constant thinking. She wanted to scream at him to just fucking say it already, but she managed to keep that primal, furious response inside.

"Okay." He paused, then he stood up. "Listen, Keeley..."

Oh *fuck* no. She thought she could stand here, let him say the words, and be okay with it. After all, she'd managed to stay and listen to those horrible words from Kayden.

"Mom and Dad aren't coming home. Their plane...the storm..."

She couldn't do it this time.

"It's over," she said for him.

Rafe frowned, for just a split second, clearly surprised by her words. Then he nodded. "I think it's better for everyone if we don't let the affair continue."

Affair.

She hated that word as much as the word *crush*. Because what they'd shared had felt like so much more.

He rubbed the back of his neck, something he did whenever he was stressed out, and she could tell that it was bothering him. She'd given him a massage one night when he confessed his shoulders had been tight for months.

"You and Gio want different things," he began. "And I think the two of you have a chance at making something real, something good. I think...we were wrong to give in to the attraction."

He thought what they'd done was wrong?

The most incredible time of her life was *wrong*?

"I'm holding you and Gio back. If I step away now, the two of you can begin the rest of your lives together. He's crazy about you, Keeley. Head over heels. I've never seen him like this."

Keeley nodded, her voice failing her. She wanted to yell, "What about you?!" but the words wouldn't come.

They held each other's gazes for a long time, neither of them speaking. She'd always marveled over the way Rafe and Gio were able to say so much without talking.

She wished she could manage the same because right now, all she saw was a stone wall, nothing to give her the slightest hint to what he was thinking or feeling.

When the silence drifted for too long, she went for broke.

"I love you," she whispered.

Rafe winced, as if her admission had physically hurt him.

He didn't return the sentiment. Didn't say a damn thing.

She waited as long as she dared, then turned away because tears were starting to blur her vision.

"I'll go pack then. Goodbye, Rafe," she said as she walked out of the room. Part of her waited—hoped—for him to call her back in, to offer her one of those amazing hugs of his, but he said noth-ing. Just let her walk away.

She went upstairs to get her things, swallowing hard to dislodge the lump in her throat. She didn't have a clue what Gio would say. One look and he'd know what had happened.

He had experience with this part, so would he take it in stride? Or, like her, would he be pissed as shit, hurt as hell?

When she entered the bedroom, she could tell it was empty. She checked the bathroom, but Gio wasn't there either. Walking to the window that overlooked the backyard and outbuildings, she spotted him walking into his workshop.

Typically, they all ate breakfast together before going to work.

What the hell was going on? Did Gio know this was coming? Had he tried to make himself scarce?

She quickly packed her things, somewhat surprised by how much stuff she'd brought over from her apartment. It took her half an hour to gather it all up. Walking downstairs with her bags, she glanced through the open door to Rafe's office. It was empty.

He'd made a quick escape.

Coward.

Then she acknowledged that she'd intended to play the same card, staying away from the mansion until she could face him without falling apart. She suspected she would be good to go in about five to ten years.

Keeley loaded her stuff in her car, then walked around the house just as Gio was coming out of the workshop.

She needed to know where he stood before she went home and cried her eyes out.

"Hey, gorgeous. Tony needed some specs on the cabinets, so I came out really quick to—" He stopped mid-sentence. He'd been reaching out for her, his original intent a kiss. She knew him well enough to know that, but he pulled up short when he saw her face. "That motherfucker."

She blinked a few times, wiping her eyes, willing the tears to stop. "You didn't know?"

Gio scowled. "No. Keeley—" he started.

"I'm okay," she lied.

"No, you're not. He really broke it off?" he asked, clearly needing confirmation.

She nodded, unable to say the words.

"Without me there."

She gave him a sad smile. "I'm kind of glad you weren't. You've witnessed enough of my dating rejections."

"Goddammit. This is bullshit! He's not getting away with this." Gio started toward the house, and Keeley was suddenly glad Rafe had cleared the premises. In his current state of mind, Gio was looking for blood.

"He left," she said quickly.

Gio stopped and turned back toward her. "It wasn't supposed to end." He paused, then hastily added, "Not this way."

Keeley had suspected Gio wanted the same as her, and with those words, he'd confirmed it. He'd come into this affair—fucking shitty word—hoping for the same thing she had. And after three amazing, perfect weeks, Keeley had truly believed Rafe would change his mind. How could he not see how good the three of them were together?

"We knew it wasn't forever. He told us that. Point-blank."

"He did, but I still..." Gio raked a hand through his hair, mussing it up.

"Me too," she confessed.

Gio looked equal parts resigned and angry. Then he tilted his head. "You think he heard us last night? Heard us say..." he mused.

Keeley hadn't considered that. She shrugged. "It doesn't matter if he did. I told him I loved him...just now. God, you should have seen his face. He acted as if I'd plunged a dagger straight into his heart."

"You said it?" Gio mused.

She nodded, then forged on. "We knew this was temporary, Gio. We all sort of agreed to this day as the deadline."

Gio shook his head. "No, we didn't say this was the deadline. We said we'd reevaluate and decide what to tell people. I thought these last three weeks would have convinced him. Made him see —" Gio's hands clenched into fists. "Fuck!"

Keeley took a shaky breath, and Gio noticed.

"Aw, little one. Come here." He wrapped his arms around her, and she clung to him, needing his warmth, his comfort.

"He told us it was just sex. That it wouldn't be more," she said, her voice muffled as she pressed her face against his chest. "It's my fault for—"

"No, it's not," Gio interrupted. "I don't give a shit *what* he said. Because I was there for those past affairs, and Rafe didn't act like this with our other lovers. He was different with you, Keeley. I really thought..."

He didn't finish, and she wasn't sure if that was because he'd been blindsided or if he was protecting her feelings. Probably both.

"I think we set our expectations too high. Rafe has never been in love. After so many years of watching his mom suffer heartbreak after heartbreak, it makes sense that he'd view that emotion as something negative."

Gio considered that for a moment. "He told me once that he didn't think he was capable of falling in love."

Keeley rejected that outright. "He's wrong. He probably loves more deeply than anyone I know. He just refuses to acknowledge it."

Gio gave her a rueful grin. "I think you're right. Love is hard for Rafe, but it's the relationship part that's harder. His childhood was one guy after another playing dad. Rafe doesn't talk about it much, but the first couple stepfathers were decent men, ones he'd wished had stuck. The worst part was that when they left his mom, they left him too. He's not in contact with any of them. So here's this kid with a rotating door of dads who cut and run every three to five years, leaving him fatherless once more with a devastated mother."

Keeley didn't know much about that part of Rafe's history. Then something else occurred to her. "I don't think it helped that Grandpa Albert was so madly in love with Marta that he chose to live alone for fifty years rather than open himself up to someone else. He hid himself away with a ghost story."

"You're right," Gio said. "He associates love with pain and leaving. That's all he's ever learned from his role models."

"So it's hopeless?"

Gio shook his head. "No. I don't think so."

She appreciated his optimism, the tears she couldn't hold at bay finally drying up. Although Rafe's departure was only one of the things upsetting her. "What if we can't convince him to come back, Gio? What does that mean for us?"

He frowned, and she got a sense he was mad at the question. "Are you seriously asking me that? I'm not going anywhere. You're mine, Keeley. *Mine*," he stressed, cupping her cheeks, forcing her to hold his gaze so she could see that he meant business.

"Yeah, but—"

"No buts. I know what you're thinking, what you're afraid of, but I need you to put those fears away and listen to me. *Really* listen to me. I love you. I'm in love with you. And I'm here for the long haul."

She smiled. "I love you too, but...you haven't given up on him, have you?"

Gio shook his head. "No. I haven't. I think—"

Her phone rang, and he stopped speaking.

She pulled it out of her back jeans pocket, hoping perhaps it was Rafe, praying he'd had a change of heart, that he regretted breaking things off.

"Kayden," Gio said before she'd even glanced at the screen.

Of course, it was. She was so upset, she hadn't even realized it was her brother's ringtone.

She started to put it away, but Gio grasped her wrist. "Answer it or he'll worry."

Keeley answered the phone. "Hey, Kayden. Didn't expect to hear from you so early. You on the road?"

"Actually, I'm home. Aldo and I decided we'd had enough of the sleeping bag life, so we left Vermont after dinner, got in at one a.m. Gotta tell you, there's nothing like a good night's sleep in your own bed." It was good to hear her brother's voice. He always knew how to cheer her up, how to make her feel better. Part of her was tempted to drive to his house right now, to unload every miserable feeling, so that he could hug her and reassure her that everything would be okay.

She forced a carefree laugh. "I can't believe you thought sleeping on the ground for three weeks was ever a good idea."

"So what are your plans for tonight? Because I was hoping we could do dinner together. I've missed you like crazy, kiddo."

"Dinner? Tonight? Um, yeah. That would be great. I missed you too."

Gio gave her an encouraging smile. She knew there was a lot they needed to say to each other, but maybe taking a night away would help. Kayden would distract her with stories of his great adventure, then she'd crawl into her own bed—unlike her brother, she hadn't missed hers at all—and sob her heart out. Then tomorrow, she'd figure out where to go from here.

"Awesome," Kayden replied. "Why don't I swing by your place to get you? Six o'clock okay? I know you've been working long hours."

That wasn't going to be a problem for the foreseeable future. She didn't have a clue how long it would take for her to be able to work around Rafe again. She'd been such a fool.

"Six works just fine," she replied.

"You can pick the place," Kayden said. "See you tonight."

They said their goodbyes and hung up.

"Dinner with your brother, huh?"

She nodded. "Yeah. I know the timing isn't great, but..."

"Actually, I think it's pretty good. You, me, and Rafe have been in each other's faces for three solid weeks. We need a reboot."

She gave him a curious look. "A reboot?"

Gio nodded. "A night away from each other to clear our heads. And then tomorrow, we come up with a plan. I'm taking you on a date."

"What are we planning?" she asked.

"Before I answer that, tell me something. Do you want us to go it alone from now on? Or do you want Rafe to be a part of this?" Gio waved his hand between them, and she loved it. She'd never really been part of a "this."

"I told you, I'm in love with Rafe too."

Gio grinned, and she marveled at his complete lack of jealousy. "Well then, you and I are going to lay a little groundwork. But we can discuss that tomorrow night."

He wrapped his arm around her shoulders, the two of them walking back toward the house. She pointed to the driveway. "My stuff is in my car."

He sighed. "I hate that."

"Me too. I'm going to work from my office at Eclectic today."

"Okay." Gio gave her a quick squeeze. "We'll figure this out. Together."

They stopped when they reached her car. Gio cupped her cheeks and gave her a soft kiss, full of promise and love.

And as sad as she was at the moment, she couldn't deny that she was also hopeful.

The next week flew by, but not in the same way as the previous three. After their date on Tuesday, Gio and Keeley had decided to keep their dating a little closer to home...something that had obviously caught Rafe off guard.

It was clear he'd expected to be odd man out, expected them to carry on their romance somewhere out of his line of vision.

Too bad, so sad. Because that wasn't what he was going to get.

Gio had told Rafe outright last Monday that he was going to continue to see her, that he was in love with her. Rafe had reassured Gio he would be fine, pointing out that he always had been in the past. They'd counted on that response, perfectly aware that Rafe was determined to treat this just like one of his and Gio's past affairs.

What Rafe didn't know was that Gio and Keeley planned to put that resolve to the test.

Last Wednesday, she'd shown up after work with a couple of pizzas and told them they needed to continue working on the renovation videos. Rafe—shocked by her appearance—had gone along with it, and in the end, she'd gotten some amazing footage. She'd uploaded five videos so far. None of them had gone viral, but the views were adding up slowly and steadily, just as she'd hoped. Neither Rafe nor Gio were hard to look at, and once they'd gotten into talking about the house and the ghosts, they were quite funny.

She'd sent an email to Joey, along with the link to the videos, asking him if he had any advice for future shows. Joey—God love him—had responded immediately, telling her what she'd done was great and promising to promote the videos on his show, which was set to begin airing in a month. And while that was exciting, it meant they needed to get more videos up quickly.

Gio had congratulated her privately on devising the perfect reason for the three of them to spend lots of time together.

Thursday, Friday, Saturday, and Sunday had passed in the same way—with Rafe and Gio working on the office, while she filmed it and kept them talking and laughing.

Things felt exactly as they had when the three of them had been together. It was all so effortless between them...the conversation, the teasing banter, even the way they tackled household chores.

Keeley didn't mind washing dishes, so she took on that chore while Rafe dried and Gio put them away. Rafe cleaned one hell of a bathroom, while Gio, who'd been too long without a lawn to care for, took over mowing and weed eating.

Because Rafe insisted on believing their relationship was

merely a physical one, based on lust, not love, Gio and Keeley had decided to take that out of the equation for now. Every evening, after they finished filming or hanging out, Gio gave her a sweet good-night kiss, then she'd steal a hug from Rafe.

Rafe's responses to those hugs had been stiff the first couple of nights, but he'd quickly reverted back to giving her the amazing, warm embraces they'd shared when they had just been friends.

Then she drove home.

Alone.

Which sucked.

This last Monday, they'd taken a break from the renovations, opting for a lazy night in front of the TV with Chinese takeout. She and Gio had forced Rafe to watch *Crime Scene Kitchen*, and while he grumbled about it, she noticed he'd had strong opinions about what the mystery dessert was.

The three of them had settled on the couch, just as they had the month before, Cricket nestled on the cushion between her and Rafe. Their hands brushed once or twice when they reached to pet the sweet dog at the same time. Keeley had wished every time that he would take her hand in his, but he'd simply pulled away.

Rome wasn't built in a day, she told herself, seeking some consolation.

They hoped that by recreating everything they'd shared—minus the sex—Rafe would realize that what the three of them had wasn't just an affair. It had been so much more.

Last night, she'd gone out to dinner with her brother again, so she hadn't seen either of her guys. She refused to think of them any other way. She still hadn't told her brother about Gio or Rafe. Not that she thought he'd be angry or upset, and not because she wanted to keep it a secret. It was just that until things were settled —*please, let them settle the right way*—she wanted to wait. She wanted to be able to look at Kayden and tell him that she was madly, deeply, truly in love with Gio and Rafe, and know that they felt the same way.

So now, it was Wednesday night again, and they were back in the office, after putting the finishing touches on the room. Thus far, Keeley had shown bits and pieces of the office on video, but hadn't given a total panoramic, waiting until the work was finished so she could do a big reveal show.

Tonight, they were finally there, and the three of them were thrilled with the end result.

"And that's a wrap," she said, hitting the red button to stop recording. She spun around once more, marveling at the room. "I can't believe this is the same room! When I started working for you, Rafe, this was floor-to-ceiling boxes with little more than a path to the desk."

"I know." Rafe's smile was huge and contagious. "I can't... Jesus, I never imagined." He looked over at Gio. "You outdid yourself."

Gio waved the compliment away. "*We* outdid ourselves. You were right beside me every step of the way, man."

"Yeah, but I never could have come up with this. My idea for renovating it was slapping some paint on the walls. This..."

Gio's vision had gone quite a few steps further and included stripping and refinishing the molding and hardwood floor, adding a vintage rug they'd found at an antique shop, repairing the gorgeous bookcases that lined two walls, removing the heavy curtains to let in more natural light, replacing the gross, dusty lamps with recessed lighting that worked with a dimmer switch, making the useless fireplace functional again...and *then*, slapping some paint on the walls.

In addition to restoring the historical aspects of the room, Gio had updated it with some hidden, contemporary touches, because this room—once the inn opened—would serve as the business center.

"Well, one room down, forty-seven more to go," Gio joked as

he slapped Rafe on the shoulder. "At this rate, we should have the inn ready to open by our ninetieth birthdays."

"We could break all the records for longest-running renovation show on Facebook," Keeley joked.

Rafe chuckled, but before he could respond, his phone rang. He answered it, turning his back to them and walking to the window.

Keeley could tell it was his mother. Rafe had a "mom voice," which was sort of similar to the tone he used to use on her, when she was flirting shamelessly.

Patience and affection.

"Oh, Mom, I'm sorry to hear that," Rafe said.

Keeley and Gio exchanged a glance, both of them coming to the exact same conclusion. Rodney, the stepdick, had left. Keeley felt the slightest twinge of panic because, while there was no love lost between Rafe and Rodney, she couldn't help but wonder what that would mean for the three of them. Would this set Rafe back? Restrengthen his convictions that love and relationships were bad things?

"I'll come by tomorrow morning to see you, promise." Rafe paused, then said, "It's all going to be okay. Bye, Mom."

After hanging up, Rafe stared out the window, into the darkness.

Keeley studied his reflection, hating the heaviness that replaced what had been genuine happiness just a few minutes earlier.

"Rodney leave?" Gio asked, breaking the silence.

Rafe nodded as he turned around. "Does it make me a terrible son that I'm glad the asshole is gone?"

Keeley shook her head and walked over to him. "I think it makes you a good son. From what you've told me about the guy, he was a total jerk and not good to your mother."

Rafe lifted one shoulder miserably. "And yet, she loved him."

Keeley acted on instinct, hating how sad he looked. She stepped closer, wrapping her arms around him. "I'm sorry, Rafe."

Unlike the past couple of nights, Rafe didn't immediately return her hug, his arms remaining by his sides. Keeley didn't care. She wasn't letting go.

Once that became apparent, Rafe lifted his arms, wrapping her up, holding her tightly. She breathed in his scent, relishing this too-infrequent closeness.

When his grip began to loosen, she lifted her head from his chest, turned her face up to his. She could feel his breath, could see all those emotions he'd been trying so hard to hide written in his eyes.

"Rafe," she whispered.

He lowered his head and kissed her. Kissed her with the same passion and power she'd come to expect from him. Rafe never merely claimed. He consumed. And she loved it.

Their lips parted as the kiss deepened. Her fingers closed in his shirt, while his found her hair, his fist closing around it tightly until her scalp stung under the delicious intensity. He used his grip to twist her head, to control her, to put her exactly where he wanted her.

And then, as quick as it started, it ended. Rafe broke the kiss and took two steps back. She started to follow him, but he held his hand up, and she knew she'd let this go too far, too soon.

It was just...he'd been hurting.

Rafe's expression was one of regret and apology, especially when he turned to look at Gio.

Keeley followed his gaze, took one glance at Gio, then her eyes flew back to Rafe, perfectly aware he wouldn't like what he'd seen.

The apology lingering on Rafe's lips died the moment he saw Gio's smile, his pleasure at watching the two of them kiss. After all, Gio had allowed his best friend to assume they'd moved on, that they were fine with following the standard protocol of Rafe walking away and Gio continuing the relationship.

Gio's smile. Her kiss. It gave them away.

Rafe's eyes narrowed.

They'd overplayed their hand. Revealed their true intentions, hopes, desires.

"That won't happen again," he said coldly.

Four words. That was all Rafe said before he left the room.

Gio sighed heavily. "Fuck."

"Yeah," Keeley agreed. "Fuck."

Chapter Sixteen

"Anybody home?" Keeley called out from the front door.

Rafe sighed. He had hoped to make his escape before she arrived this evening.

He'd tried to be pissed about last night, about that kiss the two of them had shared, but he couldn't work up a single speck of anger. Because it had become immediately, painfully clear that Gio and Keeley hadn't truly accepted his decision to step away from the relationship.

Instead, they'd joined forces, trying to bring him back into the relation—

Shit.

He sighed heavily.

Affair. It was a fucking *affair*.

Or at least, he'd let himself pretend it was. For an entire week, things had continued the same as they'd been the previous weeks. Only without the sex.

And it had been just as amazing, just as terrific.

But they'd been tricking him, playing a game, making him believe they were a happy couple, fine with moving on without him because that had been the plan all along.

Then he'd fucked up. Kissed Keeley because he missed her so bad, it was a physical ache that never left him. He'd reached for her before his brain could engage. When it had, he'd looked over, expecting Gio to be pissed. After all, Rafe had broken things off, had basically given Gio his blessing to make Keeley his girlfriend, assuring him he'd be fine, just like he always was.

Rafe had been lying.

But so had Gio.

Because instead of anger, Gio had been smiling, looking at Rafe with that same open expression that held back nothing, that proved Gio hadn't accepted the so-called status quo. His best friend had no intention of moving on alone with Keeley.

Not this time.

So why wasn't he furious at them for trying to trick him?

Because this is what you want, you fucking idiot.

Keeley loved him. That had been the catalyst, had been the trigger, his downfall.

She'd said those words and Rafe had shut down, panicked. No woman had ever said those three little words to him because he'd held every woman he'd ever dated at arm's length, made sure to walk away before they could.

The worst part was that Rafe was so fucked up in the head, he hadn't even believed her, certain that Keeley was mistaken.

Then he'd kissed her last night...

And he'd felt...

Fuck.

He'd felt all of it. Her love, his love...Gio's.

The truth crashed in on him until he thought he'd suffocate beneath the fallout.

And he'd run again because at the back of it all, he'd just heard his mother's voice when she told him her marriage was over...again.

Love. Leave. Love. Leave. It was one of the few absolutes in life. Right?

He started down the stairs, stopping halfway when Gio

drifted in from the kitchen. He used the back door there to go to and from his workshop.

Keeley lifted a bag. "I brought over homemade Italian hoagies and chips for dinner." She looked up and gave him a hesitant, hopeful smile.

It made what he was about to do feel a million times harder.

"I can't stay for dinner," he said.

"Going to your mom's?" Keeley asked.

Rafe shook his head. "No, I stopped by her place this morning. She's fine."

"Fine?" Keeley asked in surprise. Not that he could blame her. Rafe had talked about his mom's previous four divorces. About how she fell apart and it took a long time, and a lot of consoling, to pick her back up again.

"*She* kicked *him* out," Rafe explained.

"No shit!" Gio exclaimed, as shocked as Rafe had been this morning when he'd walked into his mom's house and found her humming as she cleaned the kitchen.

"She'd had enough of him grumbling about the inheritance and bad-mouthing me, accusing me of preying on Grandpa's illness and tricking him into rewriting his will."

"What a jerk," Keeley said. "You would never do that."

"I know. And so did Mom. I didn't realize how bad he'd gotten since Grandpa's death. I should have called her more, but first, I was afraid she wouldn't want to talk to me. And then..."

"We distracted you," Gio finished for him.

"She told me she understood why Grandpa left his business, his house, everything to me. I reassured her I'd take care of her, but..." Rafe smiled, recalling their conversation. "She said she didn't want me taking care of her. Said she didn't want *any* man to do that anymore. She's made some new friends in a book club, who've apparently inspired her to find her own happiness rather than thinking she needs a man or material stuff to make her life good."

"Wow," Keeley said, grinning widely. "That's awesome."

It was awesome. But Rafe was afraid to trust it. His mom had managed to break the pattern, and he was happy, albeit tentatively. For the first time in her life, it felt like she'd found the strength to do what made her happy rather than focusing on someone else's happiness.

The smile on her face this morning had stuck with him all day because...he'd never seen it. Not like that. Not that bright, that absolute, that sure.

"So where are you going?" Gio asked. "Got a hot date?" The last was a joke, which made Rafe's response all the worse.

"Yeah. I do." He started down the remaining stairs—and tripped when he reached the last one.

He grabbed the handrail to steady himself, pausing. It felt as if someone had...*pushed* him.

He considered all the times Keeley had almost fallen, he or Gio reaching out to catch her. Rafe took a deep breath, then mentally told his grandpa to cut it out.

"You do," Gio muttered, clearly surprised by his response.

He tried to focus on Gio, unwilling to see Keeley's reaction.

On the way to his mother's this morning, he'd called Dana, a part-time employee from the flower shop he'd inherited, inviting her out for dinner and drinks tonight. It had been an impulsive, knee-jerk decision that he'd regretted five seconds after she'd accepted.

This was why he thought shit out. Because as soon as he didn't, he was opening an inn and indulging in a menage with Keeley and Gio and...fucking up everything in his life.

"Oh," Keeley said quietly. She managed to pack quite a punch with that single syllable.

Rafe glanced her direction, forcing himself to acknowledge the deeply hurt expression he'd put on her face. "Her name is Dana. She works at the flower shop. I met her last week when I was going around to check in on all the businesses. I thought..."

He'd thought moving on and dating someone else would show Keeley and Gio just how serious he was. Because there was still a small part of him that didn't believe he belonged, that she really didn't love him, that they would be better off without him.

He'd made that call to Dana, which had been a huge fucking mistake, and he'd hated himself for it ever since. He'd picked up the phone a dozen times since this morning to cancel, but...apparently, he was his own worst enemy.

"It's just drinks and dinner. I'm taking her to that new Italian place, Roma's, that Tony was telling us about a couple weeks ago. Near Rittenhouse." Rafe had no idea why he was still talking. He needed to get out of here. "Anyway, I should probably get going or I'll be late. Enjoy your hoagies. I'll see you both tomorrow."

A large part of him—the foolish part he'd only just discovered —wished they'd stop him, tell him they wanted him to stay.

Neither Keeley nor Gio said a word as he left.

Looked like he'd not only slammed the door closed this time. He'd locked it as well.

Rafe forced a smile as Dana shared a story about an encounter with a customer. The man, a husband, was looking for a way out of the doghouse. Dana had reassured him a dozen roses would probably work just as well as a hundred.

"A *hundred*," she exclaimed. "Can you imagine? And it wasn't even infidelity. The guy had just forgotten their anniversary. I had to wonder if he was married to Atilla the Hun."

"So what I hear you saying is, you could have sold a hundred roses, but you talked the guy down to twelve," Rafe joked, aware it was the first thing he'd said since they sat down that wasn't a single-word response. He felt guilty for being such a shitty date, especially considering he'd been the one to ask her out.

Dana was nice, an easy companion. At any other time in his life, he would have felt an attraction, would have asked for a second date in hopes that things would progress to the bedroom. But every single part of this evening had been hard work so far... and he hadn't even been putting much effort into it.

"Guess I shouldn't have confessed that to the boss."

They fell silent again, Dana sneaking yet another peek at her phone, probably wondering how much longer she would have to endure his less-than-stimulating company.

If he'd been smart, he would have simply invited her out for drinks. What had he been thinking, tacking a whole meal onto the deal?

They'd finished their first round of drinks and an appetizer, and were just about to order, when two familiar faces caught his attention.

Rafe fought to restrain a relieved grin when Keeley and Gio approached their table, both of them feigning absolute amazement over running into him in the exact place he'd told them he would be.

"Rafe," Gio said, stopping next to him. "What a nice surprise. How long has it been, buddy?"

It was on the tip of Rafe's tongue to give him the honest answer of "less than an hour," but instead, he ignored the question. "Dana, these are my friends, Keeley Gallo and Gio Moretti."

Gio's gaze narrowed briefly at the word *friends*, but he recovered quickly. Rafe keenly recalled how *he'd* felt when they'd crashed Keeley's first date, and she'd introduced them that way. He'd hated it...though he had refused to admit it at the time, even just to himself.

"Nice to meet you," Keeley said, shaking Dana's hand.

Dana smiled and returned the greeting.

Gio looked around the restaurant, which was doing a pretty good business but was by no means overly crowded. "This place is packed," he exaggerated. "Hey, what do you say we get the waiter to pull a couple chairs over and we'll join you."

Rafe covered his mouth, quickly trying to pass his laugh off as a cough.

Dana, who really *was* very nice, looked at him and shrugged like she was game. She was probably grateful there would be someone else at the table to talk to, since he hadn't been carrying his weight.

Gio, the cocky bastard, didn't even wait for them to give their approval. He'd already waved the waiter down and requested the chairs. He and Keeley sat down with them, ordering drinks and looking at the menus.

Keeley, a master at first dates, led the conversation throughout the meal, engaging Dana in discussions about their favorite wines, what books they were currently reading, then debating the best-smelling flower—Dana was in the hyacinth camp, Keeley in the lilac one.

Then they told Dana about the renovations they were doing to the mansion, and Keeley pulled out her phone, showing her a bit of one of the videos. Dana asked for the link, promising to watch later.

If Dana thought it was strange that he and Gio were currently making videos together, yet pretended they hadn't seen each other in a long time, she had the good grace not to mention it.

While the date had felt eternal at the beginning, Rafe was surprised by how quickly the time passed, the four of them enjoying the meal and each other's company.

Several times, he felt Keeley's foot brush against his leg. The woman was playing footsie with him...and given his friend's smoldering looks, he'd say she was teasing Gio the same way.

Near the end of the meal, Dana excused herself to go to the ladies' room.

"Seriously," Rafe said, once she was out of earshot. "You crashed my date?"

Gio grinned. "You wanted us to, bro. I mean, you all but drew us a map to the place."

Rafe rolled his eyes. "I'm pretty sure I was just making conversation. Is this going to become a thing between the three of us? The date-crashing?"

"Jesus, I hope not." Gio was rarely without a smile, but there was no mistaking the misery in his tone, the sadness in his eyes. "I mean, dude, I'll crash as many dates as I have to, but...fuck. I don't think my heart can take too much more of this. This last week..."

Keeley pointed toward the lobby, where the hostess station was set up. "We were standing near the door for a full five minutes, watching you. This date wasn't working, Rafe, and you know it. You *needed* us to crash it."

Rafe didn't bother to deny that. It was the truth.

He had proven pretty decisively over the course of the past week that he needed help.

He'd spent the entirety of his adult life letting his mother's life choices impact his. Watching her run toward love, and ultimately heartache, had taught him to run the other direction.

But Mom had finally seen the disastrous effects of that and she'd made a change. She'd found the strength to kick Rodney out, to do what was best for her, to seek her own happiness—however she could.

What if he did the same? Grabbed what would make him happy.

He'd told Gio and Keeley that he didn't want love, so he'd pretended what they'd shared was nothing more than lust. Which was total bullshit.

While they'd been careful not to say the words lest they spook him, Keeley and Gio had shown him how much they loved him through a million more meaningful ways. Gio's care and attention to remodeling Grandpa's home, Keeley's steadfast support as he learned how to navigate his business, the way they cuddled, and laughed, and ate together, and kissed good night.

The way they'd crashed this date.

Jesus. If he couldn't trust these two with his heart—his best friend and the girl he'd watched grow into a woman—then who could he trust?

So yeah.

He needed them to crash a hell of a lot more than his date. If he hadn't screwed things up beyond repair, he wouldn't mind if they'd go ahead and crash his life too.

"I need *you*," Rafe said, simplifying Keeley's assertion, breaking it down to the most, *only*, essential part. "I just...need you."

Keeley sucked in a surprised gasp. She reached over and grasped his hand. "Do you mean that?"

Rafe nodded. "Yeah. I do. I really do."

Gio smiled. "You finally figured it out, didn't you? Figured out the only place you belong is with us, Rafe. Nowhere else. The three of us...we work. It's perfect."

Gio wasn't exactly yelling, but he was talking loud enough that Dana, who'd returned to the table, heard him loud and clear.

"Us?"

The three of them looked up, probably resembling deer in headlights.

"Dana," Rafe started, wondering how in the hell he could explain this to her. "Listen, I—"

She raised a hand to stop him. "It's okay, Rafe," she said, letting him off the hook easily. "I just got out of a relationship myself. When you called, I knew I wasn't mentally ready to put myself back out there. I just felt like I should. I could tell something was... not exactly *off* about the three of you. Just different. There was a closeness that I didn't quite get, especially when you pretended you hadn't seen each other in a while. But I do now. And it's cool."

He stood up. "Thanks for being so understanding."

She smiled. "I think I'm going to let the three of you finish this date without me," she said, giving Keeley a wink. "You're a lucky woman."

"Thanks," Keeley said sincerely.

Dana and Rafe shook hands, and she said her goodbyes.

"Damn," Keeley said. "Now I sort of feel bad for crashing the date. She was super nice."

"She was. But, Keeley..." Rafe said, resuming his seat so he could reach for her hand. He didn't want to talk about Dana right now. He had too many things to make right. "I'm sorry. More sorry than I can possibly say with words. I never meant to hurt you."

Keeley blinked rapidly, fighting to keep the tears at bay. "I know that."

Then he glanced at Gio. "I owe both of you an apology. A big one."

"Bro—" Gio started, but Rafe shook his head.

"Let me say this, Gio. The last time we were all in bed, well...I heard you, Keeley. After you thought I'd gone to sleep. Heard you tell Gio you loved him."

"I was afraid of that," Gio muttered.

"And because I'm an idiot, I thought..." Rafe ran his hand through his hair, unsure how to explain. "I thought you'd waited until I was asleep because you didn't feel the same way about me."

"Rafe...I told you the very next day, but—"

Rafe raised his hand, cutting her off. "I know you did. But because I still wasn't finished fighting this—fighting myself and my own feelings—I didn't believe you."

"Didn't believe me?" Keeley asked, aghast. "Oh my God, Rafe. I love you so much I can barely breathe."

Rafe smiled, touched by her words. "I was a fool. Working overtime to convince you both that I was only in it for sex."

"Which we knew that was a lie," Gio said quietly.

"It was," he agreed, still addressing Keeley. Now that he was coming clean, he let all his fears, all his anxieties out. "But let's face it, Gio was openhearted and minded, always talking about the future, not afraid to let you see how much he cared about you. While I'm...Jesus. I'm fucking clueless when it comes to love and relationships."

"We can show you," Keeley said, squeezing his hand. "I wish I'd told you how I felt that night instead of letting you believe—"

"It wouldn't have changed the outcome," Rafe reassured her.

"I was still in denial. Plus, I'd convinced myself that the two of you are the natural couple. You're like-minded, compatible."

"What the fuck are you talking about?" Gio asked. "Haven't you ever heard the expression opposites attract? Keeley and I are *too* alike in some ways, which is why you balance us out."

Rafe had never considered it that way, but he liked the idea of it. "Gio, in the past, I've always walked away. I thought maybe you were expecting—even waiting—for that to happen."

Gio scoffed, letting him know exactly how crazy that fear was. "This time was completely different. I know you felt it too. We've shared women before, but it was nothing like what we have with Keeley. You've sworn off relationships for as long as I've known you, and if I'd grown up watching the shit you've seen your mom go through, I might have felt the same way."

"I've been using my past as an excuse. That stops now. And while I've never seen forever up close and personal, and I sure as shit have never been around a relationship that was perfect, my eyes have been opened." He recalled Keeley's comment that, while she personally had no experience with love, she knew what it looked like because her parents had shown her. "Because what the three of us have...this is it, isn't it?"

Keeley nodded, the tears on her lashes in direct counterpoint to her huge-ass smile. "This is it. I'm sure of it, Rafe. And I'm sorry you spent a single second questioning my feelings for you. I love you," she said, stressing every single syllable so that there could be no denying her feelings.

He grasped her hand and pulled it to his lips, kissing her knuckles. "I'm in love with you too."

"Good. Then it's settled," Gio said, raising his hand and gesturing to the waiter that they wanted the check. "Let's go home. I'm horny."

"Just like that?" Rafe asked.

Keeley shook her head. "Duuuude. You really need to work on your romantic side."

"I'll romance the hell out of you, little one. Once we're naked. This was the longest week of my life."

Rafe shook his head in amusement, though he didn't disagree. "Felt like a hundred years."

"A million," Keeley corrected.

After paying the check, they decided to leave Rafe's car in the restaurant parking lot, none of them willing to separate even for the short drive back to the mansion. Instead, they climbed into the bench seat of Gio's pickup, Keeley and Rafe making out like a couple of desperate teenagers while Gio drove. They were probably lucky to make it home in one piece, considering Gio's eyes had been on *them* more than the road.

Rafe held Keeley's hand, the three of them heading directly to the stairs, to his—their—bedroom, after she'd kicked off her shoes at the door first.

Cricket had become accustomed to sleeping in her doggie bed in the corner until the wee hours, even after Gio and Keeley stopped coming to bed with him. She lifted her head, acknowledged them all with a sleepy yip, then went right back to sleep.

"Holy heat," Gio murmured when they walked in. "It's gotta be eighty degrees in here."

Rafe laughed. "Clearly we're wearing too many clothes for the ghosts."

Gio looked around, pleased. "Albert and Marta for the win."

Keeley released Rafe's hand so that she could begin to unbutton his shirt.

"Getting right down to business, I see," he murmured.

"It *is* warm in here," she teased.

Rafe let her strip his shirt off, loving the feeling of her fingers stroking his bare chest. Unlike Gio, Rafe didn't have a single tattoo. He chalked it up to a lifetime of overthinking. He'd never been able to decide what ink he'd like.

But now...as he watched Gio tug off his shirt, saw the appreciative way Keeley looked at him before turning to draw her tongue in swirling patterns over the artwork on Gio's arm, Rafe thought it might be time to give a tattoo serious thought.

Gio reached for the hem of her sweater and pulled it over her head, then lost no time tackling her bra.

"I don't want to go slow. I've missed you. Both of you," Keeley said, stripping her pants and panties off, adding them to the pile. To accentuate her point, she climbed onto the bed seductively, crooking her finger at them.

Rafe frowned as he considered her words. "The two of you really didn't..."

"We were waiting for you," Keeley admitted.

"God, I love you," Rafe said again. Now that the words were out there, he couldn't stop saying them. "You're probably going to get sick of hearing me say that."

She shook her head. "Never."

For the first time in his life, Rafe was seeing a future he'd never imagined for himself...and he sent up a silent prayer that Keeley's brother would be okay with this because Rafe knew what his end game was.

It was them.

Rafe took off his pants and joined Keeley on the bed. Kneeling, he reached for her hand and pulled her in front of him.

Rafe prided himself on his control and restraint in the bedroom. Both, however, were seriously lacking at the moment. He shifted Keeley into the position he wanted, kneeling in front of him, facing away, both of them right at the edge of the bed. Then he lifted her hips, lined up his cock, and pulled her back down.

They both gasped, then groaned.

Once she was fully seated, he tightened his grip, holding her in place before looking at Gio and hitching his chin in a "get on with it" manner.

Gio grinned as he dropped his pants and kicked them off.

"Commando?" Rafe observed.

"Figured it would save time," his friend joked.

Rafe grinned. "Cocky bastard."

"If there's one thing I knew for sure, it was that our determination was way stronger than your stubbornness."

"And for once…it appears you were right," Rafe said, loving the way his playful jab made Keeley laugh.

"Buuuurn," she said, giggling.

"You want to burn?" Gio asked, stepping close to the bed, right beside them, his erection jutting out.

"Bend forward, beauty," Rafe directed, gently pushing her down.

She reached out for Gio's cock, but Rafe grasped her wrist firmly, halting her.

"Grip the base. The way I showed you. But just take the tip of him in your mouth, tease him a little," Rafe demanded.

Gio's heated look promised retribution, and Rafe looked forward to whatever attempt his friend made.

Keeley did exactly as he asked, wrapping her hand around Gio's dick while sucking on just the head. She was a sexy, giving lover, her ministrations fueling her own arousal as her pussy clenched, tightening around Rafe's erection.

They weren't even moving, yet Rafe knew it was going to take a lot of multiplication tables in his head to hold his climax at bay. There was no way he was going to let this end too quickly.

Gio groaned, raking his hands through Keeley's hair. He gathered it up in one fist, creating a ponytail that left Rafe an unobscured view as Gio's cock slid in and out of those pretty pink lips of hers.

Gio started to take control, to thrust more deeply.

Rafe reached down and cupped Keeley's chin, drawing her away slightly. "What did I say, Keeley? Just the tip, remember?" he warned.

Gio panted and shook his head. "Dammit, Rafe."

Rafe grinned, then pushed his thumb into Keeley's mouth, alongside Gio's dick. "Suck on my thumb, beauty. Get it nice and wet for me."

Keeley's tongue slid over his thumb and Gio's dick. Rafe ran his thumb over Gio's slit, then down until he hit the sensitive spot just beneath the head.

Gio groaned, then cursed. "Fuck me!"

Rafe still wasn't sure what kept prompting him to touch Gio sexually. It certainly hadn't been something he'd wanted or tried before, with their previous lovers. All he knew was that boundaries he'd always respected were falling away. He'd given his heart to Keeley. She'd claimed it hook, line, and sinker. But now...well... if he could give his love, his heart and soul and body to one person...why not two?

Gio didn't push him away, didn't tense up, or give him any indication that these new, sensual touches were unwanted. Just the opposite, in fact. He could tell they turned Gio on. As much as they did Rafe.

"Keep Gio in your mouth, take him deeper."

Keeley shifted, opened her mouth wider. Gio took advantage of his hand in her hair, pulling her closer, pushing more of his cock inside her mouth.

Rafe pulled his thumb out, then reached for Keeley's hand, guiding it between Gio's legs. He encouraged her to grasp Gio's balls, using his own hand to show her how to play with them. He tightened his fingers around hers so that she was cupping his balls firmly. They lifted them slightly, stroking downwards together as they tugged.

The massage was having the desired effect as Gio's cursing grew louder, more pained. "Mother. Fucker!" he gasped. "That feels...fuck. *Fuck*."

Rafe was nowhere near finished. He loosened his grip, and Keeley started to pull her hand away.

"No," Rafe commanded. "Keep hold. Gio's ready for you. And he likes it rough, just like you."

She resumed her strokes, while Rafe reached farther back. Finding the taint, he caressed the area gently before pressing more firmly.

Gio jerked, as if struck by lightning.

Keeley released him for a moment, looking curiously at Rafe over her shoulder. "What did you do?"

Rafe reclaimed the hand she was using to play with his balls and guided her fingers back, showing her where he'd touched. "Self-destruct button," he joked.

Neither Keeley nor Gio laughed—Keeley too fascinated, and Gio too aroused.

She increased the pressure on his taint, taking Gio back into her mouth. She was a quick study, evidenced by the absolute pleasure on Gio's face.

Aware Gio wasn't going to last much longer, Rafe decided to up the ante. Using the thumb Keeley had wet with her mouth, he slipped between her ass cheeks and ran it over her anus.

She grunted, the sound drawing Gio out of his blissed-out state, his eyes opening as he sought out the reason for her sudden twitching.

When his gaze landed on Rafe's thumb, Gio grinned wickedly.

Now that he had an audience, Rafe pushed his thumb deeper. Keeley was still sucking on Gio's dick, but her motions were jerkier now as he breached her virgin ass.

She whimpered once the whole digit was inside her, and he wiggled it. Unbeknownst to Keeley, she was fucking the hell out of Rafe right now, the continual clench and release of her pussy around his dick, driving him mad.

Fucking hell. She was doing Kegels on his cock.

"Rafe!" Gio gasped. "I can't..."

Gio was there, and no matter how much Rafe wanted to draw this out, there was just no fucking way. It would take years of sex with these two before he ever managed to find his self-control. "Do it."

Gio began to thrust into Keeley's mouth in earnest, using his grip in her hair to drive the pace and speed. Rafe mimicked that rhythm, fucking her ass with his thumb, stretching the too-tight hole.

Keeley pushed back against him, silently demanding more. Rafe tilted his hips, the need to pound inside her growing too great.

Gio went over first, his eyes closed, his face contorted in what might have looked like pain in any other circumstance. Keeley, their incredible woman, came as well.

Rafe held still, watching them both in the throes of pleasure, loving their sexy cries and the ways their bodies trembled.

He wondered how in the fuck he'd ever managed to walk away from this.

Gio and Keeley had reached out to him, even after he'd hurt them, and pulled him back in. He was never going to hurt them again.

Gio withdrew from Keeley's mouth, the fingers that had been clenched in her hair now loose, stroking the strands from her face with a newfound gentleness.

Keeley shifted slightly, moving to her hands and knees, signaling she was ready for more.

"Wait," Gio said, climbing onto the bed. He claimed the middle, lying on his back. Reaching for Keeley, he pulled her over him, giving her a quick kiss.

Then his friend looked at him and graced him with a wink. "Back where you were," Gio said.

Rafe resumed his place behind Keeley...*inside* Keeley.

Gripping her hips, he set the raging beast inside free, pounding, thrusting, pounding, thrusting. He felt, rather than saw, when Gio began to stroke her clit. He didn't shy away from the area, his fingers reaching lower, to feel the place where Rafe penetrated her. It looked like his voyeur best friend had found a new way of watching...with his hands.

Keeley cried out, coming hard. Rafe wanted to hold back. God, he really fucking wanted to, but in the end, there was no hope for him.

He climaxed hard, every muscle in his body tensing up under the avalanche, the impact.

Rafe had no idea how long they remained there, locked together. But it was Gio who stirred first, now, as always, finding a way to make them laugh. "Everybody still with me? It got kind of quiet."

Keeley laughed breathlessly, her strength giving out. The arms and knees she'd locked in place loosened, and she slowly slid down, lying fully on top of Gio.

Rafe collapsed to the side, watching as his friend engulfed Keeley in his arms.

"Love you," Gio murmured, gaze locked with Rafe's as he kissed the top of Keeley's head.

Rafe smiled.

Yeah. So it happened.

The man who thought himself incapable of love had just fallen hard, not with one person but two. It had been a rough ride, but Rafe was finished fighting.

He was ready for the next part.

Come what may.

Because he was impulsive like that.

Chapter Seventeen

Gio stood up from the recliner, put his iPad down, and stretched as Rafe walked into the office. He'd been sketching out some ideas for the upstairs bedroom renovations set to begin next week.

"Keeley's in the kitchen, whipping up some hoagies," Rafe said as he walked across the room to glance at a piece of paper on the desk. "You about finished with the designs? Everybody will be getting here soon."

Gio nodded. "Yeah. Just put the finishing touches on. I'll show you my ideas tomorrow. I'm ready to just kick back and relax for the rest of the night."

Rafe nodded. "We've been going full-steam ahead for weeks, what with the renovations, the date-crashing—"

"The marathon sex every night," Gio added to the list, grinning. It had been a week since Rafe stopped being a stubborn ass and came to his senses. The best week of Gio's life. Every single night, the three of them had come together in a rush of almost desperate lovemaking. Gio wondered how long it would take before they all felt secure enough in the knowledge that this was for real, that it would last. Considering none of them had ever managed a long-term relationship in their lives, he figured their concerns were valid.

Rafe winked. "Tonight was a good idea."

They were throwing an old-school hockey night party. Keeley had confessed a few days earlier that she missed the way they all used to get together to watch Elio play back when she was in high school.

Gio decided it was a good time to bring the weekly get-together back. He also figured this was the perfect way to come out to their friends about their change in status. Keeley had already told Liza, but tonight...they wanted to tell everyone else.

Starting with her brother.

"Nervous about talking to Kayden?" Gio asked.

Rafe started to shake his head, then changed his response to a shrug. "Yes and no. I mean, Kayden's a reasonable guy about pretty much everything. Except—"

"Keeley," the two of them said in unison.

"If it was just one of us," Rafe continued, "I think he'd be cool with it. But the truth is..."

"Two of his closest friends are banging his sister," Gio finished for him, grinning.

"Fuck. Think we should frisk him when he gets here? Make sure he's not carrying his gun?"

Crossing his arms, Gio leaned against Rafe's desk. "I don't know. Maybe we should—"

Before he could finish his statement, the desk slid a good six inches across the floor.

"Jesus!" he cried out, wobbling.

Rafe reached out, grabbing Gio's upper arm to steady his friend. "You okay?"

"What the fuck?" Gio scowled. "That desk weighs at least two hundred pounds." They'd learned that fact the hard way when they'd had to move it out of the room so they could refinish the floors.

"Yeah. Apparently, the floor in here is made of ice on occasion. That, or Grandpa wants the desk somewhere else. It's not the first time it's slid that easily. Keeley nearly fell once, as well, when she leaned on it." Rafe was still gripping Gio's arm, their proximity close. Neither of them bothering to separate.

"We gonna talk about the touching thing?" Gio asked, before he could think better of it.

Rafe had become less restrained in the bedroom, in terms of he and Gio. After introducing Keeley to Gio's taint, the "instruction" had continued as Rafe revealed every secret of the male anatomy, giving her hands-on demonstrations...using her hands *and* his.

Rafe should write a goddamn book because Gio had always considered himself to have some decent staying power, but this week, with Rafe tutoring Keeley, he'd been popping off like an untried schoolboy.

"Do you want me to stop?" Rafe asked.

"Fuck no. It's just..." Now that he'd started the conversation, Gio realized he didn't have a clue what he wanted to say.

"We're both adventurous in the bedroom," Rafe said, taking over for Gio. "Both open to trying new things. I'm not proposing we jump straight to fucking each other, but...forever is a long time. We've got time to do a little investigating. Why not explore a few things, see how we feel about it, figure out where our lines are?"

Gio smiled, relieved and pleased by Rafe's suggestion. He hadn't been able to make sense of his jumbled-up feelings regarding this new facet of their sexual relationship. He'd witnessed the closeness between Layla's guys, Finn and Miguel, both of whom were bisexual. Gio had never felt that tug, never felt like that word applied to him. But lately...with Rafe...

Thankfully, Rafe's suggestion resonated with him, managed to break it all down in a way that suited Gio just fine and made him comfortable. This was why it was smart to have a best friend who was a thinker.

"That sounds pretty damn good. Can't wait to see what we

discover." Gio turned to look at the desk. "And I don't give a shit if Albert wants the desk here. It doesn't work this close to the wall."

He and Rafe started to push it back into place, but something peeking from the bottom corner of the heavy piece of furniture caught Gio's eye.

"What's this?" He reached down and pulled a thin piece of paper from beneath the desk. His eyes widened. "Holy shit, man. It's the combination to the safe!"

"How the hell did that get there? We've moved this desk at least half a dozen times while we were renovating the room." Rafe took the paper from him.

"Maybe it was stuck to the bottom," Gio suggested. "Or maybe Albert was finally ready for you to find it. Either way, open the damn safe! I'm dying to see what's inside."

Rafe took the combination over to where the safe was hidden behind a portrait of Marta. Pulling the frame, which was on hinges, away from the wall, Rafe spun the dial to the appropriate numbers, then turned the latch.

"Well..." Rafe said, blocking Gio's view. "That's anticlimactic."

Gio pushed Rafe over so he could get a glimpse inside. The safe, in direct opposition to the boxes, which had been stuffed to the gills, was pretty much empty, containing nothing more than an envelope and a small box.

Rafe reached for the box at the same time Gio grabbed the envelope.

"It has your name on it," Gio said, handing it to his friend.

"That's Grandpa's handwriting." Rafe took the envelope and box to his desk. Setting the box down, he opened the letter.

Gio shifted so he could read it over Rafe's shoulder. Rafe glanced back and chuckled at his nosy crowding. "Here." He put the letter down on the desk between them so that they could both read it easily.

· · ·

Rafe,

The cancer came too soon, stealing away so much of the time I thought I would have with you. As I sit here, writing this, I am overwhelmed by all the things I wish I'd told you. But upon consideration, I can see that only one of those missed conversations truly matters.

You told me a few weeks ago at dinner that you didn't plan to marry, that you couldn't see yourself ever falling in love. To close yourself off to that emotion, my dear grandson, would be the biggest mistake of your life.

If there is only one last thing I can teach you, let it be this.

Don't be afraid to give your heart to someone else.

Find a girl like my Marta. Fall in love. Give her a ring. Buy her a home. Make babies. And never—never—let work and money mean more than the people you care about.

Do those things, and you will be the richest man on the planet.

Enclosed in this safe is the best thing I ever bought. The thing that made my life worth living. It's yours now. Use it!

Grandpa

"Your grandpa was a wise man," Gio said.

Rafe grinned. "Yeah. He was."

"What's in the box?"

Rafe opened the small box, revealing a beautiful engagement ring. Gio glanced at the portrait of Marta. The same ring sparkled on her finger. "Your grandma's ring."

Rafe followed his gaze. "Think Keeley will like it?"

Gio gripped his shoulder. "I guess we'll find out one day when we give it to her. How long should we wait? A year? A month? Tomorrow?"

Rafe laughed and closed the box, putting the letter and the ring back in the safe. "What do you say we leap the first hurdle before we start renting the reception hall and booking the band."

"The first hurdle?" Gio asked.

"Kayden."

Gio sighed. "Shit. Yeah. Kayden."

"Rafe? Gio? Can you guys give me a hand in the kitchen?" Keeley called out.

"You move the desk, I'll help our girl," Rafe said, leaving the room.

Gio shifted the desk back into position, then looked around the office and smiled. "Thanks, Albert," he whispered to the silence.

Walking toward the kitchen, he detoured when he saw head-lights. Glancing out the front window, he spotted Kayden's car.

"He's here," Gio yelled out.

Rafe and Keeley walked out of the kitchen, each with a platter in their hands. Keeley carried a tray of hoagies, while Rafe's was laden with wings.

"He just pulled in." Gio took the platter from Keeley, carrying it to the living room and putting it on the coffee table. Rafe placed his next to it.

Keeley went to open the door when they heard the knock. He and Rafe exchanged a glance, Rafe giving him an encouraging grin.

Kayden strolled in with a twelve-pack of beer. "Am I early? You guys said six, right?"

They'd given Kayden an earlier time than the rest of their buddies so they could break the news to him alone.

"Yeah, everyone else will be along in a half hour or so. We invited you early because we wanted to talk to you about some-thing," Rafe began.

"Oh?" Kayden was clearly curious. "Okay."

"Here." Keeley took the beer from her brother. She opened it, handing each of them a bottle. "You guys sit down, and I'll put the rest of these in the fridge. Be right back."

Kayden grabbed one of the recliners, while Gio and Rafe dropped down on opposite ends of the couch, leaving room for

Keeley in the middle. She returned with her own beer as well as four koozies. She tossed each of them one, then sat down.

"So," Keeley began. "I guess you've noticed from your Find My Friends stalking that I've been over here a lot."

Kayden rubbed his jaw...and Gio realized they weren't going to have to explain as much as they'd thought. "I knew it. Told Aldo something was going on while we were on the trail one night, when neither one of us could sleep. You were over here at two a.m., and when we started walking the next morning at seven, I checked the app and you were *still* here. So, which one of you is it?"

"Kayden," Rafe started. "Listen—"

Kayden frowned. "Seriously? Wow. My money was on Gio."

"Gio?" Rafe asked. "Why him? Why not me?"

Keeley elbowed Rafe. "That's not really the point, is it? I'm sure he thought it was Gio because you never date anyone. Walk away, remember?"

"I'm just saying, I don't think I'm *that* long of a shot." Rafe wasn't finished arguing his case.

Keeley rolled her eyes. "You've gotta be kidding me. Were you not paying attention last week?"

Rafe scowled. "Keeley, all I'm say—" he started.

Gio snorted. "Jesus. Can we start this over because you two are doing a shitty job. Kayden, Rafe and I are dating your sister. Both of us."

"Both of you?" Kayden repeated, dumbfounded.

Rafe quickly added, "We don't want you to think this is a casual affair. Because it's not. We've asked her to move in with us while we work on the inn, and once that's finished, the three of us are going to buy a house together."

"Right," Gio continued. "And at some point, we're going to figure out the marriage thing, and then we're gonna make a pile of kids."

"By the way, you need to redefine *pile*," Keeley said. "Because five ain't happening."

Gio considered that. "Three?"

She tapped her chin. "I think I could go three."

"Wait!" Kayden said, raising his hand. "The niece and nephew conversation is one I'll be happy to revisit with you at some point, but first...the three of you? Like Tony, Jess, and Rhys?"

"And Layla, Finn, and Miguel," Keeley added. "And Erin, Oliver, and Gavin."

Kayden took a second to let that soak in. "What the *fuck* is up with Baltimore?"

Keeley burst out laughing, while Gio and Rafe looked confused. "Liza said the exact same thing. Kayden," she said, standing up, placing her beer on the coffee table before crossing over to her brother and kneeling in front of him. "I love them."

He put his beer on the side table and took her hands in his. "I can see that."

"And they love me."

Kayden rolled his eyes. "I'm not blind, Kee. I see that too. I think I've *always* seen that. You know there was never a bro-code, right?" he reassured her. "They're my friends because they're good guys. Why would I make the best men I know promise to stay away from you?"

"Kayden," Keeley said, tears in her eyes.

"My biggest fear was you'd end up with one of those yahoos from the dating websites."

"Does this mean no more stalking me on Find My Friends?"

Kayden laughed. "Don't get carried away."

Keeley and her brother stood up and hugged. Then Kayden looked at them. "Were you worried about telling me?"

Gio shrugged. "My family notwithstanding, this isn't exactly a normal thing. We weren't sure how you'd feel about it being both of us rather than just one of us."

"I told you guys the day we moved you in here, Gio. All I wanted for my sister was a man who would love her, take care of her, treat her the way she deserved. I know you guys, know you're exactly those kinds of men. For God's sake, I asked you to look after her when I was gone. If that wasn't me giving my blessing, then I don't know what is."

Rafe smiled and rose. Gio followed suit. The three of them shook hands, which morphed into guy hugs with some firm back-slapping.

"Couldn't ask for better men for my sister. And, well, I've always considered you guys brothers. Now it'll be for real. So... about those nieces and nephews...when's that starting? Because I'm going to be the world's greatest uncle."

Keeley swatted her brother on the arm. "This relationship is five minutes old. Give us a year."

"Or, you know, six months," Gio added, winking at Keeley.

Rafe put his arm around Keeley's shoulders, giving her a kiss on the cheek. "Or three."

Keeley shook her head. "If you propose that soon, you're going to have to apologize to Penny for accusing her of going too fast."

"So noted," Rafe replied.

Kayden glanced around the house. "Since we've got a little while before everyone else shows up, how about you show me the work you've finished?"

The three of them took Kayden to the office, then to the rest of the rooms on the first-floor level, telling him their plans for the inn. The tour ended once the rest of the gang began to arrive.

Liza and Gianna showed up with a huge bag of tater tots that Keeley immediately threw in the oven.

Aldo and Luca, like Kayden, showed up with beer.

When Keeley returned to the living room, Gio reached out and grabbed her, giving her a big kiss.

Luca honed in on it fast, gaze flying to Kayden. Either ready to break up a fight, or pull up a chair to watch the fireworks.

"The fuck?" Aldo said, when Rafe stole Keeley from Gio, wrapping his arms around her from behind, nuzzling the side of her head.

"We wanted to let you guys know," Gio announced, "that me, Rafe, and Keeley are dating now."

Liza grinned. "It's about time you told everyone. That was *not* an easy secret to keep."

"You knew about this?" Aldo asked.

She nodded.

"And you didn't tell me?" Gianna was obviously annoyed at missing out on first dibs of the gossip.

"Hey," Liza said, with no remorse. "You were invited to dinner with us the night Keeley told me. You were too busy—as always—cleaning your bedroom."

Gianna grimaced. "Oh. Yeah. Shit."

"When did you find out?" Aldo asked Kayden.

Kayden glanced at his phone. "About forty-five minutes ago."

Aldo gave Gio and Rafe a quick once-over. "Well, considering there's no blood or bruises on either one of them, I'm going to go out on a limb and say you're okay with it," he directed to Kayden.

Kayden gripped Rafe's shoulder. "Of course I am. They're great guys. And they know if they ever do anything to hurt my sister, I'll plant evidence on them, arrest them, and throw them in jail with the biggest bruiser I can find, for the rest of their lives."

Keeley brightened up. "Hey, points for creativity, Kay. Usually you just intimidate my boyfriends by cleaning your gun in front of them. I like the extra effort this time."

"Figured something this big called for a fresh threat."

They all settled in around the TV to watch the game. Elio's team was taking on the Bruins, which ensured a lot of trash-talking.

Fucking Boston.

The living room, like everything else in the mansion, was over-sized, so there was room for two couches, a love seat, and a recliner, perfect for entertaining. Plus, Rafe's grandpa had spared no expense on his big-screen TV.

During a commercial break, Gio overheard Keeley ask Gianna how she was doing. Gianna Duncan had been dating Sam

Mannarino for as long as Gio could remember, and he'd always figured they'd be the first in their group of friends to get married. Their break-up had surprised the hell out of everyone.

"Oh, I'm fine," Gianna said, as if she didn't have a care in the world...hadn't just lost the only man she'd ever loved. "My apartment is spotless right now. I had no idea how much of a mess Sam made until I didn't have to clean up after him anymore."

Keeley had confessed that she and Liza were worried about Gianna's lack of emotion about the break-up. Both women feared their friend was in for a fall at some point.

"That's great," Liza said, giving Keeley a look behind Gianna's back that seemed to indicate the opposite.

"Is it just me, or is it chilly in here?" Keeley asked the room at large.

Liza, Luca, and Gianna were sharing the other couch, and all three agreed they felt fine.

Gio agreed with Keeley. He grabbed a blanket from the back of the couch, shaking it open to drape over the two of them. "There's definitely a draft over here."

Rafe slid his feet under the blanket, trying to steal his own bit of heat. "Grandpa Albert and Marta seem determined to make this stick."

At everyone's curious glances, Rafe, Keeley, and Gio filled them in on all the ways they thought Rafe's grandparents had been playing matchmaker. Gianna and Liza, like Keeley, were convinced the ghosts were real, while Aldo and Luca seemed more skeptical.

"Second quarter is starting," Aldo announced, grabbing a handful of napkins, his hands covered with barbeque sauce from the wings. "Tonight is awesome, by the way. I've missed the weekly hockey nights."

Everyone agreed.

"Should we take turns hosting?" Kayden asked. "Or keep having it here so Albert and Marta can fuck with us?"

Luca laughed. "The ghosts do add an extra element of excitement to the game. Plus, there's plenty of room for all of us."

Five minutes before the end of the second quarter, Elio took a bad hit. Liza jumped up from her spot on the couch and raced to the TV as if she could step through it and onto the ice, worried about her brother.

"That dirty motherfucker!" she cursed, pointing to the Boston player. "There's no need to check someone that hard into the boards. And from behind too."

Liza paced, despite her brother Aldo trying to calm her down. "He's going to be okay, sis," he reassured her. "Elio's taken harder hits than that and gone right back out on the ice."

Liza wasn't appeased. Especially when Elio was helped off the ice, clearly in pain.

They were a bit more subdued as they watched the rest of the game, and even more so when the announcer gave an update toward the end of the game, reporting that doctors suspected Elio had suffered a broken collarbone.

Gio whistled low. "That could put him on the bench for a while. Weeks. Poor Elio. That's really gonna fuck up his season."

Liza stood up and pulled out her phone. She walked into the kitchen, but not before they heard her asking Elio how he was doing.

Aldo sighed. "She worries about him a lot. He's taken some nasty hits the last few seasons. Two concussions, a broken finger, now this."

"She told me she wished he'd just quit for good and come home," Gianna added, petting Cricket, who had curled up on her lap.

"He's played professionally for ten years. That's a hell of a career for someone in the NHL," Luca said.

"Yeah, but what will he do if he retires?" Gianna asked.

Aldo shook his head. "I have no idea. That boy has lived and breathed hockey from the second he was old enough to strap on a pair of skates."

Liza returned and informed them that while Elio was still awaiting X-rays, the doctor was certain it was a broken collarbone, which meant—best case—six weeks in a sling. "He's not happy, but like he said, it's the nature of the game," she added, pointing out what they all figured was pretty obvious. "Then he said, on the bright side, he might be able to come home for a longer visit while he's healing."

The game, despite the drama, ended with a Baltimore win, which cheered them up a little bit. Losing to Boston would have added too much salt to the wound.

They all tidied up, then headed out, confirming that they wanted to do hockey night again.

Once everyone was gone, Gio wrapped his arm around Keeley's waist.

"We have great friends," she said.

"Your brother's pretty awesome too," Gio said, giving her a quick kiss. "Not gonna lie. I had some concerns about how tonight might go down."

Keeley waved his apprehension away. "Oh, I knew that was going to be okay. My horoscope today told me so."

Rafe chuckled. "What did it say?"

"That I'm ready to embrace a challenge of a personal nature and my support network will come through for me."

"And you took that to mean Kayden would approve of our relationship?" Gio asked.

Keeley gave him a look like he was six eggs short of a dozen. "Of course."

Rafe reached for her hand and pulled it to his mouth, kissing her knuckles before drawing his tongue along them suggestively. "What else did your horoscope say?" he asked, before sucking her pointer finger into his mouth.

Her eyes darkened with arousal, but her mischievous grin never wavered. "It said I was going to encounter two tall, dark, and handsome men who would seduce me, lure me to their lair, and give me a very, *very* happy ending."

Gio ran his hand along her spine, loving the way she shivered in response. "Is that right? Well, we wouldn't want to thumb our noses at fate, would we?"

Rafe released Keeley's finger. "Or piss off Grandpa Albert."

Keeley laughed, wiggling her way out from between them as they'd begun to close ranks. When she reached the bottom of the stairs, she looked over her shoulder and laughed when she yelled, "Race ya!"

Ready for more Italian Stallions? Book four (Elio and Gianna's story) releases February 2023! It's one-night stand, surprise pregnancy, hockey romance. What more could you want? And you can preorder it now!

Wild and Wicked

Be sure to be on the lookout for the rest of the Italian Stallions series.

Down and Dirty
Hard and Fast
Hot and Heavy
Steady and Strong
Tempted and Taken
Kiss and Tell

Want to see how Layla Moretti met her guys, Finn and Miguel? Want to see how the Moretti brothers got their Italian Stallions nickname? What to find out what's up with Baltimore?! Check out these books, standalone within the Wilder Irish series!

Wild Side
Wild Dreams
Wild Chance

· · ·

Calling all fans of Mari Carr AND Facebook! There's a group for you. Come join the Mari Carr's Facebook group for sneak peaks, cover reveals, contests and more! Join now.

And be sure to join Mari's mailing list to receive a **FREE** sexy novella, Midnight Wild.

About the Author

Virginia native Mari Carr is a New York Times and USA TODAY bestseller of contemporary romance novels. With over three million copies of her books sold, Mari was the winner of the Romance Writers of America's Passionate Plume award for her novella, Erotic Research. She has over a hundred published works, including her popular Wild Irish and Compass books, along with the Trinity Masters series she writes with Lila Dubois.

Follow Mari:
www.maricarr.com
mari@maricarr.com

Join her newsletter so you don't miss new releases and for exclusive subscriber-only content.

9 781958 056189